AUNT BESSIE INVITES

AN ISLE OF MAN COZY MYSTERY

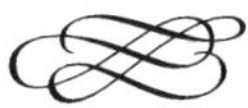

DIANA XARISSA

ISBN: 1523633034
ISBN-13: 978-1523633036

❀ Created with Vellum

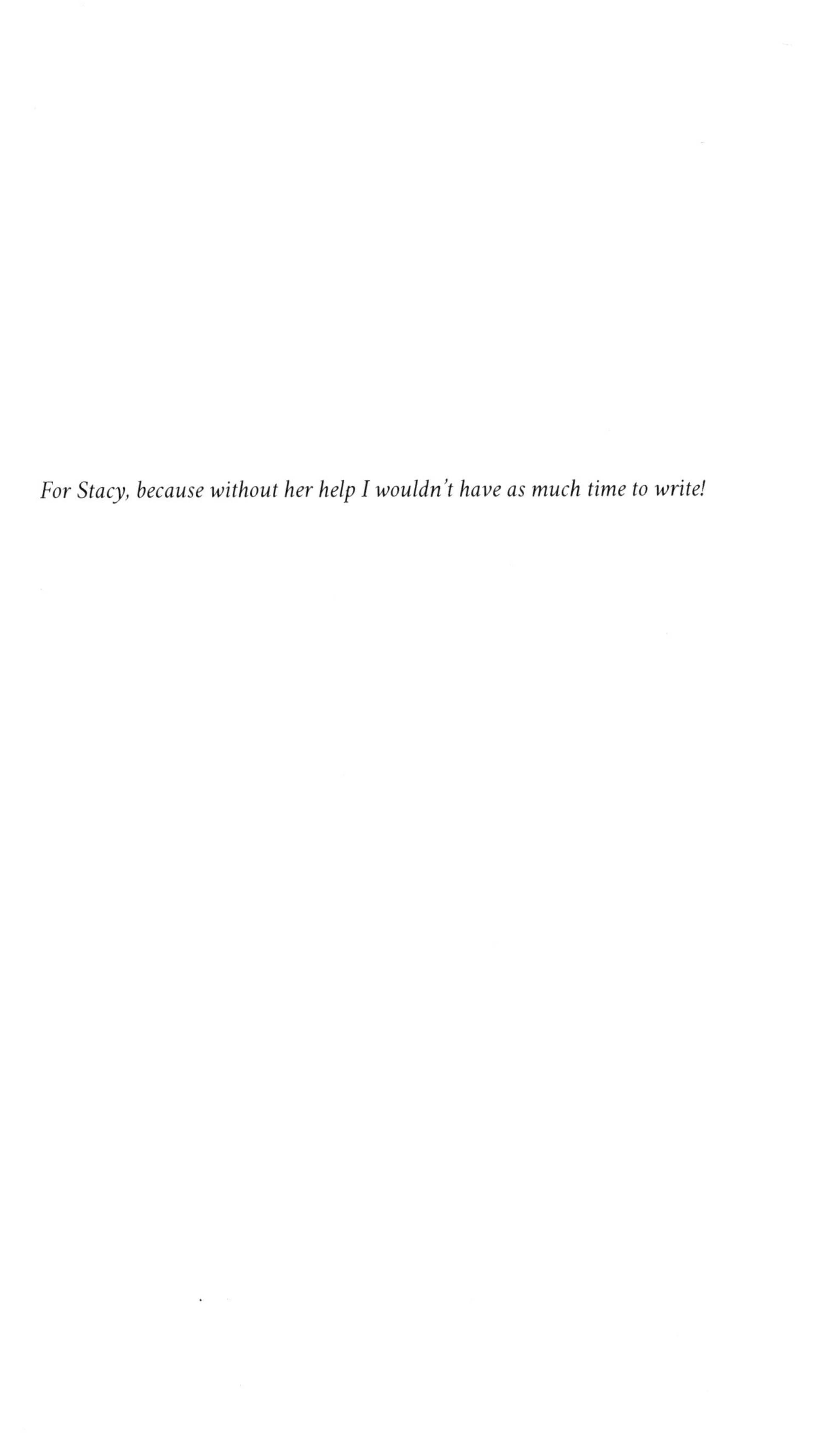

For Stacy, because without her help I wouldn't have as much time to write!

AUTHOR'S NOTE

Welcome to the ninth book in the Isle of Man Cozy Mystery series. I try to make each book stand on its own, but as the series progresses, it gets more difficult. My characters are changing and developing, and I really do recommend that you read the series in order (alphabetically by the last word in the title).

Most of the characters continue throughout the series, and I had great fun with this book by inviting almost everyone we've met thus far to Bessie's Thanksgiving feast. Some of the characters also appear in my Isle of Man Romance Series, although they are about fifteen years older there than in the Bessie books. (Bessie had just passed away in *Island Inheritance*.)

This is a work of fiction and all characters are entirely fictional. If they bear any resemblance to any real person, living or dead, that is entirely coincidental. The island businesses mentioned are also fictional, although the historical sites are all real. Manx National Heritage is also real and is tasked with preserving and promoting the island's amazing history. The employees of Manx National Heritage in this story are all fictional creations, however.

The photo on the cover is of the Ramsey Harbour Swing Bridge. It was built in 1892 by the Cleveland Bridge and Engineering Company and takes both road and foot traffic across the Sulby River. It was refitted and painted in 2013-2014, so it wouldn't have looked exactly as it does in the photo when this story takes place.

As ever, I have used British spellings and terminology as much as I can. There is a glossary in the back of the book for readers outside of the British Isles who might not be familiar with some of the English and Manx terms used. No doubt some Americanisms have slipped into the text as well, and I do apologise for those to my readers who are in the British Isles!

I'd love to hear from you. My contact details are in the back of the book.

CHAPTER 1

"Thank you again for driving me around today," Bessie said to Doona as they drove slowly along the road towards Ramsey Harbour.

"It's the perfect day for being out and about," Doona replied. "It's cold, but clear, and the sun is shining. I don't mind the cold nearly as much when the sun is out."

"It looks lovely shining on the water, doesn't it?" Bessie asked.

Doona slid her car into a space and looked out across the harbour. "It's beautiful," she replied. "And I love all the little boats. Maybe, if I really do inherit millions, I'll buy a little boat. Would you like to come sailing with me?"

Bessie shook her head. "I'm not much for sailing," she told her friend. "The ferry isn't too bad, if I need to get across for some reason, but otherwise I'm quite happy to stick to dry land."

The pair climbed out of the car. Bessie headed towards the pavement that ran in front of a row of small shops, with Doona on her heels. Anyone going past who noticed the pair might have imagined that they were mother and daughter, rather than friends.

Doona was in her early forties. Her brown hair was highlighted, and today she was wearing her glasses, rather than her usual coloured contact lenses which gave her bright green eyes. After some rather upsetting events the previous months, she'd lost some weight, but she still had curves, unlike her companion.

Bessie was probably around twice Doona's age, but she didn't like to talk about such things. Her grey hair was short and almost exactly matched her eyes. She was only a couple of inches over five feet tall, while Doona was a few inches taller than Bessie. Bessie had always been slender and age hadn't changed that. She kept herself fit by walking daily along the beach where she lived, often venturing out two or three times each day to enjoy the sea air and the exercise.

"Here we are," Bessie said, stopping at the last shopfront. "The Swing Bridge Restaurant. No creativity in the name, as the swing bridge is right outside their windows, but the food is delicious."

Doona followed Bessie into the small restaurant. It felt dark inside after the bright sunlight outdoors, and Bessie found herself blinking as her eyes worked to focus.

"Ah, Bessie, we were just wondering when you would arrive," a voice greeted her from behind the hostess stand.

"Lisa, I hope I didn't keep you waiting," Bessie replied. She gave the woman a quick hug before introducing Doona.

"Doona, this is Lisa, the assistant manager here. She's coordinating everything for our feast," Bessie told her friend.

"It's nice to meet you," Doona said politely.

Lisa was slim and was neatly dressed in black trousers and a matching shirt. The red jacket she was wearing was the only thing that differentiated her from the waiters and waitresses. She was probably no more than thirty, with long brown hair in a neat ponytail.

"I do hope you're planning on having lunch with us today," Lisa said to Bessie.

"That's why we timed our visit as we did," Bessie replied.

Lisa showed them to a small table in a quiet corner and left them with menus.

"I must say it's a treat having a day off on a Monday," Doona said after the pair had ordered their lunch. "I could get used to this."

"I don't suppose you have enough holiday time saved up to let you take every Monday off for a while?" Bessie asked.

"Anna would like it if I did," Doona replied. "She's very keen on getting us to use up our holiday time."

"Why?" Bessie asked bluntly.

Doona shrugged. "Maybe it's a lot of bother for her, keeping track of it all. Or maybe because she just likes telling us all what to do."

Bessie sighed. She knew Doona wasn't fond of the policewoman who'd recently been assigned to the Laxey station where Doona worked at the reception desk, but it was increasingly clear that Doona really disliked Anna Lambert. "It isn't getting any better, then? Working for Inspector Lambert, I mean."

Doona shook her head. "I don't know why they even assigned her to Laxey," she complained. "John was doing an excellent job without her. I know she's supposed to handle the administrative duties and leave John with the investigative work, but really she just seems to get in the way of everything.

John Rockwell had originally moved to the island to work as an investigator in the Ramsey branch of the CID, but various circumstances had led to his being put in charge of the Laxey station. Anna Lambert's appointment was meant to give him more time to work in the area he loved, investigation, rather than having to sit behind a desk all day figuring out the staff schedule and ordering supplies.

"So she isn't helping John?" Bessie asked.

"I suppose she is," Doona admitted with a frown. "But she seems to pick and choose how she helps so that John still ends up with a lot of jobs that she really ought to be doing."

"How does John feel about her?"

Doona shrugged and then looked away. "I haven't, that is, John's awfully busy at the moment," she muttered.

Bessie didn't press the point. John was in the middle of a fairly civil divorce and Doona had her own complicated personal life. Bessie was pretty sure that John and Doona were attracted to one another, but the timing wasn't quite right for them to get together. It seemed as if they weren't even really speaking at the moment, though, something Bessie hoped she could help them sort out eventually.

After a delicious lunch, Lisa joined them at their table. "Here's the final menu," she told Bessie. "Please let me know if we've missed anything."

Bessie ran her eyes down the printed card. "Turkey and gravy, stuffing, mashed potatoes, sweet potatoes, cranberry sauce, assorted vegetables, bread rolls, pumpkin and apple pies," she read slowly. "I think it's all here.

"And thank goodness we had lunch before you read through it," Doona said with a laugh. "Even with a full tummy, that list made me hungry."

Bessie smiled. "It does sound good. A good, traditional Thanksgiving feast. I can hardly wait."

"It makes a change for us every year," Lisa said. "We're usually getting ready for Christmas dinners through most of November. Your Thanksgiving meal is very like a Christmas one, of course."

"When we were in Ohio, we always had ham for Christmas dinner," Bessie replied. "But I really love turkey and all the trimmings. I'm more than happy to have it for both meals."

Bessie had been born on the Isle of Man, but her family had moved to the United States when she was a toddler. They'd returned to the island when she was seventeen. Now, many years later, Thanksgiving was one of the few American traditions she still observed. There was just something special to her about a day set aside to be grateful for all of your blessings.

Because she liked to spend the day surrounded by as many of her friends as possible, she had her Thanksgiving celebration on the Saturday after the official feast in the US. That way no one generally had to take time off work to attend. For many years she'd cooked the meal herself in her tiny cottage by the sea, but as the years had passed the celebration had grown. Now she hosted the event at a local restaurant, letting them handle the cooking while she enjoyed the day. This was the third year in a row that she was having the meal at The Swing Bridge restaurant, and she was anticipating another delicious feast.

"I'll just take you upstairs for a quick look at the banquet room," Lisa told her.

Bessie and Doona followed the woman through the restaurant and up the stairs. The first floor room was large enough to hold several round tables. In total, the tables could seat around fifty guests.

"Do you have any idea on numbers yet?" Lisa asked.

"I'll get back to you," Bessie said. "I'm still waiting to hear back from a few people. At this point, I expect there will be about forty of us."

"Are there going to be any children, and do you want to do a separate table for them if there are?"

Bessie shook her head. "There might be a few children, in fact, we might even need a highchair or two, but the children can sit with their parents. I can't imagine they'd enjoy being all lumped together at one table."

Lisa nodded. "And you're going to get us the turkeys we need, right?" she asked. "Our farmers don't start delivering turkeys until December."

"I'm going out to the Clague farm from here," Bessie told her. "I'm going to make sure that Eoin has my turkeys just about ready."

"And you really don't want any holiday decorations in here?" Lisa asked. "We could put a Christmas tree in the corner, just to brighten up the space a bit."

"Absolutely not," Bessie said firmly. "When I was a child, Christmas decorations didn't go up until after Thanksgiving. It was almost magical in the shops. The day before Thanksgiving they'd be just as plain and boring as ever. Then, on the Friday after, the first official shopping day for Christmas, there would be Christmas trees and fairy lights everywhere. I know some poor people had to work late into the night on the Wednesday to make it happen, but as a child it felt magical."

"It must be nice to have that clear start date for the Christmas season," Doona said. "Over here shops just start putting up their decorations whenever they feel like it, so it seems like some are dripping in fairy lights from October, while others barely manage to get anything up before mid-December."

"I understand that things aren't necessarily still done that way in the US," Bessie told her. "Apparently many of the shops now decorate earlier than was traditional when I was a child."

"But we won't," Lisa assured her. "If you don't want any Christmas decorations, that's fine."

"Last year you did a lovely job with the leaves and pumpkins," Bessie told her. "It was very autumnal and exactly right for Thanksgiving."

"Great. I have some good ideas for this year as well," Lisa said.

Bessie walked slowly around the room, imagining it full of her friends. While many of the guests would be old friends, she had invited a number of people for the very first time. If everyone came, it would be her largest Thanksgiving ever.

"Thank you again for coming by," Lisa said as she escorted Bessie and Doona back down the stairs. "Please ring if you have any questions or concerns."

"I know everything is in good hands," Bessie told her.

"I'm just sorry it's nearly two weeks away," Doona said as she and Bessie walked back to Doona's car. "The menu sounds amazing."

"The time will fly past," Bessie assured her.

Back in the car, Doona headed north. "You'll have to give me directions," she said after a short time. "I still get lost outside of Laxey Village." Doona had grown up in the south of the island, moving to Laxey only a few years earlier during an unpleasant divorce.

"With all the new roads going in, I'm not sure I'm much better," Bessie said with a laugh. "But the old Clague farm is a landmark property. It's been there for hundreds of years."

"And they farm turkeys?" Doona asked.

"They farm wheat and oats," Bessie told her. "And they keep some animals as well. They used to only keep animals for their own consumption, but many years ago, not too long after I first returned to the island, I persuaded Niall Clague to sell me a turkey from their farm. It's pretty impossible to buy turkeys in November, you see.

Nearly everyone has turkey for Christmas dinner, which means all of the farmers, both here and across, are working to that time frame. They're still busy fattening up their birds in November."

"But Niall sold you a turkey?"

"Actually, he gave me a turkey," Bessie told her. "I went all over the area, to just about every farmer, and begged and pleaded for a turkey. For the first few years I just ate chicken, but it wasn't the same. I really missed the US in those early years after my return, you see."

"But you stayed here anyway."

"I didn't feel as if I had any choice," Bessie replied. "Travelling back would have been expensive and young women didn't make trips like that on their own. Anyway, if I had gone back I would have had to go and stay with my sister, and she was already being overwhelmed with children. There wasn't room for me there."

"So you went around and begged for a turkey," Doona repeated.

"I did," Bessie replied. "There weren't actually many farmers that even had turkeys, and those that did were mostly raising them for themselves. Niall didn't even have any turkeys, but I went around in the spring, figuring that one of the farmers might be willing to get them and get one ready early if I asked at just the right time. Anyway, Niall had just found himself with half a dozen baby turkeys that were sent from across by mistake with some chickens he'd ordered."

"That was lucky," Doona said.

"Our turkeys for this year are descendants from those original birds," Bessie said. "Niall decided to have a go at raising them and they've done really well for him. The farm sells quite a few to the big grocery chain on the island every year at Christmas, but he always gets some ready for me for Thanksgiving."

"Did I hear you say you've ordered four?" Doona asked.

"Yes, I think that's about right," Bessie said. "They should be nice and plump, around fifteen to twenty pounds each, so they should feed forty or so people, especially with all the trimmings."

"Now I'm getting hungry again," Doona laughed.

Bessie told her friend where to turn. "The entrance to the farm is about another four or five miles along here," she told Doona. "But then it's another mile or more from the road to the farm house."

"Is Niall Clague still running the farm?" Doona asked.

"No," Bessie said. "Unfortunately, he isn't very well. Physically he's still reasonably fit, I understand, but mentally he's not doing well."

"How sad," Doona replied. "How old is he?"

"Oh, somewhere near eighty, I think," Bessie replied. "His parents had the farm before him, but his father died young. Niall pretty much took over when he was eighteen or nineteen and ran the place for fifty years or more."

"So this Eoin that you mentioned, he's Niall's son?"

"Eoin Faragher is his son-in-law," Bessie corrected her. "Niall and his wife, Marion, only had one child. Their daughter, Fenella, was only two or three when her mother died. Niall never remarried."

"How old is Fenella?"

"She must be sixty," Bessie said thoughtfully. "Eoin is a few years older. He'd been working on the farm for a few years before he married Fenella."

"And do they have children ready to take over?" Doona asked.

"They don't, actually," Bessie said. "Fenella always wanted children, but they simply never arrived. I remember when she and Eoin first got married everyone teased her about when the babies might start arriving, but for some reason they never did."

"And medical science couldn't do much about it in those days," Doona added.

"No, there wasn't much that could be done, and women didn't feel comfortable talking about such things with their doctors either. If you didn't get pregnant you just accepted it and got on with your life. I'm sure it was hard for Fenella, maybe for Eoin as well, but it was just how it was."

"So what happens to the farm when Fenella and Eoin pass away?" Doona asked. She shook her head. "What a morbid question," she said. "Maybe you should just ignore me."

Bessie smiled. "It's a natural question, after the conversation we've been having," she said. "I told you the farm has been in the family for hundreds of years, but I'm not actually certain who might be in line to inherit it after Fenella and Eoin. Of course, they're still relatively young. I'm sure they'll be around for many years to come."

"Did Niall have any brothers or sisters?" Doona asked.

"Actually, he was an only child, the same as Fenella," Bessie said. "His mother nearly died delivering him and I gather she couldn't have any more children afterwards. As I said, his father passed when Niall was in his teens."

"What about Eoin? Does he have brothers or sisters?"

"You're quite worried about this, aren't you?" Bessie teased her friend.

"Having been unexpectedly named the main beneficiary of someone's will quite recently, the question of inheritance is probably on my mind too much," Doona replied.

"Yes, well, that makes sense," Bessie told her. "As for Eoin, he had a brother and a sister. His sister died in childhood of some sort of fever. I don't know that I ever heard more than that, really. It happened when I was in the US, but it wasn't unusual in those days before antibiotics were readily available."

"And his brother?"

"His brother led a very colourful life," Bessie said. "He moved across as soon as he was eighteen and managed to get himself into all manner of trouble."

"What sort of trouble?"

"Mostly with the law," Bessie said. "Now you're really testing my memory, though. I haven't thought about Nicholas Faragher for years."

"Is he still across?" Doona asked.

"I'm not sure," Bessie said, trying to remember events from many years earlier. "I heard that he spent some time in prison. I think he'd stolen a car and some other things. There was some talk about him moving to the US or even Australia, so that he could start over once he was out, but I'm not sure that I ever heard what happened to him."

"He didn't marry or have children?" Doona asked.

Bessie looked curiously at her friend. "You're very curious about all of this," she said.

Doona flushed. "I'm being nosy," she said. "I think I'm just talking to keep my mind off my own troubles."

"Is everything okay?" Bessie asked.

"It's fine, really," Doona said. "There's just a lot going on with the solicitor from across coming over on Friday, and having to work with him and my advocate here. Then there's Anna at work, which isn't fun." Doona sighed. "I suppose hearing about other people's problems make mine seem less serious. Just ignore me."

"Of course, I won't ignore you," Bessie replied. "As for Nicholas, I don't know if he ever married or had children. Niall and I weren't exactly friends. Farmers are very busy people and he was bringing up Fenella on his own. I only really ever saw him around Thanksgiving time, and he wasn't the sort to spread stories about the younger brother of one of his farmhands."

"But I thought everything that happened on the island became common knowledge," Doona teased.

"Nearly," Bessie replied. "Most of the farms are quite remote, so they had a measure of privacy. And then Nicholas moved across or maybe even abroad. Fenella never spoke of him when I happened to see her in town and I probably went years at a time without seeing Eoin except for when I visited my turkeys."

"So we don't know what happened to Nicholas," Doona concluded.

"I'm sure he's alive and well somewhere," Bessie said emphatically. She couldn't help but think of another person who everyone had thought had left the island many years earlier. That young man's body had recently been found and there were still unanswered questions about his death.

"I'm sure he is," Doona agreed quickly; no doubt her thoughts were running along the same lines as Bessie's. "The turning is coming up, right?"

"Yes, just beyond those trees," Bessie pointed.

A moment later Donna signaled to no one and turned slowly

through the open gates. They passed over a cattle grid and through a second open gate.

"You probably want to turn left here," Bessie said. "You can go the other way if you'd like to drive all the way around the farm, but if you turn left the road goes straight to the farmhouse."

"Left it is," Doona said.

"It's still a mile or more and you'll need to go slowly, as the road isn't paved," Bessie warned her. After a moment she sighed. "You know, the more I think about it, the more you have me wondering who Fenella and Eoin will leave the farm to. I'm sure there must be distant relatives. It's possible that Marion had brothers or sisters, but I can't recall any. Then again, my fortune, such as it is, will all go to my family in America, even though I've never met any of them. Perhaps Nicholas is settled there now and he and his children will inherit."

"And then you'll have to persuade them to sell you turkeys," Doona said.

"Yes, well, as Fenella is probably twenty years younger than I am, I suspect I'll still be getting my turkeys from her for the rest of my life."

"But where will I get mine?" Doona asked. "I'm getting to quite like the whole Thanksgiving idea."

Bessie laughed. "I'm sure you'll work something out," she replied.

They crossed another cattle grid and then found themselves driving through a large field full of sheep. Doona slowed down to a crawl as the sheep wandered back and forth across the dirt road.

"I thought you said they only kept a few animals," she said to Bessie as half a dozen sheep walked in front of the car and then stopped.

"Last year Fenella said that they were considering taking on more sheep," Bessie said. "These are Manx Loaghtan. Their meat is considered a delicacy in some circles and their wool is valuable as well."

Doona narrowed her eyes at a sheep that was slowly advancing towards the now stopped car. "Those four horns make them look quite dangerous," she said to Bessie. "I don't want to get into a fight with a sheep."

"I'm surprised Eoin hasn't come out and rescued us," Bessie said. "I told him we were coming."

"Maybe I should get out and try to encourage them to move," Doona said after a minute or more.

"But I can't drive," Bessie reminded her. "I'm sure by the time you got back in the car they'd have wandered right back into the road. Why don't I get out and see if I can persuade them to go?"

Doona glanced at Bessie. Bessie could see the doubt in her eyes. "You don't think I can scare a couple of sheep away?" Bessie asked, lifting her chin. "I can be quite scary, really."

Doona patted her friend's hand. "I'm sure you can be very scary," she said. "But those are pretty large sheep and I don't want them to trample you if you do frighten them."

Bessie put her hand on the door handle. There had to be a way to get the sheep out of the road. She was about to open her door when one of the nearby sheep suddenly stepped closer and pressed its nose to the passenger side window. Bessie gasped.

"That's a big sheep," Doona said.

"Much bigger than it looked when it was a few paces away," Bessie agreed; glad now that she'd stayed in the car.

They sat for a few minutes, nervously watching the sheep as they strolled around the pasture. Occasionally a small gap would open on the road in front of Doona and she would inch forward

"Perhaps we should have gone the other way," Doona muttered as she was forced to stop again.

"Maybe we should go home that way," Bessie suggested. They both silently watched a large ewe as she nibbled on the grass in the centre of the road.

After a few more minutes, the sheep suddenly seemed to tire of the game and they all moved away together. With the road clear, Doona quickly made her way through the field and across another cattle grid.

"Well, this part is just boring," Bessie said a moment later as they bounced along the road. Along both sides of them were immense fields that had been ploughed and were now sitting empty for the winter.

"I prefer boring to dodging sheep," Doona told her.

Bessie wasn't sure she agreed. The sheep had been fascinating to watch, and Bessie wasn't really in any hurry today.

A few moments later Doona pulled up in front of the farmhouse.

"This isn't at all what I was expecting," she said. "This looks new."

"They tore down the original farmhouse about ten years ago and built this one in its place," Bessie told her. "That was when Niall was still well. He suddenly decided that his daughter deserved a more modern home than what they had before. Repairing the old house would have cost about twice what building this one did."

Doona nodded. She and Bessie climbed out of the car. "Did they put it in the old house's footprint?"

"They did," Bessie said. "And it really looks a lot like the old house, just brand new. In another ten or twenty years no one will know it isn't the original, at least not from the outside."

She walked towards the front door of the large house. Doona caught up to her and took her arm.

"Careful in the mud," Doona cautioned.

"It isn't too bad," Bessie told her. "I'm fine."

Doona nodded, but didn't let go of Bessie's arm. Bessie swallowed a sigh. She hated when Doona fussed over her, but she knew it made Doona feel better, so she tried not to complain too much. At the door, Bessie pressed the bell.

"Maybe no one is home," Doona said after a minute had passed.

"Someone is always home," Bessie countered. "Anyway, I have an appointment." She pressed the bell again and then knocked loudly.

"Perhaps everyone is working in the barns," Bessie said after another minute passed.

"Do we go and hunt for them or wait here?" Doona asked.

Bessie shook her head. "I'm not thinking clearly," she said. "I'll just ring Fenella's mobile. Wherever she is, she should have it with her."

Bessie found her phone in her handbag and then found the number in the small notebook that was also in her bag. After a few rings, Fenella answered.

"Ah, Fenella, it's Bessie. We're here to talk to you about the turkeys," Bessie said.

"The turkeys? Yes, of course, but well, I'm sorry. I'm rather flustered," was the reply.

"Is something wrong?"

"I don't know," Fenella said. "Or rather, yes, I think there is something wrong, but I don't know what to think."

"Where are you?" Bessie asked.

"Where am I? Oh, I'm at the lower barn. Maybe you should come down. You'll know better than I do what I should do next, I suppose."

"Whatever is the matter?"

"Just come down to the lower barn," Fenella said. She disconnected before Bessie could ask any more questions.

"Fenella's at the lower barn," Bessie told Doona. "Something's wrong, but she wouldn't tell me anything more than that."

Bessie had Doona turn around and then follow the road past the farmhouse. "There are several barns scattered around the site. As far as I know, they use the lower one for storage."

"Storage for what?" Doona asked.

"Old equipment and furniture, mostly," Bessie said. "I remember Niall taking me in there one day to look at an old wardrobe that had been in his father's bedroom. I had mentioned that I was looking for a wardrobe for my spare room. That one was far too massive for the space I had, but I remember the barn being stuffed with furniture and boxes. I've no idea what is in the boxes."

"So what could possibly be wrong?" Doona asked.

"I haven't the slightest idea," Bessie said, forcing herself to ignore the feeling of dread in her stomach.

"You don't think..." Doona trailed off.

"I don't know what to think," Bessie replied.

Doona pulled the car off to the side of the road in front of the barn. Fenella was sitting on an old milking stool near the doorway. Bessie and Doona crossed to her.

Like many women who farmed, Fenella had a weathered and worn look about her. She looked older than her sixty-odd years, watching Bessie through tired brown eyes. Her clothes were worn and had been carefully mended in several places. A long grey plait of hair hung down her back, and Bessie thought that she'd never seen the woman with her hair done any other way. Fenella didn't get up as the other women approached.

"Fenella, how are you?" Bessie asked when they reached her side.

"I've been better," Fenella replied. "Eoin had to go across for some tests. The doctor sent him yesterday after he went in to get his knee checked out."

"That left knee still giving him trouble?" Bessie asked. She remembered hearing about the tractor accident about five years earlier that had severely damaged the man's knee.

"Aye. It's worse when the weather's damp and cold, but the new doctor said there might be other problems with it and sent him off to Liverpool to get it checked properly."

"You could have rung me to reschedule," Bessie said.

"Aye, but if you don't see the birds soon, we'll have to get them ready. Eoin likes to have your approval on his choices."

Bessie nodded. Somehow it had become tradition for her to visit the farm about a week before the turkeys were due to be killed. In the early days, Niall had quite enjoyed her annual visit to see the birds. Once Eoin took over, the tradition had carried on. Really, all she ever did was agree with Eoin, but they'd done it that way for many years now and there seemed little point in changing things at this stage.

"So what's wrong?" Bessie asked.

Fenella rubbed her forehead with a dry and callused hand. "I've been after Eoin for years to sort through all of the junk in here, but he's always too busy with other things," she told Bessie. "I thought, while he was away, that I'd start going through some of the boxes, just to see what we have down here."

"And?" Bessie asked after a long pause.

"There are several boxes of Christmas things, actually," Fenella said. "They must have been my mother's. My father never bothered to do any decorating for the holidays."

"What a lovely thing for you to find," Bessie exclaimed. "But I'm sure it's been something of a shock as well."

Fenella shrugged. "Not half as shocking as the skeleton that was behind the boxes," she said.

CHAPTER 2

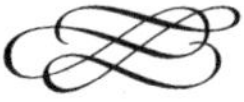

Doona gasped, but Bessie simply nodded. While she hadn't exactly been expecting the other woman's words, they didn't surprise her as much as they might have a few months earlier.

"Where's the skeleton?" Bessie asked in a resigned tone.

"In the back corner," Fenella replied. "You'll see it."

"Maybe we should just ring John," Doona suggested.

"I'm just going to have a quick look," Bessie replied. "Before we drag the police in unnecessarily."

Doona looked at Bessie and then nodded. "That's probably wise," she said.

Bessie walked slowly into the barn. She could see the route Fenella had taken, as furniture and other items had been moved and stacked together to clear a path to the very back of the room. Carefully, Bessie and Doona made their way through the piles.

"You think she might be, um, confused?" Doona whispered.

"I'm hoping she's found the remains of an ancient burial mound or something," Bessie whispered back. "Or old cattle bones or just about anything other than recent human remains."

Doona nodded. "Let's hope," she muttered.

Bessie stopped and then sighed deeply. "Time to ring John," she said, gesturing towards the far corner of the room. All that was visible, half buried in the soil floor, was part of an arm, but the watch on the skeleton's wrist suggested that the burial was anything but ancient.

Doona and Bessie quickly retraced their steps to the front of the barn. Fenella was still sitting where they'd left her.

"Going to ring the police, then?" she asked, sounding bored with the whole thing.

"Yes, I think we'd better," Bessie told her.

"I reckoned you'd know who to ring, seeing as how you find dead folks all the time," Fenella said.

Bessie swallowed an angry retort. On some level the woman was right; Bessie had found rather a lot of bodies lately, and she did know whom to ring. Doona took care of that detail, however, pulling out her mobile and tapping in some numbers.

"John? It's Doona. We're just out at the Clague farm and we've found, well, it might be a body," she said when the call was answered.

Bessie wished she could hear John's reply, which seemed to take a while. Eventually, Doona continued. "We're at the lower barn," she said. Bessie listened as her friend gave the police inspector directions to both the farm and the barn itself.

"What did he say?" Bessie asked as soon as Doona disconnected.

"Something along the lines of 'not again,' of course," Doona told her.

Bessie shook her head. Ever since March her life seemed to have taken a very strange turn. Was she going to keep finding bodies everywhere she went?

"This is nothing to do with you," Doona said quietly to her friend. They both glanced over at Fenella, but she was staring off into the distance and didn't seem to be paying any attention to them.

"I know. It was just an accident of timing," Bessie agreed. "But for everyone else on the island, this will be more evidence that I'm cursed or something."

Doona shook her head. "Of course you aren't cursed," she began. Bessie held up a hand.

"I know that, but persuading others might be difficult once word of this gets out," Bessie said. "But frankly I'm more interested in who we've found than in my reputation."

"I think I was assuming it's Nicholas Faragher," Doona said. "He certainly seems most likely, based on everything you've told me."

"What are you two whispering about?" Fenella demanded suddenly. "I hope you aren't suggesting that I had anything to do with whatever happened."

"Of course not," Bessie said soothingly. She walked across to where Fenella was sitting.

"Pull up a stool," Fenella suggested. "Or a folding chair, whatever you can find."

Bessie glanced at Doona. "I'm not sure we should be moving anything out of the barn."

"There are more stools right by the door," Fenella pointed out. "We just put them in there last month when we replaced the ones in the milking barn. They can't have anything to do with what's in the back of the barn."

"How long has it been since you put anything back there?" Bessie asked as Doona pulled out a couple of stools for them.

"I haven't ever been back there," Fenella told her. "My father put all of my mother's things in the very back after she died. I never felt like it was the right time to look through them until now."

"So the body has been back there since when?" Doona asked.

"Mum passed in nineteen-forty," Fenella answered. "But I'm not sure that proves anything. It wouldn't have been hard to shift the boxes around and put the body under them, I don't think."

"I don't suppose there could be any innocent explanation for someone being buried back there?" Bessie asked.

Fenella shrugged. "I suppose there could have been an old cemetery here and the barn was built on top of it, but it would have had to have been a long time ago. There's been a barn on this site for at least a couple of hundred years, at least that's what my father always said."

"I don't think the body has been here for that long," Bessie said thoughtfully.

"Do you have any idea who it might be?" Doona asked after a long pause.

"Maybe some vagrant managed to break into the barn and hid in the back, and then died of old age or something," Fenella suggested.

"I suppose that's a possibility," Bessie said. "The police will have to start going through all of their missing person reports for the last fifty or so years."

"Do you remember anyone going missing in the area?" Doona asked.

Fenella shrugged. "Young men used to disappear all the time," she said. "We didn't have mobile phones and the like. If a boy grew up and decided to move across, he would just go. Sometimes he wouldn't even bother to let anyone know. The next you'd hear would be when he'd made some money and came back to show off, or sometimes if he got arrested, we'd hear about that."

Bessie nodded. "Young women sometimes went as well," she added. "For a lot of people moving across represented all sorts of wonderful opportunities."

"But surely their family would miss them eventually," Doona said.

"The police might have a big job on their hands figuring out who we've found," Bessie said.

Doona looked as if she wanted to say something, but she didn't speak. Bessie was trying to work out how to ask what she knew Doona was thinking.

"How is your father?" Bessie asked after a moment, choosing to change the subject.

"He's okay," Fenella replied with a shrug. "He doesn't remember me, mostly, but sometimes he recognises Eoin and gives him jobs to do. Eoin's really good about visiting him regular, like. It makes me sad when I go to see him and he thinks I'm the nurse or a stranger."

"I'm sorry," Bessie said softly.

"I should probably ring Eoin," Fenella said. "Let him know about the body and the police coming. I'm sure half the island will be talking about it before he gets home."

"Maybe he'll have some idea who it is," Doona suggested.

"That probably depends on how long it's been there," Fenella said. "He didn't start working here until the mid-fifties, long after my father put my mother's things in the barn."

"What about Nicholas?" Bessie asked.

"What about him?" Fenella said, looking confused.

"He worked here for a while, too, didn't he? Maybe he'll have some idea about the body," Bessie said.

"He did work here for a short while, just waiting for his eighteenth birthday so he could go across. Eoin had high hopes of convincing him to stay on the island, but Nicholas hated it here. He was something special, was Nicholas."

"I seem to remember that he got himself into a lot of trouble when he did go across," Bessie said.

"A little bit of trouble," Fenella corrected her. "He fell in with a bad crowd and they led him astray a bit, but once he did his time, he'd learned his lesson. He turned out just fine, our Nicholas did."

"Where is he now?" Bessie asked.

"He and his wife have a little farm in Derbyshire," Fenella replied. "Funny that he ended up farming. He couldn't wait to get away from it here."

"Do you see him often?"

"Farmers are too busy to go visiting. We send cards at Christmas and for birthdays. He's been suggesting that he and his wife might visit for years, but we haven't seen them yet."

"What's his wife like?" Bessie wondered.

"I've never met her. Eoin went across for the wedding. That was, oh, thirty-odd years ago. He said, at the time, that she was a pretty little thing, but not very bright. I gather she had a small inheritance and that was what they used to buy their farm."

"Do they have children?" Doona asked.

Bessie smiled to herself. Doona was still strangely worried about who might inherit the farm, it seemed.

"Aye, they had five, but lost one young. The other four are all over the world now. Only the oldest boy, Ned, he's called, is at all interested in farming. I hear he runs the place for Nicholas now, at least that's what Nick says in the letters."

"So he and his wife should be able to visit," Bessie said.

"I suppose," Fenella shrugged. "That's between Eoin and Nick, that is."

The conversation was interrupted by the arrival of a police car. Bessie smiled as Hugh Watterson emerged from behind the wheel.

"Good afternoon," he greeted the trio of women.

Bessie got up and gave the man a hug. He flushed but returned the affectionate gesture.

"I do believe you're taller again," she told him as she sat back down. He was still blushing as she looked him up and down. Now in his mid-twenties, Hugh should have stopped growing, and Bessie supposed it was just because he was somewhere over six feet tall and towered over her that made her think he hadn't. The fact that he looked no more than fifteen, at least in Bessie's opinion, may have also been a factor. His brown hair looked as if it had been recently cut and Bessie noted that it was styled differently to Hugh's normal, slightly untidy look. Sunglasses hid his brown eyes, but now he slid them off and looked towards the barn.

"John said you found a body," he said. "I gather it's in there?"

"Yes, in the very back corner."

Hugh nodded. "I'll just take a quick look while we wait for the inspector," he said.

Bessie and the others were silent while Hugh was gone. He returned in less than a minute.

"We're going to have get a crime scene team here," he said. "There's an awful lot of stuff to move out of there, as well."

"I can have an empty lorry brought down," Fenella offered. "We can load everything into it and move it to another barn."

"That sounds like a good idea," Hugh said. "Not that we'll move anything before the inspector arrives, but at least we can be ready."

Fenella nodded and then rose to her feet. She pulled her mobile out of her pocket and walked a few steps away from the others.

"How's Grace?" Bessie had to ask Hugh while Fenella was occupied. Hugh had been going out with Grace Christian, a pretty blonde primary schoolteacher, for several months now.

Hugh blushed and looked at the ground. "She's good," he said after a minute.

"Still thinking about proposing at Christmas?" Bessie asked.

Hugh nodded. "I'm saving up for a ring," he told her. "I want everything to be just right. I thought maybe I'd ask after I go with her family to midnight mass. Or I might wait until all the presents are opened and then tell her that I have one more thing for her and give her the ring. Or maybe I'll wait until Christmas night, after dinner when everyone is just relaxing and enjoying themselves."

Bessie shook her head. "Just don't wait for Boxing Day," she said, a little sharply. "The occasion doesn't matter nearly as much as the question, anyway, remember."

"I know," Hugh nodded. "But I want it to be special for her. I'm hoping I'm the only one who will ever ask her that question, after all."

Bessie smiled. "You could always ask her at our big Thanksgiving feast," she suggested.

"I won't have the ring by then," Hugh replied. "I love my job, but sometimes I do wish it paid a bit better."

Hugh's mobile phone rang, interrupting the chat. He frowned as he turned away from Bessie to answer it. She couldn't hear anything from his end except monosyllables. After a moment he disconnected and turned back to the women.

"The inspector should be here in a minute," he said. "Then we'll see where we go from there."

A moment later a large lorry rumbled down the road. Hugh had a word with the driver, who then drove well past the barn and parked on the side of the road. He handed the keys to the vehicle to Fenella and then headed back up the road on foot. He was just out of site when a plain black car rolled into view. Bessie watched as the driver parked behind Hugh. The passenger door opened, but the person who climbed out was a stranger to Bessie.

Beside her, Doona gasped. "What's she doing here?" she whispered.

Bessie studied the new arrival. She was dressed in a black suit with a long straight skirt. A dark grey shirt was just visible under the jacket. Her low-heeled shoes were black. Grey hair was twisted into a tight bun on the top of her head and her grey eyes were cool and appraising as she approached them.

"Ms. Moore," the woman said. "I would have thought you'd have found more pleasant things to do with your day off than finding dead bodies."

Bessie could almost see Doona biting her tongue.

"And you must be Miss Elizabeth Cubbon," the woman continued. "Of course finding bodies is nothing new for you, is it? Inspector Rockwell has quite an extensive file on you, I must say."

Now Bessie found herself swallowing hard before she said something she might regret later.

"What have you found?" the woman snapped at Hugh.

"Exactly what was reported," Hugh said. "In the back of the barn there is a part of a skeletal arm visible on the ground. Not wanting to compromise the crime scene, I did no more than verify the initial report."

"So we might have just found someone's old medical school training skeleton or an old movie prop or something," the woman said.

No one spoke. After a moment she sighed deeply. "Let's see what we have then. Watterson, bring a torch."

As the pair disappeared into the barn, Bessie let out a long breath.

"And now you've met Anna Lambert," Doona said quietly.

"I thought she was meant to be handling the paperwork while John did all of the investigating," Bessie whispered.

Doona shrugged. "I'm not going to ask," she said.

"Me, either," Bessie agreed.

Hugh and the inspector were back a moment later.

"Right, who found the, um, remains?" she asked.

"I did," Fenella replied.

"I'll start by talking to you, then," Anna told her. "Ms. Moore, Miss Cubbon, if you'd like to wait here, please, I'll get to you in a few minutes."

Bessie exchanged glances with Doona while Anna led Fenella over to the police car.

"She's going to interview people in her car?" Bessie asked after the pair climbed into the backseat.

"I suppose there aren't a lot of options out here," Doona replied.

Bessie looked around. She could just make out another small building in the distance. Besides that, fields surrounded them in every direction.

"John's tied up in Douglas at a meeting," Hugh whispered out of the side of his mouth, his eyes never leaving the car where Anna had gone.

"He didn't tell me he was in Douglas when we spoke," Doona said.

"I gather he's going to try to get here soon, but obviously this sort of investigation can't wait," Hugh said.

"Whoever it is has waited a long time already," Doona replied. "I'm sure they wouldn't mind waiting another hour or two for a proper investigator."

"Inspector Lambert is an excellent investigator," Hugh said. "I, well, I rang a friend of mine across who used to work with her. She's very good at police work, she just isn't always the easiest person to get along with."

"I still don't know why we got stuck with her," Doona complained.

Before Hugh could reply, Anna emerged from the back of the parked car. Fenella came out after her.

"I have a farm to run," Fenella was saying angrily.

"And I have an investigation to conduct," Anna told her. "It looks as if it might just turn into a murder investigation, at that. I'm sure you can spare a few hours for the sake of the poor man or woman who was buried in your barn, can't you?"

Fenella pressed her lips together. Anna turned and said something to the young police officer who had driven Anna to the site. He nodded and walked a few steps away to ring someone on his mobile.

Anna turned towards the others. "Miss Cubbon, I might as well talk to you next. Ms. Moore won't mind waiting."

Bessie winked at Doona, knowing that her friend normally hated waiting. In this instance, though, the policewoman was probably right. The longer Doona had to wait, the better the chances were that John would arrive in time to take over. Bessie frowned as she climbed into the car. John was going to take over, wasn't he?

"I'm not sure I identified myself, but I'm sure Ms. Moore corrected my oversight," the inspector said after she'd shut the car door. "Please call me Anna. I know you have a good working relationship with John Rockwell and I'd like to think that we'll be able to work well together as well."

Bessie was suspicious of the woman's friendliness, but she smiled anyway. "You must call me Bessie," she said. "Everyone does."

Anna nodded. "I hope you don't mind if I record this conversation." When Bessie shook her head, the woman continued. "Why don't you tell me why you're here?"

Bessie took a deep breath and then launched into an explanation about her traditional Thanksgiving feast. After no more than a sentence, Anna held up a hand.

"I'm sure there is a lot of very interesting history behind today, but I'm not really interested in that. Can you tell me why you're here in no more than, say, a dozen words?"

Bessie swallowed several replies before clearing her throat. "I came to see the turkeys I have ordered," she said succinctly.

Anna made a note. "You had an appointment?"

"I did."

"With whom?"

Bessie shrugged. "I've always met with Eoin in the past, but I was happy enough to see Fenella or just about anyone, really."

"With Eoin, then?"

"I suppose so," Bessie agreed, just resisting the urge to sigh.

"What time did you arrive?"

"Around half one, I think. I wasn't really paying close attention."

Anna frowned. "What time was your appointment scheduled for?" she demanded.

"Oh, any time this afternoon," Bessie said, waving her hand. "I told Eoin that I would be up after lunch."

"So he didn't know exactly when to expect you?"

"I suppose not," Bessie said.

Anna shook her head and Bessie wondered if she lived her entire life to a strict timetable. Clearly the vague nature of Bessie's appointment bothered her for some reason.

"Where had you arranged to meet with Eoin?" Anna asked now.

"We hadn't really discussed it," Bessie said. "I'd planned on just stopping at the house. Fenella was always home and she could have rung Eoin and asked him to meet us at the turkey pens."

"But you didn't plan to meet at the turkey pens?" Anna checked.

"No, because I wasn't sure when I would get here. I didn't want Eoin to have to spend the day at the pens waiting for me. He has a very large farm to run."

"Why didn't you set a specific time? Surely that would have been more efficient for both you and Eoin?"

Bessie smiled to herself. This was clearly a woman who never made last-minute plans. "I wasn't sure how the day was going to go," she explained. "I didn't know for certain that Doona was going to do the driving. I don't drive and Doona usually works on a Monday. Things might have gone very differently if I'd had to catch a taxi out here."

"And you didn't mind keeping Eoin waiting for your arrival?"

"He didn't mind leaving the appointment time vague," Bessie corrected her. "I knew that once I arrived I might have to wait a bit for him to join me, but that was fine with me."

"I seem to recall from your file that you don't work," Anna said. "Perhaps that's why you have such a casual attitude towards time."

Bessie simply stared at her for a moment. She felt as if she'd been insulted, but she wasn't sure why. "Perhaps," she murmured eventually.

"So you arrived around half one and then what happened?"

Anna was silent as Bessie told her about the drive to the farmhouse, finding it empty, and the subsequent phone call to Fenella.

"Were you surprised that Eoin wasn't here?" Anna asked when Bessie paused.

"I suppose so," Bessie replied. "I didn't really think about it. Everyone knows about the problems with his knee, so I wasn't too shocked to hear that he'd gone across for treatment."

"Has he ever been absent when you've visited before?"

Bessie sat back in the seat and tried to think. After a few minutes she shook her head. "I have no idea," she said. "For many years, I used to see Niall about the turkeys. Sometimes Eoin would be with him, but not every time. Then when Niall started having health problems, I started to see Eoin more. But really, I only visit once a year and I've simply never paid that much attention to who was here or not here."

Anna nodded and made another note. "I don't suppose you keep any record of such things," she said.

Bessie nearly laughed. "I don't," she said firmly.

"What happened after you rang Fenella?" Anna asked.

Bessie told her about the drive down to the lower barn and everything that she could remember happening before Anna herself had arrived.

"What did you and Fenella discuss while you were waiting for the police to arrive?" Anna asked when she'd finished.

"I asked her if she had any idea who she'd found," Bessie admitted.

"And did she?"

"If she did, she didn't share it with me," Bessie told her.

"What about you? Do you have any idea who's been buried in that barn for all these years?"

"I couldn't begin to guess," Bessie replied.

"Surely you know of a missing person or two?" Anna pressed her.

"There was little Myrtle Kincaid," Bessie said. "But she was only a child when she disappeared."

Anna nodded. "I've been tidying up old files at the station," she said. "I read through the one on that case. I don't think that's who we've found."

"I can't think of anyone else it might be," Bessie said after a moment. "Fenella was saying that young men and women often left the island for across and many weren't good about staying in touch. I suppose it could be anyone who said they were going to go and then were never heard from again."

"I know Rockwell spent a lot of time going through old missing person reports during a recent investigation. Perhaps he'll be able to suggest some likely candidates," Anna remarked, almost to herself.

"If the family ever filed a report," Bessie said. "If they thought their loved one had moved across, they might not have done so, or they might have tried to file one over there, rather than over here."

Anna nodded. "But all of that is our worry, not yours," she said firmly. "Just one last question, I think. Who might want to get Eoin and Fenella Faragher into trouble by hiding a dead body in their barn?"

Bessie tried not to look shocked at the idea. "I don't, that is, I mean," she stammered. She took a deep breath. "I hadn't thought of that," she said. "But I can't imagine anyone would do something so awful. Eoin and Fenella are nice people who work hard and stay out of trouble. Why would anyone, I mean, it simply doesn't make sense."

"Thank you for your time, then," Anna said coolly. "I'll be in touch if I have any more questions."

Bessie nodded and then followed the woman out of the car. Her mind was racing as she considered the woman's last question. Was it possible that someone was trying to frame Eoin and Fenella? But how could they have known that Fenella was going to start trying to clear out the barn? Surely the idea didn't make sense.

Outside, there seemed to be people everywhere. Crime scene technicians in their white coats and gloves were moving back and forth from their mobile lab. Doona was sitting with Hugh, watching the scene. Bessie took a step towards her.

"Ah, Miss Cubbon, I'd like you to go home now," Anna Lambert said. "I'm going to have to interview Ms. Moore and that could take a while."

"I'll have to ring for a taxi," Bessie told her. "I don't know how long it will take for one to get here."

"I'll have someone take you home," Anna said. She looked around and then waved to a young constable in uniform. "Ah, Williamson, will you please drive Miss Cubbon home?" she asked. She spun on her heel and walked towards Doona without waiting for a reply.

"Aunt Bessie? How'd you get mixed up in this?" the young man asked Bessie.

Bessie shook her head. "I've absolutely no idea," she told him.

CHAPTER 3

Bessie followed the man to his police car. He held open the passenger door and helped her climb inside.

"I hope this is okay," he said. "I didn't want to put you in the back, like you were under arrest or anything."

Bessie laughed. "I'm quite happy up here with you," she assured the man.

He drove carefully along the road through the farm. Bessie listened to the police radio, but she couldn't really understand much of what was being said.

"What are they saying?" she finally asked as the young man turned onto the main road.

He listened for a moment and then translated the codes for her. "There's been a minor accident on the A2 at Church Hill. No injuries, but one of the cars needs to be towed."

The radio fell quiet for a moment. Bessie turned to her companion.

"Anyway, it's nice to see you again, Joe. Your mother told me you'd moved back to the island," she said. "I'm sure it seems quiet after your time in Liverpool."

The man nodded. "It was crazy over there," he said. "It started to get to me. It seemed like every time we arrested a guy, two more would come along to take his place. I loved it when I first started, but after a while I found I really just wanted to come home."

"The island often has that effect on people," Bessie replied.

"My wife loves it here, too," he told her. "She grew up in Liverpool, and after spending her whole life in a city, the island is a big change for her."

"I gather your mother is hoping for grandchildren now that you're back," Bessie remarked.

The man laughed. "Jen, my wife, is on Mum's side on that one. Jen's a hairdresser, and I keep encouraging her to start looking for work here, but she's dragging her feet. She wants to stay at home with the kids, if and when they start arriving."

"It's a good thing for the children, if you can afford it and it suits you," Bessie said. "But it's a very tough job, being home with small children all day."

"I suppose we'll have to see how it goes," Joe replied.

He pulled up outside Bessie's cottage and parked his car. "I'll just walk you to the door," he said.

"Do you have time to come in for a quick cuppa?" Bessie asked.

Joe glanced at his watch and then frowned. "Maybe a very quick one," he said. "Inspector Lambert shouldn't mind if I take a few minutes out."

Bessie opened the door to the cottage and stepped inside. In the small kitchen she switched the kettle on and then pulled out a box of biscuits.

"I'm sorry to say I haven't baked anything in the last few days," she told the man as he sat down at her small kitchen table. "I'm rushing about getting ready for Thanksgiving and I haven't had time."

"I thought Thanksgiving was an American holiday," Joe said.

"It is," Bessie replied. "But I grew up in America and Thanksgiving holds very fond memories for me."

"Really? Don't you just eat a turkey?"

"You do," Bessie agreed. "But if I remember correctly, it's the busiest travel time of the year. I reckon more people make the effort to be together at Thanksgiving than at Christmas. Our Christmases were mostly spent with our immediate family, but Thanksgiving was about getting together with every relative we could find."

"That's nice," Joe said. "Although I have a few relatives I wouldn't really want to see, even once a year."

Bessie laughed. "Every family has those," she told him. "We used to have dinner at my father's cousin's house. When everyone made it, there would be thirty or more people to feed. My mother took the pies every year. She'd bake every day for a week leading up the big day, and my sister and I weren't allowed to have any. The anticipation made those the best pies of the entire year."

"Are you going to be baking pies this year?"

Bessie shook her head. "I used to have the dinner here, and I used to do all of the cooking, but now I have too many friends and not enough space. I'm letting The Swing Bridge restaurant handle the food and the pies this year."

"They do great food," Joe said. "I took Jen there for a meal a few weeks ago. Everything was delicious."

"How is your sister?" Bessie asked as she poured the tea.

"Jane's fine," he said. "She's still in London, studying chemistry and engineering."

"Good for her," Bessie said. "She's so smart. I'm sure she'll do great things."

"She's much smarter than me, anyway," Joe laughed.

"I remember her staying here one night, a few years ago now, and she'd brought some school work with her. I couldn't understand the math problems, but she flew through them."

Bessie had never married or had children, but she enjoyed spending time with young people. Over the years, her cottage had become a favourite destination for teenagers who needed a break from their parents. Bessie had been used to welcoming overnight guests fairly regularly, but such visits had become increasingly rare lately, as she'd found herself mixed up in several murder investigations.

"Your cottage was always my favourite place to run away to," Joe told her. "Even when I wasn't fighting with my folks, I used to love coming here. It just feels so cosy and warm here."

Bessie smiled and then looked around the kitchen. Of course, cosy could be considered just another way of saying small, but her cottage had been home to her for all of her adult life and she loved it very much.

Before she could reply, Joe's mobile buzzed. He pulled it out of his pocket and then frowned at it.

"Yes, I'm just on my way back now," he said to his caller. He disconnected and frowned at Bessie. "Clearly the inspector noticed my absence after all," he said glumly.

"Surely you're entitled to a quick cuppa," Bessie replied, getting to her feet. "I'll just put a few biscuits into a bag for you to take with you."

The man quickly swallowed his tea and then took the offered bag from Bessie. "Thank you so much," he told her. "It was wonderful to see you again. I shall have to bring the wife over to meet you one day."

"I'd like that," Bessie told him. She stood in the doorway and watched him drive away. He'd always been a nice young man and she was pleased to see him back on the island, working hard and happily married.

She shut the door and then tided up the kitchen. It was nearly time for her evening meal, but after her restaurant lunch and recent biscuits, she wasn't especially hungry. Outside the sky was overcast, but it wasn't actually raining. A long walk in the fresh air was exactly what she needed, Bessie decided.

She had the beach to herself. The holiday cottages that were her nearest neighbours sat empty now, waiting for spring. Unable to help herself, Bessie found that she was looking inside each cabin as she walked along. Several of them looked as if they were getting ready to be painted, with covers on the furniture and drop cloths on the floors. Bessie wondered if Thomas Shimmin, the owner of the cottages, was doing the work himself or if he'd hired a local firm. She knew he'd had a very successful summer, with full occupancy and extra income from offering a shopping service and even some limited catering.

Beyond the cottages, Bessie strolled along the beach, watching the waves. It wasn't long before she came to the stairs that led to Thie yn Traie, the mansion that was perched on the cliff above. As far as she knew, the property was still on the market, and Bessie felt that it was a shame that no one had purchased it. She was hoping someone might buy it and live in it year-round, even though the original owners had built it as a summer home. Glancing up at the sprawling estate, Bessie shook her head. The longer it sat empty, the less likely it seemed that anyone would ever purchase it.

She continued on for a short while longer and then turned back towards home. She was just beginning to feel hungry and began to plan a light evening meal as she walked.

"Hullo, Bessie," a voice called as she approached the holiday rentals.

"Good afternoon," she said, smiling at Thomas Shimmin as he climbed down off the deck of one of the cottages and headed towards her. "How are you today?" she asked.

"Oh, I'm fine," he replied. "But what's this I hear about you finding another body? Maggie rang me and said it's the talk of the island."

Bessie squelched a sigh. Thomas's wife, Maggie, loved a bit of skeet. If she'd heard about the body on the Clague farm, there probably wasn't anyone else on the island who hadn't heard as well. "I didn't find anything," Bessie said firmly.

"Well, that isn't how Maggie heard it," Thomas said with a chuckle. "And you know as well as I do that Maggie is never wrong, at least not in her mind."

Bessie grinned. "Yes, well, she's wrong this time, but please don't tell her I said that."

Thomas nodded. "But something's happened," he said, suddenly serious. "Are you okay?"

"I'm fine," Bessie replied, touched by the genuine concern she could hear in his voice. "Fenella Faragher was moving some boxes around in one of their barns. Underneath one of the boxes was at least part of a skeleton."

Thomas winced. "Poor Fenella. That must have been upsetting for her."

"The police have to work out how long it's been there, of course, but the boxes were her mother's, so it might have been there for fifty or sixty years or more."

"Well, that's something," Thomas said. "If it's been there that long, I suppose no one is still missing whoever it is."

"It's still very sad. I don't suppose you have any idea who it might be?"

Thomas looked shocked. "How on earth would I know?" he asked.

Bessie couldn't help but smile at his reaction. "It was just a random thought," she said soothingly. "Like maybe you had a friend forty years ago who suddenly disappeared one day after telling you he was heading up to the Clague farm, something like that."

"I'm not sure I'd remember something like that if it did happen," Thomas told her.

"I suspect the police are going to be asking everyone to search their memories," Bessie told him. "Someone has to know who the person was."

"I'm glad that isn't a job for me," Thomas said stoutly. "I'll stick to painting and the like."

"I was wondering if you were going to do the painting yourself or hire someone," Bessie told him.

"Oh, Maggie would have a fit if I hired anyone," he replied. "These cottages were my idea and we spent pretty much every penny we had in savings to buy the land and build them. We had a good summer, but we'd have to have made at least double what we did before Maggie would even consider hiring anyone to do anything. They're our cottages and I did quit my job to look after them. Painting every winter is my responsibility."

"I do hope you're going to take time off to come to my Thanksgiving dinner," Bessie said.

"Oh, we wouldn't miss that," Thomas assured her. "We had such a nice time last year and the year before that. It's one of our favourite holidays now, even if it is an American one."

"Well, if I don't see you before, I suppose I'll see you at The Swing Bridge, then," Bessie said.

"Yes, indeed, although I'm sure you'll see me before. I plan to start painting tomorrow and it will probably take a couple of weeks to do the whole lot."

Thomas headed back to cover more furniture while Bessie continued on with her walk. She was nearly home now and as she reached her door she stopped to run her fingers over the sign on the side of the house. "Treoghe Bwaane," it read.

"Widow's Cottage," she murmured to herself. Of course she wasn't a widow, having never married, but when she'd found the cottage all those years ago when she'd first returned to the island, she'd felt as if she were. Matthew Saunders had swept her off her feet, and she'd been devastated when her parents insisted that she return to the island with them rather than let her stay in the US and marry Matthew. She was only seventeen; she wasn't really given any choice in the matter. Matthew had followed her a short while later, but illness had swept through the boat he was sailing on and he'd died just before his arrival in Liverpool.

Bessie smiled sadly as she remembered how she'd been convinced that her life was over when she'd heard. She'd not been able to forgive her parents, and thanks to a small legacy from Matthew, she'd bought herself her very own home. The legacy had provided just enough income, thanks to some very clever investing by her advocate, for Bessie to live frugally in her small cottage ever since. In the last few years, she'd been able to be less careful with her money and had mostly indulged herself with an ever-growing collection of books. While there were times when she wondered what her life might have been like if Matthew had survived, for the most part she was satisfied with the way her life had turned out. She loved her small home and she was content with living on her own.

Now she made herself a bowl of soup and ate that with a few pieces of toast and a cup of tea. By the time she'd taken care of the washing up, it was quite dark outside, so rather than think about another walk, Bessie curled up with an old Sherlock Holmes novel that she hadn't read for many years. Holmes was just explaining things to Watson when someone knocked on her door. Bessie slid a bookmark into the book and walked to the door.

She'd never worried about opening her door at any time, day or night, until rather recently. Now she stood and stared at it, wishing that there were a window in the door.

"Of course, if there was, whoever it was would see you standing here, talking to yourself," she muttered to herself. Taking a deep breath, she pulled the door open.

"Inspector Rockwell, how lovely to see you," she said, smiling delightedly at her visitor.

The man on the doorstep smiled back. "Surely, after all this time, you can call me John?" he asked as she ushered him inside.

Bessie grinned. "Sometimes you look more official than others," she told him. "Tonight you look quite inspectorial, if that's a word."

"I've just come from an entire day of meetings," John replied. "I almost stopped home to change, but I wanted to see you and I was afraid that if I did stop at home I might not want to go back out again."

Bessie smiled. John was a very handsome man in his early forties. He had brown hair and stunning green eyes that Bessie was certain were natural. He'd lost weight recently, as he worked his way through his relationship troubles, but Bessie was pleased to see him looking more like his old self tonight. The expensive suit he was wearing fit him well, although Bessie fancied that she could see tension in shoulders and his eyes were tired.

"You should have gone home and changed and gone to bed," Bessie scolded the man. "You look tired."

"Moving is hard work," John replied. "And the kids are coming next weekend, so I've been cleaning a lot as I go, not to mention shopping."

Bessie nodded. John was in the middle of moving from a small rental property into a renovated home in the same neighbourhood. Sue, his wife, had taken most of their furniture back to Manchester, where she'd moved with the pair's two children after she'd filed for divorce. Now John was trying to furnish his new home as inexpensively as possible on his far from generous police salary.

"I'm so glad that Thomas and Amy are going to be able to join us for Thanksgiving," Bessie said. "It's always nice to have children there."

"I'm not sure you'll want Amy at the moment," John said with a catch in his voice.

"What's wrong with Amy?"

"She's taking the divorce badly," John explained. "And she seems to think it's all my fault, even though her mother is the one who, ah, never mind."

"Children can't possibly understand all of the things that go into a marriage or why marriages fail," Bessie said.

"And I can't exactly tell my daughter that her mother never really loved me, she just married me because the man she did love didn't want to marry her," John added.

"Perhaps you can tell her, one day, when she's much older," Bessie said.

"If I survive her teens, you mean."

"I thought she was only twelve," Bessie said.

"She'll be thirteen in February," John replied. "But she's definitely behaving like a teenager. Worse, actually, Thomas is nearly fifteen and nowhere near as much trouble."

"I'm sure she misses you," Bessie suggested.

"I miss them both terribly," John replied. "But my career is here now and I can't afford to get that wrong."

"And they'll be here for Thanksgiving," Bessie said.

"They will. I just hope they're both on their best behaviour."

Bessie laughed. "We used to have thirty or more for dinner every year when I was a child," she told him. "There was always a fight, someone always had too much to drink, and at least one of the teens always shouted that they hated everyone at some point in the day."

John grinned. "That sounds like a family occasion."

"But you didn't come to talk to me about Thanksgiving," Bessie guessed. "What can I really do for you?"

"I spent half an hour with Anna hearing about what she found on the Clague farm. I was hoping you might be able to fill in some background before tomorrow."

"Are you taking over the case?" Bessie asked, holding her breath while she waited for his reply.

John hesitated and then shrugged. "Let's say Anna and I are sharing the responsibility for this one," he said. "While she's meant to be doing much of the paperwork associated with running the station, she does want to keep her hand in in terms of investigative work as well."

Bessie frowned, but nodded. "I suppose that makes sense," she said. "But let me make some tea and then we can talk about everything."

While Bessie refilled the kettle and switched it on, she had a sudden thought. "I haven't heard anything from Doona," she said. "I'm surprised she didn't ring me once she left the farm."

"She's at the station," John told her. "Anna asked her to go in and start digging out missing person reports."

"But it's her day off," Bessie argued.

"I'm sure she'll get paid for any overtime," John replied. "Obviously, we're anxious to get the remains identified as quickly as possible."

"Of course," Bessie agreed. She poured the tea and set a plate of biscuits down in front of her guest.

"Ah, this is a treat. I didn't have time to eat this evening."

Bessie pulled the plate away from him. "Then you need something a good deal more substantial than biscuits," she said.

John tried to protest, but Bessie ignored him as she dug through her cupboards and refrigerator. "I have some chicken breasts, if you'd like me to make one quickly. Everything else will take too long, I think. Otherwise, I can do some tinned soup and toast."

"Soup would be fine," John replied. "It's perfect for a cold and damp night."

Bessie opened a tin and poured the contents into a pan. She set the pan on the heat and then pulled down a toast rack. When the bread was in the toaster, she turned back to John.

"So, what can I tell you about the Clague family?" she asked.

"Anything and everything, really," John told her. "I've never actually met any of them. That's my first job tomorrow. I'm going to drive up to the farm in the morning and talk with Mr. and Mrs. Faragher."

"Is Eoin back?" Bessie asked. "Fenella said he was across for some medical tests or something."

"He flew back late this afternoon, which was as scheduled. Fenella insisted that we not tell him anything about what was happening over here until he returned, which, considering the age of the remains, seemed a reasonable request. Anna stayed at the farm to have a quick chat with him when he got home, but according to her, he was simply shocked and confused by the news. Our first job is figuring out how long the remains have been there, of course."

Bessie nodded. "The farm has been in the family for hundreds of years," she said. "When I moved back to the island, Niall Clague and his wife Marion had just taken over the farm. I remember when Fenella was born. Marion was very poorly after and I'm not sure she ever properly recovered. She passed away a few years later and left poor Niall to bring up Fenella on his own."

John nodded. "This is exactly what I need," he told her. "The more background you can provide, the better."

Bessie slid slices of toast into the toast rack and set it on the table next to John. She added the butter dish and a jar of strawberry jam to the table and then poured hot soup into a bowl. John was already halfway through his first piece of toast when Bessie set the bowl in front of him.

"Go on," he encouraged her after he'd swallowed a bite.

"I didn't see them more than once or twice a year," Bessie said. "Like most of the farmers, they kept to themselves, really. Fenella went to school here in Laxey, but I suspect she missed as many days as she attended. Book learning wasn't really a priority for farmers' wives in those days."

"When did Eoin arrive in the area?" John asked.

"He grew up on a nearby farm," Bessie said. She frowned as she struggled to remember. "His father was the livestock manager for the

Kelly farm, which was just to the north of the Clagues. I think he retired back across when Matthew Kelly sold the farm. He didn't like the new owners or they didn't like him, one or the other."

"But Eoin stayed here?"

"Oh, yes, he and Fenella were married by then. They started seeing one another almost as soon as Fenella turned eighteen, and were married by the time she was twenty."

"No children?"

"No, they were never blessed with children," Bessie said. "I'm sure Fenella wanted them, but it just never happened."

"I know Fenella was an only child; what about Eoin?"

"He has a brother, Nicholas. I actually asked Fenella about him today. Apparently he's happily settled across with a wife and some children."

"Just the one brother?"

"Just the one," Bessie confirmed. "I didn't know the families well, but I knew them well enough to know they didn't have any more children than that."

"No chance either family was hiding a mentally ill relative in a disused barn?"

Bessie shook her head. "First of all, they couldn't have kept such a thing secret, and besides, there is no such thing as a disused barn on Manx farms. The one where the body was found was being used for storage, even back then. It was used for farm machinery for many years, until Marion passed. Then Niall packed up all of her things and moved them to the barn."

"What year was that?"

"Nineteen-forty, I believe," Bessie replied. "You'll have to check the records, but it was around then. Fenella was two or three, so I think that's about right."

"So who have we found?" John asked.

Bessie stared at him. "Is that a serious question?" she asked. "Because if it is, I have no idea."

John frowned. "It was a serious question," he told her. "The last time we found a skeleton, you were able to put a name to it almost immediately."

"In that context, it seemed the most likely answer," Bessie said. "But for this, I have no idea. I don't remember anyone going missing from up there. They've had any number of farmhands over the years, of course, but I don't recall any disappearing suddenly."

"What about anyone who might have caused trouble?" John asked. "Maybe someone who was caught stealing something or mistreating the animals?"

Bessie shook her head. "Oh, whenever I was there Niall or Eoin would often have a good moan about the quality of the help they could get," she said, thinking back. "The farmhands never worked hard enough or fast enough to make them happy. But I certainly don't recall any serious problems with any of them. I'm going to give it some thought, though, that's for sure."

"It sounds like you weren't already considering that possibility," John said, his tone curious.

"It was the watch," Bessie replied. "I just glanced at it, but it looked as if it might have been valuable. Farmhands don't own such things."

"Maybe the dead man stole it," John suggested.

"Then why bury it with him?" Bessie asked.

"Why bury him with it anyway?" John retorted. "Assuming someone killed the man, why not take the watch?"

"Perhaps it was too distinctive," Bessie suggested. "Maybe the watch will be the key to identifying the remains."

"I certainly hope so," John told her.

"You're talking about the remains as male; does that mean you're sure it was a man?"

"As sure as we can be at this point. The coroner's preliminary examination of the remains suggests a young male, somewhere between eighteen and thirty, but that could change after a more thorough exam. It took most the day to carefully dig up what's there. He barely got a look at it before we called it a night."

"Has Doona had any luck with the missing person reports?"

"Not so far," John told her. "She's found several that might be relevant, but it was a long time ago and the records aren't exactly complete. We'll have a few constables ringing all over the island and across in the next few days trying to track people down, but we have to hope the watch will help."

"What about clothing?"

"Nothing significant was left," John told her. He opened his mouth to say something else, but Bessie held up a hand.

"I think I'd rather not know," she said.

John nodded. "If there were anything to tell you, I would, but you don't need all of the details that amount to nothing."

John had finished his soup, and now Bessie cleared away the bowl and replaced it with the plate of biscuits. John grinned at her and took several. She handed him a small plate to put them on.

"Did you have any more questions for me?" Bessie asked.

"Oh, several," John replied. "Tell me about Niall, to start with."

Bessie frowned. "He lives in a care home in Douglas now," she told him. "He suffers from dementia of some sort. I'm not sure of the exact diagnosis, but he's been there for many years now."

"So interviewing him about the body might not be very helpful," John said with a sigh.

"Even if he told you something, I don't think you could trust it to be true," Bessie said sadly. "I went to visit him over the summer and he didn't have any idea who I was. He, well, it's just very sad."

"I think I'll leave him for Anna, then," John said. He looked at Bessie and then winked. Bessie hid a smile behind a chocolate biscuit. Perhaps John was finding Anna as difficult to work with as Doona was.

"So what else can I tell you?" Bessie asked.

John glanced at the clock and shook his head. "I don't want to keep you all night," he said. "Until we can get a better idea of when our victim died, I'm not sure there's much else you can tell me. I'm sure I'll need a lot more background after that."

"You know where to find me," Bessie said with a grin.

"I do," John agreed. He stood up and then sat back down. "How's Doona?" he asked.

"Surely you saw her today," Bessie replied in confusion.

"I did, but at work, when we were both focussed on other things. I was just wondering how she's dealing with everything that happened last month."

"I think she's getting through it all," Bessie said slowly. "I'm sure she'll feel better when all of the legal issues are sorted, of course."

"And she might end up being quite wealthy," John added.

"She's engaged a solicitor across," Bessie told him. "He's coming over to meet with her on Friday to discuss things."

"I wish she'd told me the truth about her divorce," John said.

"That makes two of us," Bessie replied. "But I know she did it to avoid talking and thinking about it rather than to mislead anyone."

John nodded and then shrugged. "We're, well, things are a bit awkward between us at the moment, but I'm glad she's okay. Please let me know if she needs anything."

Bessie bit back a dozen replies and settled for simply nodding. John stood up and walked to the door. As Bessie joined him to let him out, she had a thought.

"I still have that painting," she reminded him. A few months earlier she'd been given a painting of Laxey Beach that she adored. She hadn't wanted to accept the gift, as the painting was expensive and the giver wasn't someone she wanted to feel indebted to. Now the man who'd given her the painting was on the run from the police and Bessie really didn't feel right keeping it.

"Ah, I forgot to tell you," John said. "There is going to be an auction at the weekend. It will be well advertised now that we've received clearance to hold it. Many of Grant Robertson's things are going to be auctioned off and all of the proceeds are going into a fund to reimburse the people he stole from over the years."

"What a good idea," Bessie said.

"Yes, well, it took some considerable time to get it organised, but it's set for Saturday, I think."

"The painting should be included," Bessie said.

"The painting was given to you before witnesses," John countered. "It's legally yours."

"It was purchased with stolen money," Bessie told him. "I don't feel right keeping it under the circumstances. I'll probably come to the auction and bid on it, though, as I do love it."

John shook his head. "Just keep it," he urged her.

"I can't," Bessie said softly. "It simply isn't right."

Before John could argue further, Bessie went upstairs and got the painting from where she'd stored it in a spare bedroom. It was still wrapped up, as it had been when Grant had given it to her.

"Here, I'll sleep better tonight with it out of my house," she told John.

John took the bulky package from her. "Maybe I'll buy it for you," he said.

"You just bought a house," Bessie replied. "I think you have enough expenses without adding to them on my behalf. I'll talk to my bank manager and see how much I can afford to spoil myself with before I go."

"I'll probably be back tomorrow," John told her. "After I talk to Eoin and Fenella, I'm sure to have many more questions."

"I should be home most of the day," Bessie replied. "I don't have any plans for tomorrow."

"Lucky you," John said lightly.

Bessie shut the door behind him and checked that it and the back-door were locked tightly. She washed up the dishes and then switched off the lights, taking a moment to turn off the ringer on her phone as well. She'd decided a few years earlier that she was too old to be racing down the stairs in the middle of the night for a wrong number. It was one of her very few concessions to her age.

Upstairs she got ready for bed and then propped herself on pillows and read for a short while. When she switched off the lights and slid down under the duvet she found her mind racing. How did someone come to be buried on the old Clague farm, seemingly unnoticed for so many years? She felt a curious mixture of dread and excitement as she finally fell asleep.

CHAPTER 4

Bessie took a very long walk the next morning, trying to clear her head. For the first time in a very long time, she'd actually overslept. The shock of seeing her clock showing seven instead of her usual six stayed with her in the shower and as she dressed. She only began to feel like herself again as she patted on the rose-scented dusting powder that reminded her of Matthew Saunders. After a quick breakfast, she took herself for a long walk on the beach, not turning back until she was well past Thie yn Traie.

As she passed the holiday cottages on her way back, she waved to Thomas, who was just arriving as she was heading home. He returned the gesture. Bessie's heart sank a bit when she realised that his wife was with him. She kept walking, pretending she hadn't noticed Maggie, but she knew her efforts were futile.

"Bessie, there you are," Maggie shouted across the beach.

Sighing, Bessie stopped and turned to face the woman who was rapidly approaching. "Good morning, Maggie. How are you?" she asked.

"I'm fine, but I'm ever so worried about you again," Maggie said. "What's happened now?"

"I'm sure you know as much as I do," Bessie replied.

"Oh, no, you were there, on the scene. It must have been terrifying, like something out of a horror film. I can just picture it. Hidden for decades behind broken furniture in the dark and dusty barn, a skeletal hand reaches desperately out of its shallow grave, imploring someone to find him and bring the evil soul who put him there to justice."

Bessie rolled her eyes. "It was nothing like that," she told Maggie. "The barn is well-lit and the furniture they store in it is in good condition. The hand wasn't reaching anywhere, it was just lying on the ground, and it wasn't the least bit scary, just somewhat sad."

"But who could it be?" Maggie asked.

"I haven't the slightest idea," Bessie told her.

"But you must know," Maggie said emphatically. "I'm much younger than Fenella, of course, but you knew Marion Clague. I heard that the body was under her things that Niall put there when she died."

Bessie knew that Maggie was less than ten years younger than Fenella, but she let the remark go. "I don't believe the police have established a date for the remains yet," Bessie said. "They could have been there since the barn was first built, or they could have been put there rather more recently. Until they can get an idea on the date, it's rather pointless to try to guess who they've found."

"I wondered about Eoin's brother," Maggie said in a whisper.

Bessie glanced around the beach. There was no one else in sight. "Fenella tells me that he's happily settled in Derbyshire with a family."

"Ah, but has anyone seen him lately?" Maggie asked. "If Eoin killed him and hid the body, they'd probably tell everyone that he was across, right?"

"Why would Eoin kill his brother?" Bessie had to ask.

Maggie shrugged. "Why does anyone kill anyone?" she replied "I'm sure he had a reason at the time."

"I really don't think the body is Nicholas," Bessie said. "But I'm sure the police will be investigating every possibility."

"I did think it might be Harvey Snow," Maggie said.

Bessie stared at her for a moment, trying to think. "Harvey Snow?" she said eventually. "I don't think I know who you mean."

Maggie nodded. "I'm probably the only person who remembers him," she said. "He and his father moved to the island when I was sixteen. He was a year older and he went to school with me for a little while. Then he decided to move back to live with his mum instead. He promised he'd write, but I never heard from him. I told my mum at the time that something terrible must have happened to him, because otherwise I know he would have written to me."

"Well, you should definitely let the police know about him," Bessie said. "You should let the police know about anyone you think of that might be a possibility."

"I just hate talking to them," Maggie told her. "That Inspector Rockwell is quite intimidating, really."

"You should ask to speak to Anna Lambert," Bessie said. "I'm sure it would easier, talking to a female inspector, wouldn't it?"

Maggie nodded. "Harvey and I had a little romance," she told Bessie. "Another woman would understand why I'm so sure something awful happened to him. He really cared about me, you know."

"I'm sure he did," Bessie replied. "Whatever happened to him, I'm sure Anna can find out, assuming they haven't identified the body yet, that is."

"I'll go and see her now," Maggie said with determination. "Before I change my mind."

"I hope it isn't him," Bessie said. "I'm sure you'd be sad, even after all these years."

Maggie shook her head. "At least, if it is him, I'll know why he never wrote," she told Bessie. "I quite fancy the idea that he would have written if he could have."

Bessie nodded uncertainly and then continued on her way home. She was almost feeling sorry for Anna Lambert by the time she reached her cottage. No doubt Maggie wouldn't be the only person visiting the police with a suggestion about the identity of the body. It was likely that Harvey Snow would be able to be quickly eliminated, though. Bessie was pretty sure the man had simply never bothered to write.

Back at home, Bessie checked for phone messages. There were a great many, and they were all concerned with the remains on the Clague farm. Bessie listed the callers and then crossed out several that she simply couldn't be bothered to ring back. Although she hadn't rung and left a message, Bessie decided to ring Doona first.

With a cup of tea on the table, Bessie sat down and rang the front desk at the Laxey police station.

"Laxey Neighbourhood Policing, this is Joan. How can I help you?"

Bessie was so surprised that she nearly didn't reply. "Oh, I was expecting Doona Moore to answer," she said after a moment.

"Doona's on another line. Is there something I can help you with?" Joan asked in a cheery voice.

"No, I really just wanted to have a quick word with Doona," Bessie replied. "Can you let her know that Elizabeth Cubbon rang, please?"

"I'll tell her, but I wouldn't expect her to get back to you any time soon," the woman said. "We're quite busy at the moment."

"There's no rush," Bessie told the woman, even though she didn't really mean it. She wanted to speak to Doona as soon as possible, but it seemed like it might be a while before that happened.

Bessie put the phone down and frowned at her tea. "I'm sure there are lots of people ringing in with ideas about the remains," she said to the cup. "But who is Joan and why is she answering the phone?"

When the tea didn't reply, Bessie sighed and then picked up the phone again.

"Good morning, Breesha," she greeted her advocate's secretary when her call was answered. "It's Bessie Cubbon. Is there any chance Doncan has a minute?"

"I'll just put you through after I thank you for the kind invitation to Thanksgiving dinner," Breesha replied. "It's one of the highlights of my social calendar every year, you know."

Bessie laughed. "It's kind of you to say so," she replied. "Would you like to bring a guest?"

"Ah, no, but thank you for asking," Breesha replied. "I'm quite happy on my own. Now let me put you through to Doncan."

"Ah, Bessie, how are you, my dear?" Doncan Quayle, Bessie's advocate, asked when they were connected.

"I'm fine," Bessie said. "Thank you for ringing to check on me, though."

"I do hope yesterday's events weren't too traumatic for you," Doncan said. "I know you're a strong woman, but I do worry about you."

"I'd hate to think that I'm getting used to finding dead bodies, but yesterday wasn't nearly as awful as some of the things I've gone through lately," Bessie replied.

"Yes, well, if you need anything, don't hesitate to ask," he told her.

Bessie smiled. The man had handled her legal and financial affairs for many years and in that time she liked to think that they'd become friends. "You and Jane are coming for Thanksgiving dinner, right?" she asked now.

"We're planning on it," the man replied. "It was kind of you to include young Doncan as well. He said you suggested that he might bring a guest as well."

Bessie laughed. "I'm sure there are plenty of young women who would love to accompany him for the occasion," she said. "And I'm sure he'll enjoy it more with a friend than on his own."

"Well, we're all looking forward to it," Doncan replied.

"I don't suppose you have any ideas on the identity of the dead man?" Bessie asked.

There was a long pause before the man spoke again. "Really, I don't," he said. "I've been thinking about it since yesterday. There seem to be almost too many possibilities, but none of them seem likely, really. People do come and go from the island a great deal, but it seems odd that no one missed this man."

Bessie nodded and then caught herself. "Yes, that's exactly it," she replied. "I don't envy the police their job."

"I never do," Doncan told her. "I understand that the watch they found with the body is quite distinctive. I heard that the Chief Constable has agreed to put it on the front page of the local paper today to see if anyone recognises it."

"I hope they find out who he is soon," Bessie said. "And what happened to him."

After making herself another cup of tea, she picked up the phone again and read down the list of people she needed to ring back. She didn't really feel like talking to any of them. The sun was shining outside the window and Bessie thought seriously about taking another walk. A glance at her calendar reminded her that there was a lecture at the Manx Museum that afternoon that she had been thinking about attending.

William Corlett, a young researcher who was one of the driving forces behind the creation of a new Manx History Institute, was speaking about fifteenth-century pottery finds on the island. Her own fascination with the island's history tended to focus on the eighteenth and nineteenth centuries, but she enjoyed learning everything she could about the island she called home.

More to avoid returning any more phone calls than anything else, Bessie rang and requested a taxi. The driver took her into Douglas and left her in front of one of her favourite restaurants. She ate lunch with a book for company and then headed up to the Manx Museum to hear what William had to say.

Some parts of the lecture were fairly incomprehensible to Bessie, who knew very little about pottery, but she enjoyed hearing where the various pieces that had been found around the island came from. When the talk was over, she found herself having tea and biscuits with a large group of friends from Manx National Heritage, the organisation responsible for preserving, protecting and promoting the island's unique history and culture.

"Bessie, thank you for coming," William said when they came face-to-face in the crowd.

"I enjoyed it very much," Bessie told him. "Although some of it went over my head, of course."

"I tried to make it as clear as possible," William said with a frown. "Perhaps, if you have a few minutes, we could go through the talk together and you could point out what you didn't understand. I'm hoping to get this talk published and I would like it to be interesting and enjoyable for readers of all backgrounds."

Bessie nodded. "Why don't you give me a printed copy and I'll make some notes for you," she suggested.

"I'll do that," he agreed. "And thank you very much."

"It's no problem," Bessie assured him.

"If it isn't a bother, I'll bring the copy to Thanksgiving dinner," he said. "And thank you so much for inviting me, by the way."

"It's no bother at all," Bessie replied. "As long as you don't expect me to read it during the meal."

William laughed. "I'd be hugely grateful if you could get your comments to me early in the new year," he said. "And I feel rather demanding asking for that."

"I should be able to have it back to you before Christmas," Bessie said. "I've very little else going on right now."

"Except Thanksgiving," William replied.

"Except that," Bessie agreed. "Are you bringing a guest? I can't remember what you said when you replied."

"I probably said that I was bringing a guest," he told her. "But now I'm not so sure."

Bessie waved a hand. "Don't worry about it," she said. "One person either way won't make a difference."

William didn't get a chance to reply before someone shouted his name. He gave Bessie a quick hug and headed off to talk to the man. Bessie picked up another biscuit and turned to see who else she knew.

"Marjorie, what a great turnout," she said to the Museum's librarian and archivist. Marjorie Stevens was a wonderful resource for Bessie's research. The woman also taught the Manx language classes that Bessie had taken several times.

"I'm pleasantly surprised at how many people are here," Marjorie replied. "It is a Tuesday afternoon in November. I thought we'd be lucky to have a dozen people turn up."

"I suppose William is very popular," Bessie said.

"He's a very talented researcher and the Manx History Institute is going to be a wonderful resource once it gets up and running properly," Marjorie told her.

"How are things in the library?" Bessie asked.

"Fine, although I'm missing you," Marjorie told her. "It was so nice, when you were living in Douglas, having you around so regularly. Now that you're back in Laxey, no one is indexing my boxes."

"I'm sorry," Bessie said. "I have really been neglecting my research, haven't I? I'll try to do better after Thanksgiving."

Bessie had left school at seventeen, content with her American high school diploma, but she'd learned a great deal about historical research after years of working at the museum library on various projects. She worked mostly with old wills and Marjorie was always grateful when Bessie was willing to go through one of the old boxes of papers that the museum had received over the years. Bessie indexed the contents and enjoyed the excitement of finding old and interesting documents that had been long forgotten.

"Thanksgiving," Marjorie exclaimed. "I don't think I ever thanked you for inviting me to your dinner," she said. "I'd love to come, if it isn't too late to let you know."

"Of course it isn't," Bessie replied. "And I'm delighted you can make it. Did you want to bring a guest?"

Marjorie shook her head. "I'll be quite happy on my own," she assured Bessie. "Kyst t'ou?"

Bessie laughed. Marjorie never let her get away without at least saying a few words in Manx. "Ta mee braew," Bessie answered her.

Marjorie patted her arm. "You'll be fluent in no time," she told Bessie.

Bessie just laughed again and then headed for the stairs. She'd spoken to just about everyone she knew. Mark Blake, the director of special projects, caught her just before she reached the first step.

"Bessie, thank you for the invitation. I'd love to come to your dinner," he told her.

"Excellent," Bessie said with a broad smile. "Will you be bringing a guest?"

Mark shrugged. "My brother might be visiting that weekend," he said. "I may have to bring him so that he doesn't complain about being abandoned when he went to all the trouble to come across. If that's okay, that is."

"It's fine," Bessie said with a laugh. "I'd hate for him to feel left out, especially after coming such a long way."

At the entrance to the museum, Bessie stopped to chat with Henry Costain, who'd worked for Manx National Heritage since he'd left school. That had been a great many years ago, and Bessie knew he had built up an extensive knowledge of the various sites on the island in those years.

"Bessie, that's a terrible business out at the old Clague farm, isn't it?" Henry asked.

"It is, yes," Bessie agreed.

"I was starting to worry a while back that I was bad luck, you know," he told her. "I was finding dead bodies all around the place, but it turns out it isn't me. I don't seem to find any when I'm not with you."

Bessie forced herself to smile at the words, knowing Henry didn't mean to upset her. "This one has been dead for a very long time," she said.

"Aye, I've been trying to work out who it might be," Henry replied. "I can probably list half a dozen old school mates of mine who disappeared at one time or another over the years. I expect their families will know where they are though, won't they?"

Bessie shrugged. "I would hope so," she said. "I'm hoping the police sort it all out quickly. I understand he was found with a distinctive watch. It's going to be in the paper this afternoon, I gather."

Henry nodded. "Aye, ours was just delivered and it's right on the front page."

He held out the paper and Bessie quickly spread it out on the desk. The photograph of the watch took up a quarter of the page, with an appeal underneath it for information. Bessie studied it for a long time.

"Do you recognise it?" Henry asked.

"There's something familiar about it," Bessie said slowly. "I'm sure I've seen it before, but I can't think where."

"Well, let's hope someone else can remember more than you can," Henry said. "And speaking of remembering, I'd love to come to the Thanksgiving party. Thank you for asking." He stopped and looked down at the desk, his face turning red. "I'll be, that is, you said in the invitation, I mean, if it's okay, I'll be bringing a friend."

Bessie grinned. "Of course you may bring someone," she said, forcing herself to keep her curiosity in check. "I'll look forward to seeing you then."

"Thanks," he said, still not looking at her.

That conversation gave her something to think about in the taxi on the way back to Laxey. Henry seemed both excited and nervous about bringing his friend. As far she knew, he'd never had a steady girlfriend. Bessie couldn't wait to see who accompanied him to her event.

There were another dozen messages on her machine when she got back, and Bessie listened to them as she made herself a light snack that would substitute for her evening meal after the large lunch she'd enjoyed in Douglas. Most were repeats of earlier calls, but she was happy to hear Doona's voice as well.

"I'm home," Doona said. "Ring me when you get in."

Bessie was quick to place the call. Doona had sounded tired and stressed, which just added to Bessie's eagerness to speak to her.

"How are you?" she asked as soon as Doona answered.

"I'm fine," was the automatic reply.

"It's me, Bessie. How are you really?"

Doona chuckled. "I'm fine, really," she said firmly. "I ended up working quite late last night and today was total madness at the station, so I'm quite tired, but otherwise, I'm fine."

"I rang and someone called Joan answered," Bessie told her.

"She told me you'd rung," Doona replied. "She's on loan from Castletown at the moment as they were the only station that could spare anyone."

"She seemed nice enough on the phone," Bessie said.

"She's very nice, but irritatingly cheery all the time," Doona told her. "Not that I got to talk to her much. I was pretty much tied to my phone all day."

"I gather everyone in Laxey has a guess as to who was found at the Clague farm," Bessie said.

"Everyone in Laxey, Lonan, Ramsey and just about every other place on the island," Doona replied. "It was crazy this morning, and then after the paper came out, the phone lines just exploded. Joan and I couldn't keep up, and it was a huge relief when five o'clock rolled around and I got to come home."

"So people recognised the watch?" Bessie asked.

"People seem to think they've recognised the watch," Doona replied. "But I did get given different names by different people."

Bessie sighed. "It does look very familiar," she said. "I'm certain I've seen it somewhere before. I'm sure if I hear the right name it will all come back to me."

"I can bring you a list," Doona said. "I was given maybe a dozen names and I suspect Joan probably has a similar list as well. We're just handing everything over to Hugh, who's coordinating the efforts, but I bet he'd be happy to have you look through the names."

"Maybe there will be some duplicates when he compares the lists and he'll be able to start narrowing it down."

"Maybe," Doona sighed. "By the end of the day I'd just about forgotten my own name, let alone any and all of the ones people had been suggesting to me. At least I only have to talk to the people who ring, Hugh has to follow up on their suggestions."

"Poor Grace, he'll never find time to see her," Bessie said.

"She brought him lunch today," Doona said. "It was very sweet, really. She brought him a bunch of sandwiches and a cold drink, and she brought a huge box of chocolate biscuits for everyone in the station to share."

"She's a lovely girl," Bessie said happily. "I hope he realises how lucky he is to have found her."

"If he doesn't, she won't have any shortage of volunteers to take his place,' Doona remarked. "All of the other young constables were very impressed with her."

Bessie laughed. "I wish he'd just propose and get it over with."

"I think Grace would agree with you on that," Doona replied.

"Is there anything you can tell me about the case?" Bessie had to ask.

"If you've seen the evening paper, you know just about everything I know," Doona replied. "Everyone seems to think the watch is the key, but after all of the calls I took today, I'm not so sure."

"Do they know how old it is?" Bessie asked. "Surely that will help with figuring out when the man died."

"John is working on tracking that down," Doona told her. "At this point, he seems to think that the watch may be even older than the remains."

"How is John doing?" Bessie asked.

"I was going to ask you that," Doona countered. "I gather he came to see you last night."

"He did," Bessie agreed. "We had a nice chat, but mostly we talked about the dead man, rather than anything else."

"He doesn't really talk to me at the moment," Doona said.

Bessie heard the catch in her friend's voice. "He's coping with a lot right now," she said. "Moving house and the divorce are huge life changes."

"And he's angry that I told him I was divorced when I wasn't," Doona added.

Bessie sighed. "I don't want to be in the middle of this," she said firmly. "But at the same time, if you feel as if you need to talk to John and want to do it on neutral territory, you're welcome to arrange to meet him here. You could take a walk on the beach and talk it all out. You'd have the beach to yourselves this time of year."

"It's complicated," Doona said. "I like John so much. He's a wonderful boss and a great person. I hate knowing that he thinks I lied to him, but I didn't mean to lie. It was all just too difficult to explain and I assumed that the divorce was going to go through soon anyway, so I didn't think it mattered."

"At this point it might be better to wait until the Clague case has settled down before you try to speak to him," Bessie suggested. "I'm sure it's adding a lot of stress to his life."

"It's adding a lot of stress to everyone's lives," Doona countered.

They chatted for a few minutes more before Bessie let her friend go. "Get some sleep," she counseled. "Tomorrow is going to be another busy day, I'm sure."

She was just debating what to do with her evening when someone knocked on her door.

"John, do come in," she invited. "I can't remember the last time you visited me two nights in a row."

"I can't either, but it was probably in the middle of a murder investigation," John replied.

"That's a rather unfortunate comment on our friendship," Bessie said tartly.

John flushed. "I love coming to visit you," he told Bessie. "But it's difficult to find the time. During murder investigations, I can visit you and convince myself that it's work, not play."

Bessie shrugged. "I'm not sure that's much better, but let's not argue," she said. "You look tired."

"I feel as if I've spent the day chasing ghosts," he told her. "Although a great many of the ghosts turned out to be quite alive and well."

"Does that include Maggie Shimmin's old friend Harvey Snow?" Bessie had to ask.

John laughed. "He wasn't hard to track down, as he was still living at the address he'd given Maggie when he left. Unfortunately for her, he has absolutely no recollection of her, but I didn't tell her that, of course."

Bessie laughed. "Better she not know," she agreed.

"Anyway, I don't want to stay long. I'm exhausted, and I'm sure you have better things to do as well, but I wanted to show you a list of names and see if any of them rings a bell."

"Is this the list of people who might have owned the watch?" Bessie asked. "Doona said she had about a dozen names suggested to her. I'm sure I've seen that watch somewhere before, but I'm not sure I'll be able to pick out the right name."

"There are only ten names on my list," John told her. "Some are possible watch owners and others are just men that might have gone missing in the last sixty or so years. There were some duplicates on the lists that Doona and Joan took, and Hugh was able to track down some of the men quite quickly. I dug a little deeper to find a few more. What I'm left with is a list of ten names of men who may have once owned a watch like that and who can't be easily located."

"I can't be sure I'll pick the right name," Bessie said.

"If you aren't sure, that's fine," John assured her. "I'll settle for you selecting a handful that seem like they might be possibilities. There are only so many hours in a day and I hate chasing around in the dark. If you think three or four of these men might be the one you remember as owning that watch, I'll dig deeper into them first. If none of them matches up, we'll go back to the list."

Bessie nodded. "I'll do my best," she said.

John pulled out the list and Bessie read the first name. "My goodness," she exclaimed. "I haven't thought about Richard Staunton in fifty years."

"Is he a possibility?" John asked.

"Oh, goodness, I don't think so," Bessie replied. "He moved to Cumbria and started a bed and breakfast. You could try looking there for him. He may have moved a dozen times since then, of course."

John made a note and then smiled at Bessie. "I should have rung you every time we got a call," he said. "I'll bet you could have eliminated most of the names for me without any effort at all."

Bessie read the next name and shook her head. "He moved to America," she said definitely. "He actually went and stayed with my cousins there for a short time in the sixties before heading out west to look for gold. I seem to recall that he passed away somewhere in Oregon, but I'm not positive."

They worked their way down the list methodically. Bessie was able to give John suggestions for places to look for several others on the list, although there were a few that she wasn't sure about and one that she didn't remember at all. The last name on the list had her catching her breath.

"Jacob Conover," she said softly. "He's the man who owned that watch."

CHAPTER 5

"Are you sure?" John asked, his voice tense.

"I'm positive," Bessie replied. "I can't believe I didn't remember his name, now that I think about it. People used to tease him for being a 'comeover' named Conover."

"What about the watch?"

Bessie sat back in her chair and tried to remember events from forty or more years earlier. "It was his father's," she said eventually. "I remember he was very proud of it. His father gave it to him on his eighteenth birthday, if I'm remembering correctly."

"Maybe you could just start at the beginning and tell me all about him," John suggested.

"I think I need a cuppa," she said. While Bessie bustled around her kitchen, she cast her mind back and tried to remember everything that she could about Jacob Conover. She was hoping to have everything in a nice neat order for John when she began, but she wasn't sure that was possible after such a long time.

She made tea for them both and then sat down again. "He came over to the island some time in the mid-fifties," she began. "Nearly everything I can tell you is hearsay. I only met the man a couple of times myself, but he was the talk of the village when he was here."

"I'm happy with hearsay at this point," John told her.

Bessie nodded. "He had some money, but no one ever heard the same story as to where he'd acquired it," she said. "I gathered, at the time, that his family was wealthy and the money had come from his father. Supposedly, he'd come to the island to buy a farm and raise sheep. At least I think that was the plan." She shook her head. "It was a long time ago," she said.

"Don't worry if you can't remember things perfectly. I'm happy with anything and everything you can tell me. If it turns out he was planning to raise cattle instead, I would be surprised if that had anything to do with his death."

"I seem to recall that he stayed in Douglas for a while. Most people did when they came to the island. Laxey didn't have much to offer for young single men, at least not when compared to Douglas."

"But he moved to Laxey after that?" John asked.

"He did," Bessie confirmed. "He was looking at farms all over the island and there were a few in Laxey that caught his eye. None of them were actually on the market, you understand, but he moved up here and set about trying to persuade one of the farmers to sell to him."

"And the Clague farm was on his list?"

"I don't think so," Bessie said, feeling confused. "I can't imagine that Niall would have considered selling at that point. He was in his prime and the farm was thriving."

"Tell me more," John said.

"After a while, he began to develop something of a reputation for, well, having an eye for the ladies, I suppose you could say," Bessie told him.

"How old was he?"

"Maybe twenty-five," Bessie said.

"And the women he went out with?"

"I don't think it would be much of an exaggeration to suggest that he went out with just about every woman in Laxey between the ages of eighteen and thirty in the summer he was here."

"Wow, that's some accomplishment," John said.

"He was very good-looking, seemed to have an endless supply of money and he drove a new car," Bessie told him. "The girls in the village had never really met anyone like him before. He seemed worldly and sophisticated to girls and young women who'd never been further from home than Douglas."

"And how did he seem to you?"

"I was a little bit older and I'd seen a great deal more of the world," Bessie replied. "I thought he was flashy and arrogant."

"So he was trying to buy a farm and take out every woman in the village. What happened next?"

"The longer he was here, the less talk there was about him buying a farm," Bessie recalled. "He was here for three or four months and after the first few weeks I don't remember hearing any more about it. At the time I thought he'd either found a property and was keeping the negotiations secret, or he'd given up and decided to just have some fun before he went home."

"And then he disappeared?"

"That sounds so dramatic," Bessie said. "But it wasn't like that. He told everyone he was going. I think there was even a small gathering at the local pub before he went. I'm sure he sold his fancy car and packed up his things. I'd always assumed he'd simply left as planned."

"But maybe he didn't," John said with a sigh.

"He wouldn't have given or sold that watch to anyone," Bessie told him. "He loved showing it off and telling people about it. I barely knew him and he told me all about the thing. It's coming back slowly, but I think he said his father bought the watch in Germany, from a little watchmaker on a back street somewhere. Jacob seemed to think there weren't more than a handful like it in the world. I'd be very surprised to learn that someone else on the island had one like it. If that isn't Jacob that you've found, whoever it is must have stolen Jacob's watch."

John nodded. "I told you that there were some duplicate names on the lists that Joan and Doona made. Jacob's name came up several times, actually, once we'd published the photo of the watch. Everyone that I've spoken to has said the same thing. That he was very fond of that watch."

"Well, if it is him, he wasn't buried there before Niall put Marion's things into the barn," Bessie said. "Marion died many years before Jacob came to the island."

"We're working on finding the man's family," John told her. "We're hoping we can get a DNA match so we can be certain who we've found."

"I can't imagine why they never reported him missing," Bessie said. "Surely he was missed?"

"Remember, we aren't even sure it's him," John said. "Maybe the watch isn't as rare as Jacob thought it was, or maybe he was robbed before he left the island. From what you've said, he was definitely planning to leave, so maybe he did just that."

"Maybe," Bessie said, doubtfully. The more she thought about the young man, the more convinced she became that the remains were his. She closed her eyes and could picture him, walking into a small café in Laxey, some young girl on his arm. He'd taken every excuse to check the time and she could hear him bragging to his companion that his watch was never wrong. She shuddered.

John got up and poured Bessie some more tea. He handed her the cup and then squeezed her other hand. "Are you okay?" he asked.

Bessie nodded and took a sip of her drink. She set it down before she spoke. "I'm fine," she said. "I wasn't even all that upset when we found the body yesterday. Somehow putting a name to the remains makes it seem much more awful for some reason. I barely knew the man and I didn't really like him, but when I think about him I can picture him. He was loud and brash and so very full of life."

She sighed and then got up to find a tissue. After wiping her eyes, she sat back down. "I'm sorry. What else can I tell you?" she asked the inspector.

"What was his connection with the Clague farm?"

Bessie thought for a moment and then shook her head. "I don't know that there was any connection between them," she said. "As I said earlier, I can't see Niall even discussing selling the farm with him."

"What about Fenella?"

"Oh," Bessie exclaimed. She sat back in her chair and thought hard. "She would have been in her teens. I can't remember exactly what year he was here. I suppose she might have been old enough to catch his eye, but I don't remember hearing that she was seeing him. Then again, he went through women very quickly. I'm sure I didn't hear about most of them."

"He never helped out on the farm?"

"He never did any work, as far as I know," Bessie said. "He wanted to buy a farm, but he didn't intend to work on it himself. I doubt he'd have been any help to any of the hardworking farmers on the island."

"Who do you remember him going out with, then?" John asked.

"Everyone and no one," Bessie said with a sigh. "I remember that he went out with a lot of women, but I'm not sure I could put names to any of them now. I suppose, if I really work at it, I can come up with some names, but as I said, he didn't stay with anyone for long. I don't recall hearing that anything serious ever developed between him and anyone on the island."

"I'd appreciate it if you'd try to make a list for me," John said. "Hopefully, we'll be able to identify the body before I start going through it."

"It was so long ago, I can't imagine it will help, but I'll try."

"It was a long time ago," John agreed. "But someone killed the man and hid the body. Somewhere, forty or so years ago, someone felt strongly enough about him enough to kill him. My job it find out who that was and why."

"Whoever it was could be long dead themselves," Bessie pointed out. "Or they could have moved away."

"I just have to do my best," John replied.

"And, of course, Niall should be the first person you question, but he's not going to be any help."

"Anna went and talked to him today," John told her. "He wasn't very lucid."

"What about Eoin and Fenella?" Bessie asked.

"Neither of them recognised the watch," John told her. "I didn't specifically ask about Jacob Conover, because we aren't sure it's him. Neither of them could offer any explanation for why there was a dead body in the barn, either."

"Poor Fenella, it must be very upsetting for her," Bessie said.

"Thank you for your time," John said now. "I think I'd better go and let you get some sleep. Let me know when you've had time to put that list together for me."

Bessie nodded. "I'll go back through my diaries and see if I can find anything relevant."

"That would be a great help," John said.

"I'm not sure I have any from the right time period, but I'll see what I can find," Bessie promised.

She walked him to the door and locked it behind him. Mechanically, she cleared up the tea things and did the washing up. It was only as she climbed the stairs to bed that she realised she'd never offered the poor man any biscuits to go with his tea. Clearly, she was more upset than she'd realised.

Bessie's sleep was restless and she woke at six feeling tired and anxious. Going through her old diaries was an emotional job and she didn't quite feel up to it. A long walk on a cold and rainy beach did little to improve her mood. Pancakes with maple syrup, a reminder of her childhood in the US, washed down with milky tea, helped calm her.

Before she went in search of her diaries, she sat down to start the list of women whom she could recall had gone out with Jacob Conover. After listing a few names, she gave up. She'd start with the diaries and make the list from them, assuming they were any help.

Upstairs, she found the box that was full of diaries. It only took a few minutes to locate the book that started in June 1951. She skimmed through it shaking her head at her younger self. She found herself wondering why she'd ever bother to write down so much of the minutiae of her life. Still, if anyone ever wanted to know what she'd had for lunch on the 23rd of October 1952, she'd be able to tell them that she'd had a chicken sandwich.

She'd reached the 10th of May 1956 before she found what she was looking for.

Margaret Hayes has taken in a lodger. Apparently the young man, Jacob Conover, had been staying in Douglas, but he's decided to buy a farm in Laxey, so he's moved up here to consider his options. I saw him at the market this afternoon. I suppose he's attractive, but he's very arrogant and he was flirting with half a dozen girls who were hanging on his every word.

Bessie smiled as she thought about the daily market that used to take place in Laxey in the fifties and sixties. The farmers, or more typically their wives or daughters, would bring fresh fruit and vegetables, and the market became a sort of central meeting place for the residents of the village. She closed her eyes and recalled many long hours spent there, catching up with news from around the village. She turned to the next page, but there was nothing about the new arrival the next day.

A week later, though, she found him again.

Jacob Conover is working his way around the area, trying to persuade farmers to sell their property to him. He's also working his way through their daughters, it seems. Margaret Hayes told me that he's out every night with a different young lady and several have been hanging around her house in a most shameful fashion.

Of course, young ladies didn't chase after young men in those days, Bessie reflected. Things had certainly changed since then, although Bessie still thought that women should have better things to do than chase after men. A few days later she found Jacob mentioned again

I ran into Bahey Corlett in Ramsey today. She's back on the island with the Pierce family, who are holidaying here as they do every summer. She's ever so worried about her cousin, Karen. Apparently Karen has fallen quite hard for that Jacob Conover. I told Bahey everything I know about the man, which isn't much. Karen's only seventeen and last week her father caught her sneaking out to meet Jacob somewhere. I told Bahey that, from what I've heard, the man will probably soon move on to someone else.

Bessie sat back in her chair. Karen Corlett had been a very beautiful young girl, she remembered. When Karen had left school, she'd spent some time with Bahey, staying at the Pierce mansion across. Bessie had a vague recollection of hearing that she'd married very well and settled in London. She made a note to ring Bahey when she'd finished looking through her diaries and moved on.

An hour later, Bessie had a list of an even dozen women whom she'd seen with Jacob or been told were involved with him during his time on the island. Of that number, four were definitely still on the island, three were living across, three had passed away, and she wasn't sure about the final two. Fenella's name wasn't on the list, but that didn't mean much. She would have been eighteen that summer and she'd been very pretty in her youth. It was highly likely that she'd have attracted Jacob's attention, even if they'd not been seen together enough to stir up gossip.

Bessie read her entry for the 23rd of September that same year.

It seems Jacob Conover has given up on buying a farm on the island. There was something of a party for him last night at the pub. He's going back across to farm in Cumbria, or some such thing. The young women of the village are, I gather, nearly inconsolable. I must say, when I met him, I found him far too fond of himself and his wealth, but apparently that is quite attractive to the young women in Laxey.

Bessie flipped through the rest of that diary, but the man wasn't mentioned again. She sat back in her chair and let her mind wander. For several minutes, she thought about young, handsome, brash Jacob Conover and the women who'd been so flattered by his attention. With a sigh, she put her diaries back into their box and returned the box to the spare room. She'd ring John after lunch with her list and he could decide what to do with it. Of course, he wasn't in the office when she rang.

"I can put you through to Anna," Joan suggested.

Bessie bit back a sigh. She had been hoping for a few words with Doona, but had reached Joan instead. And now John wasn't available either. "Just have John ring me, please," Bessie replied.

She was eager to ring Bahey and ask her about her cousin, Karen, but she didn't want to do that without checking with John first. Curling up with a new book about Catherine the Great of Russia, Bessie soon found herself caught up in court intrigues and political upheaval. She was startled when her phone rang several hours later.

"Bessie? I'm sorry I didn't ring you back sooner. It's been a busy day," John told her.

"I've been through my diaries," Bessie replied. "I have a list of women who I'm reasonably certain spent time with Jacob Conover when he was here. I could probably add half a dozen others that he probably at least asked out, as well. Fenella Faragher would fall into that category."

"I'll come over this evening around seven to go over the list with you, if I may," John said. "I'll bring Chinese food and something for pudding."

"What about Doona and Hugh?" Bessie asked.

John hesitated for a moment. "Sure," he said eventually. "Why not?"

There were a few hours to wait before Bessie's guests would arrive. She'd lost interest in Russian history for the moment, so Bessie sat down with her lists and copied them neatly, making notes about each woman where she could. She was about half-finished with the project when the phone rang.

"Bessie? It's Bahey Corlett. How are you?"

"I'm fine. How are you?"

"Oh, I'm doing well," Bahey told her. "Howard and I are so looking forward to your Thanksgiving feast next week. After that, we're heading across to spend some time with his daughter and the grand-baby, which will be wonderful."

After working for the Pierce family her entire life, Bahey had retired some years ago. She'd never had a boyfriend in her youth and she and Bessie had both been surprised when she'd met her attractive neighbour, Howard Mayer, and begun a relationship. The pair had been together for several months now and Bessie wondered sometimes if Howard might be thinking of proposing at some point in the near future.

"That will be nice for you all," Bessie said. "It will be the baby's first Christmas. Are you going to be staying that long?"

"We're only going for a week this time," Bahey replied. "But then we're going back over in the middle of December and staying through the new year."

"How fun," Bessie said.

"Yes, well, Carla didn't really like it when her father started spending time with me, but she's come around. It might just be because I'm a big help with the baby, having been a nanny to the Pierce boys, but whatever the reason, she seems as happy as we are that we're coming."

"I'm sure you're a huge help," Bessie said. Bahey had always been a very hard worker, even if she was somewhat inclined to complain. Actually, she'd been much happier since she'd met Howard, and aside from some concerns about strange happenings in her building of flats, Bessie had heard far fewer complaints from the woman when they'd spoken recently.

"But I didn't ring to talk about that," Bahey said. "I saw the photograph in yesterday's paper and it brought back a lot of bad memories. I'm sure you know exactly what I mean."

"Which photograph?" Bessie asked, not wanting to start the wrong conversation.

"That watch of Jacob Conover's," Bahey answered, spitting the name out bitterly.

"I did see that picture," Bessie said. "I hope you rang the police to tell them you recognised it."

"Oh, aye, I rang Inspector Corkill and he came and took a bunch of notes," Bahey replied.

Inspector Peter Corkill was head of the Douglas branch of the CID. He and Bessie had met over a dead body and had taken some time to come to appreciate one another. Now they'd become something like friends and Bessie had included him in the Thanksgiving invitations as well.

"I don't really remember much about Jacob Conover," Bessie said.

"I remember him all too well," Bahey answered. "And I'm sure poor Karen does, as well."

"I did recall that your cousin Karen went out with him for a while," Bessie said. "But she's happily married and living in London, isn't she?"

"She is, but she had her heart well and truly broken by that man, and I won't forgive him for it."

"It looks as if someone murdered him," Bessie said quietly.

"Probably the father of one of his victims," Bahey said sharply.

"Would you like to suggest a likely candidate?" Bessie asked.

"I could probably come up with a few. Why don't you meet me for lunch tomorrow and we'll talk?" she suggested.

"I'd like that," Bessie said.

"I'll invite Joney," Bahey added. "You haven't seen her in a while, have you?"

"I haven't," Bessie replied. "And I'd really like to. She might be able to add to your list of suspects, as well."

"She might," Bahey said. "Although she was already in Foxdale when that man came over."

"Well, I'll enjoying spending time with you and your sister, either way," Bessie said. "I'll be there at midday and I'll bring pudding."

"No, no, let me bake," Bahey said. "Howard and I are both watching what we eat at the moment. We've both gained weight since we've been together. Let me bake something nice for our luncheon. I'll enjoy having an excuse to make something and then eat it."

Bessie laughed. "If you insist," she said.

After she'd disconnected, Bessie went back to her list. There were a handful of women about whom she was uncertain as to their current whereabouts. She reached for the phone and then stopped herself. While she could ring around and track some of them down, that job might be best left for the police. If John asked for her help, she'd be more than happy to provide it, but after her call from Bahey, it was clear that at least some people on the island had far from pleasant memories of Jacob Conover. Perhaps it would be best if Bessie didn't stir those up unnecessarily.

She sighed and walked slowly through her cottage. Reading didn't appeal and she was just thinking about baking something when someone knocked on her door.

"Doona, I wasn't expecting you until closer to seven," she exclaimed when she opened the door.

"I was just sitting around my house, feeling bored and restless," Doona told her. "I thought I'd come over early and let you entertain me."

Bessie laughed. "I was just feeling rather the same way," she confided to her friend. "I'm ever so glad you're here."

The friends hugged and then Bessie led Doona into her sitting room. "If I make tea now, we'll just start eating biscuits and ruin our dinner," she said. "Let's sit in here instead and just chat."

"What should we talk about?" Doona asked after she'd settled into a comfortable chair.

"How was work today?" Bessie asked.

Doona wrinkled her nose. "It was pretty busy," she said. "Joan was back to help, but I still feel as if I spent nearly the whole day on the phone."

"Are you still getting rung by people who think they've recognised the watch?"

"Yes, although it seems as if everyone is giving us the same name now, at least."

"Jacob Conover," Bessie said.

"That's the one," Doona agreed. "Did you know him?"

"I wouldn't say that I knew him," Bessie said slowly. "I'd certainly met him, but only once or twice."

"I really don't want to talk about work," Doona said with a sigh. "John is being, well, distant. The phones won't stop ringing and I don't think Joan likes me."

"Oh, I'm sure that's not the case," Bessie said in a reassuring voice. "How could anyone not like you? Just give her some time to warm up, that's all."

"I'm hoping she won't be here much longer," Doona said. "I miss having my desk all to myself."

Bessie nodded sympathetically. "I'm sure things will quiet down soon."

"They were quieter by this afternoon," Doona admitted. "I think John will probably send Joan back to Castletown tomorrow, unless something else comes up."

"Are you all ready to see your solicitor on Friday?" Bessie changed the subject.

"I suppose so. We're meeting in Doncan's office so that he can make sure everything is being done right," Doona told her. "The police investigation into Charles's company is still ongoing, but Doncan seems to think that some money should be coming my way very soon."

Doona's second husband, Charles Adams had recently been murdered. Bessie had been surprised to learn, during the course of the investigation into his death, that he and Doona were still married. The only good thing to come out of the whole incident was the news that Charles had named Doona as his heir. Now Bessie was hoping that her closest friend was in line for a small fortune.

"That is good news," Bessie exclaimed.

"I'm waiting to see how much I get before I get too excited," Doona commented. "I suppose even a few hundred pounds will help pay for Christmas, and if it's much more, maybe I can pay down my mortgage with some of it."

"I'm glad you changed your mind about keeping the money," Bessie said. When Charles had first been killed, Doona had insisted that she didn't want anything from him.

"After everything he put me through, I suppose I should get something," Doona said. "I still feel uncomfortable about accepting it, but if I don't, all of the money goes to his cousin in New Zealand. Charles never even met the man, so I suppose I deserve it more than he does."

"Of course you do," Bessie said firmly. "We just have to hope that it turns out to be a huge fortune."

Doona shook her head. "I wouldn't know what to do with a huge fortune," she said. "I'd be over the moon if I got enough to pay off my mortgage and have a holiday somewhere."

"And maybe a new car?" Bessie suggested.

"Oh, that would be nice," Doona agreed. "Something little and cute and sporty would be great, rather than the sensible sedan I have now."

"And some new clothes?"

Doona laughed. "I think you're having fun spending my imaginary funds."

Bessie laughed with her. "You're right," she said. "Spending your money is great fun. I think you should buy Thie yn Traie and then we could be neighbours."

"I can't imagine Charles was worth as much as that," Doona told her. "Thie yn Traie must be on the market for many hundreds of thousands of pounds."

"I just wish someone would buy it," Bessie said. "It's so sad seeing it sitting empty."

"It was empty most of the time anyway, wasn't it?"

"Yes, I know it was, but it didn't feel empty when I knew the Pierce family would be back soon. Mr. and Mrs. Pierce loved the island."

"Maybe they'll change their minds about selling if it doesn't sell soon," Doona suggested.

"After everything that happened here, I doubt it very much," Bessie told her. "If they ever do decide to come back to the island, I would think they'd want to stay somewhere other than Laxey, anyway."

Doona nodded. "How are the plans for Thanksgiving going?" she asked.

"I'm still waiting to hear from a number of people," Bessie said with a frown. "I'm going to have start chasing some of them, I think."

"Well, I'm coming for sure," Doona said emphatically.

"I'm counting on that," Bessie replied.

A knock on the cottage door interrupted the conversation.

CHAPTER 6

Bessie rushed to let John and Hugh in. They were both carrying boxes full of delicious smelling food.

"I ran out of time to get something for pudding," John said apologetically, as he put his box on the counter. "I just brought some vanilla ice cream."

"Everyone sit down and get started and I'll just throw together an apple crumble," Bessie said.

"Oh, no, you mustn't," John told her.

"It will take no more than five minutes," Bessie insisted. "By the time you've opened the boxes and filled your plates, I'll be ready to join you."

Hugh gave Bessie a quick hug and then grabbed the peeler from a drawer. While Bessie found what she needed for the crumble, Hugh peeled and sliced several apples. Within a few minutes, the pudding was ready for the oven. John and Doona had the food laid out and their own plates filled. Hugh insisted that Bessie take what she wanted before he loaded his own plate with generous portions. Doona found drinks for everyone and they all sat down together with the delicious smell of warm apples and cinnamon just beginning to fill the air.

"How is Grace?" Bessie asked Hugh as everyone began to eat.

"She's good," Hugh told her. "And very excited about Thanksgiving."

"And how is the new house?" Bessie asked John.

"It's just about ready for the kids," he replied. "I've been putting the finishing touches on their bedrooms after work every night and I think they will both be pleased when they see how they came out."

"What colours did you choose?" Bessie asked.

"I let the kids do the choosing," John said. "Thomas went for a sort of medium blue that should work well as he gets older. Amy decided on a light grey that seems way too grown-up for a twelve-year-old girl's bedroom, but it matches the bedding she had me buy her and it looks very nice."

"You'll have to invite me over so I can see it all," Bessie said pointedly.

John flushed. "I am sorry," he said. "I've been meaning to have a small get-together with friends so you can all see the new house, but I only just finished all of the painting last weekend and I'm still tidying up from that mess."

Bessie patted his hand. "You should have invited us all over when you first started and handed us paint cans and brushes," she told him. "We all would have been happy to help."

John smiled at her. "Thank you," he said. "It never occurred to me to do that, but in a weird way, I'm glad I did it all myself. That house feels like home to me more than any other place I've ever lived, at least as an adult."

"I did all the painting and decorating here," Bessie said. "And I know exactly what you mean. Even if I did end up with a much brighter pink in my bedroom than I'd intended."

"I love your bedroom," Doona said. "It's bright and cheery."

"That's why I've never changed it," Bessie replied. "And it reminds me of when I was much younger and somewhat more girly as well."

"Once we get this current case sorted, I'll have you all over," John promised.

"Except then some other case will come up and you'll get swamped again," Bessie retorted. "Don't wait; invite us around soon."

John laughed. "Okay, okay, you win. I'll have you over later this week or early next week. Just give me a day or two to hide all of the painting supplies."

"So what's going on with the case?" Bessie asked after she'd cleared away the dishes. The crumble wasn't quite ready, but she put the kettle on to make tea to go with it.

"I've been in touch with Jacob's sister, Jane," John told her. "She's coming over to the island if the body is positively identified as Jacob."

"What's she like?" Bessie asked.

"She was quite, um, that is, you have to make allowances, under the circumstances," John said. "She seemed quite upset."

"I gather, therefore, that she hasn't had any contact with her brother since he was meant to have left the island," Bessie said.

"Jane released a statement to the island's press this afternoon. It should be in the papers tomorrow, so I can tell you that she hasn't heard from her brother since before the time he was known to have been here."

"That's interesting," Bessie replied.

"What's even more interesting is that she didn't even know Jacob was on the island," John said.

Bessie and Dooona both gasped. The oven timer interrupted the dozen questions Bessie wanted to ask.

"I'll get that," Hugh said. He jumped up and switched off the timer. Then he carefully took the apple crumble out of the oven. While Bessie asked questions, Hugh served everyone generous portions of crumble and ice cream.

"Where did she think he'd gone?" Bessie asked.

"Apparently he left home intending to travel to Liverpool," John told her. "The last letter they had from him mentioned having a week in Anglesey and then moving on to parts of Wales. She had no idea that he'd actually gone from Liverpool to the island."

"So if the family did file a missing person report, they filed it in the wrong place," Bessie said thoughtfully.

"They did file one. Actually, they reported him missing several times in several different locations. I've requested copies of the police reports from a number of places across. I can't imagine there will be anything helpful in them, but they're a place to start."

"What else did she tell you?" Bessie asked.

"She's convinced that the watch proves it's her brother," John said. "She's positive that it's that unique and that he would never have parted with it."

"So she's coming over once the body is positively identified," Bessie said.

"She is, and I expect she might want to meet you. She said she's eager to talk to anyone who remembers her brother."

Bessie nodded. "Of course, I'd be happy to meet her," she said.

"This is delicious," Doona interrupted. "I can't believe you threw it together that quickly."

"Hugh was a big help," Bessie replied. She glanced down at her plate and was surprised to find that she'd nearly finished her large serving. She'd been so caught up in the conversation that she'd forgotten to taste it. Now she focussed on enjoying her last three bites. "It is really good," she said when she'd cleared her plate.

"You mean it was really good," Doona laughed.

Hugh insisted on clearing up while Bessie and John talked. Doona gave Hugh a hand with the washing-up.

"So, let's see this list," John suggested.

Bessie handed him the sheet of paper with her notes. "I've given you as much information as I have about each of them," she told the man. "The first dozen were in my diary as having been seen with Jacob. The other six are women who were about the right age and might have gone out with the man, but I don't know that for sure."

John read down the list. "Some of these women have rung the office to identify the watch," he told Bessie. "I suppose we'll have to try to find them all and see what they can tell us."

"It seems an almost impossible job," Bessie remarked. "It was such a long time ago."

"I don't suppose we can find a way to link this to Grant Robertson?" Doona asked. "He's already wanted for murder and a bunch of other things."

"I don't remember any connection between Jacob and Grant," Bessie told her. "Though I suppose anything is possible."

"At this point, I'm not ruling anything out," John said. "We aren't even certain that it's Jacob that we've found, after all. While we're waiting for the body to be formally identified, I'll be doing everything I can to find out what happened to Jacob Conover. If it isn't him we've found, I'd certainly like to ask him a few questions."

John went through Bessie's list with her name by name. He occasionally added to the notes she'd provided, and then he summarised everything.

"You've given me eighteen names altogether," he began. "Seven of the women are still on the island, although only two are in Laxey, counting Fenella Faragher. There isn't much I can do with the four who are deceased. At this stage, at least, I'll cross them off. We may need to talk to their families later in the investigation, but I'm hoping not to."

"I doubt they'd be much help," Bessie said. "I can't believe any of the women involved told their families anything about a man they once went out with very briefly."

"You're probably right," John said. "Let's hope we solve the case before we get desperate enough to try asking them."

"What about the ones who've moved across?" Bessie asked. "I've given you all of the information I have about them, but I'm pretty sure most of them still have family here who could help you track them down."

John nodded. "We'll have to have someone talk to as many of them as possible," he said. "Unless we get a lucky break in the next few days."

"And there are two that I can't tell you anything more about," Bessie said. "Anna Long and her family came over from somewhere in the Lake District and they only lived in Laxey for six months, as far as I remember. I didn't really get to know them at all and I only really remember them because I made a note in my diary that Anna and Karen Corlett got into a shouting match about Jacob in the middle of the market. Anna and her family moved not long after that, and I'm certain they left the island, but I've no idea where they went."

"And Susan Black?" John asked, reading the name off Bessie's list.

"Her parents were missionaries. They came to the island for a short holiday that summer and then left again for some third-world country. I noted in my diary that I was surprised to see Susan having dinner with Jacob, as I didn't think her parents would approve of him."

"But did they disapprove so much that they killed him and hid the body at the Clague farm?" Hugh asked.

"I highly doubt it," John said.

"I can't imagine," Bessie added. "They were incredibly devout and dedicated people. Anyway, I can't believe they'd have had any motive."

"Perhaps Jacob broke Susan's heart," Doona suggested.

"Even if he did, murder is a huge leap," Bessie replied. "And I can't believe that she did more than go out with him once or twice. Surely that isn't enough to break anyone's heart."

"If she'd been sheltered by her parents, maybe," Doona said. "He might have been her first boyfriend."

Bessie shrugged. "Anything's possible," she muttered.

"But that's a good point," Hugh said. "We always talk about means, motive and opportunity. At this point, we have no idea how he died, so we can't really talk about means. As for opportunity, I suppose we'll have to assume anyone who was on the island at the time had opportunity, at least as a working hypothesis. That leaves motive. What possible motive was there for killing a man who was moving away?"

After he'd finished speaking, Hugh sat back down. All four friends looked around the table at one another. Bessie finally broke the prolonged silence.

"Either it was something to do with his attempts to buy a farm or to do with his womanizing," she surmised. "Although I can't really see any motive in either of those."

"What could his wanting to buy a farm have to do with his getting killed?" Doona asked.

"I don't know," Bessie said after another long silence. "But I can't see why his going out with so many women would be a motive either, unless some woman was so upset when he broke up with her that she decided to kill him."

"Or someone's father or former boyfriend wanted to be rid of him," Doona said.

"He was leaving," Bessie reminded her.

"And he wasn't leaving anyone, um, in a family way?" John asked.

Bessie shook her head. "In spite of all the talk about him, I never heard worse than he was seeing too many women. No one suggested that he was taking the women to bed. Certainly none of the young women involved had an illegitimate child the next year."

"With the possible exception of Susan Black or Anna Long," John interjected.

"Well, yes, I suppose so," Bessie agreed.

"Of course, he might have been killed for some other reason that hasn't occurred to us yet," Hugh said. "Maybe he was involved in something criminal that got him murdered, or maybe he was just in the wrong place at the wrong time and he saw or heard something he shouldn't have."

"Or maybe he died accidently and someone just hid the body," Bessie added.

"All possibilities, especially at this early stage in the investigation," John said. "And on that note, I think I'd better get home and get some sleep. I have an awful lot of work piling up for tomorrow."

Bessie walked her guests to the door. Hugh and John both waved as they climbed into their cars and drove away.

"Are you okay?" Bessie asked Doona as she gave her a hug.

"I'm fine, just a little nervous about Friday," Doona told her. "Tonight was nice, almost like old times."

"It was nice, even if the subject was unpleasant," Bessie replied.

"At least whatever happened took place a long time ago," Doona said.

"And someone has been thinking that they got away with it for a long time," Bessie added.

Doona frowned. "I really do hope, if it was murder, that the killer moved away after it happened. I'd hate to think he or she is still around."

Bessie locked the door behind her friend and then double-checked that the other door was secure. Tomorrow she'd talk to Bahey. Maybe Bahey would be able to suggest a motive they hadn't considered yet.

Thursday was wet and windy, and the next morning Bessie stood in her doorway watching the rain for several minutes. Finally, sighing deeply, she pulled on her waterproofs and her Wellington boots and headed out for her morning walk. She walked only as far as the holiday cottages, waved to Thomas Shimmin, who was hard at work painting one of them, and then turned for home. An extra cup of tea and a slice of toast, thick with strawberry jam, cheered her up after she'd dried off. Her taxi was due at half eleven, so Bessie settled in with a book for the morning. When the knock came on her door, she was startled. A quick glance at the clock told her that she'd completely lost track of time.

Dave, her favourite driver from her regular service, gave her a bright smile when she opened her door. He was standing under a huge umbrella. "Did I get the time wrong?" he asked.

Bessie smiled at the question. She'd opened the door in her bare feet, not looking at all as if she had a lunch appointment in only half an hour. "I lost myself in a book," she told the man. "Please come in and give me a minute to get ready."

With Dave waiting in the kitchen, Bessie rushed up the stairs to change into something more suitable than her casual attire. She ran a comb through her hair and applied a quick coat of lipstick. A glance in the mirror told her that she looked pretty much the same as always. That would have to be good enough, she thought as she hurried back down the stairs.

Dave smiled at her. "Now you look ready to go out," he said. Bessie grabbed her handbag and followed Dave out of the cottage. He held his umbrella over her head as she locked her door. After tucking her into the passenger seat, Dave was quick to climb behind the wheel.

"Douglas, right?" he checked.

"Yes, I'm having lunch with my friend who lives on Seaview Terrace," Bessie told him.

They chatted about nothing much on the journey into Douglas. When Dave pulled up in front of Bahey's block of flats, he parked the car. "I'll just walk you to the door," he said. He had the large umbrella open and was at the passenger door before Bessie could object.

"Thank you so much," Bessie said as she pressed the buzzer for Bahey's flat. The lock on the door clicked open and Bessie pushed the door. Inside, she turned back to thank Dave again.

"Make sure you bill me for all of your time," she told him. "I made you wait at my cottage and now you've walked me to the door as well."

"Ah, I almost forgot, I'm so sorry the wife and I can't make it to your dinner on Saturday," he said. "I'm sure she rang and told you, but I wanted to thank you myself for including us."

"I'm sorry you can't make it," Bessie replied. "It should be a nice afternoon."

"No doubt," Dave said. "But we always go across for a short holiday in late November. It's my wife's sister's birthday, you see, and we always go over and take her out for a meal."

"That's lovely," Bessie said. "I hope you have a wonderful time."

"Ring for me when you're ready for home," Dave told her.

"I will," Bessie promised.

She walked past the desk where the manager was sitting. The man was a stranger to Bessie. He glanced up from his magazine and then went back to it, ignoring Bessie. She shrugged and headed for the lift.

Before it arrived, the door to the section of ground floor flats opened and two of her former neighbours walked out.

"Ah, Elizabeth Cubbon, what a wonderful surprise." Simon O'Malley smiled his dazzling smile at her.

Bessie smiled back at the very attractive man. "It's lovely to see you, Simon," she said. " And you, Tammara," she added, including Tammara Flynn in her greeting.

"We are so excited about next Saturday, I can't even tell you," Simon enthused. "Aren't we, Tammy?"

The girl grinned. "We are, actually," she agreed. "We've never been invited to a Thanksgiving dinner before and it sounds quite delightful."

"I'm glad you're looking forward to it," Bessie said. "I must say, a few of your neighbours seem less enthusiastic. I've actually not heard from some of them."

"That doesn't surprise me," Simon said with a shrug. "Tammy and I are the only fun ones around here. Except for Bahey and Howard, of course. You may have to go door-to-door to find out who's planning to attend."

"I might just do that," Bessie said. "But not until after lunch with Bahey."

Simon laughed. "I like a woman who has her priorities in order," he told her. After giving her a hug, he and Tammara swept past Bessie on their way out. Bessie boarded the lift that was now waiting and pressed the button for the first floor.

When the lift doors opened, Bahey was standing in the upstairs corridor. "My goodness, that lift took ages," she said as Bessie hugged her.

"I ran into Simon and Tammara," Bessie explained.

"Ah, that explains it," Bahey said with a laugh. "Anyway, come in."

Bessie followed her friend into Bahey's small but comfortable flat. Joney was settled on a chair in the small sitting area, but she got up when Bessie entered.

"Bessie, it's been too long since we did this," she said.

Bessie hugged her tightly. "We must make more of an effort," she said.

"Of course, we'll see you again at Thanksgiving," Bahey said.

"I'm looking forward to seeing Howard, as well," Bessie said.

"You might not have to wait until Thanksgiving for that," Bahey replied. "I've sent him away while we have lunch, but he'll probably be back before too long."

"You two are like teenagers," Joney said. "You can't bear to be apart for more than an hour or two."

"Yep," Bahey said happily. "It's both weird and wonderful."

Bessie laughed at the change in her friend. "I always like to see Howard," she said.

Bahey served homemade steak and kidney pie with treacle sponge for pudding. While they ate, Joney brought Bessie up to date on her life in Foxdale. As she spooned up her last bite of treacle, Bessie decided to bring the conversation around to Jacob Conover.

"So, when you rang, you said you recognised Jacob's watch," Bessie reminded Bahey. "What do you remember about him?"

"He was bad news," Joney said harshly.

"In what way?" Bessie asked.

"He nearly got our Karen into trouble," Bahey said.

"What sort of trouble?" Bessie wondered.

"Not that sort," Joney told her. "She wasn't, that is, she was a good girl. But she was only seventeen and very innocent. When he told her he loved her, she believed him."

"I didn't realise he stayed with anyone long enough to start telling them he loved them," Bessie said.

"Oh, he and Karen were together for about two months," Bahey said. "He went out with a lot of other women at the same time, but he told her they were just window dressing, like, to hide the fact that he'd fallen in love with her."

"But why would he need window dressing?" Bessie asked.

Bahey shrugged. "Maybe so Karen's family wouldn't worry?" she suggested. "But we did, and when we heard that he'd asked her leave the island with him, I took her away."

"He asked her to leave with him?" Bessie asked in surprise.

Bahey nodded. "I rang Karen last night and had her tell me the story again," she told Bessie. "They went out for a while and then he said he going back across and asked her to come with him. She actually considered it, but then she told her mum and her mum rang me and I arranged to take her with me back to my work."

"I never heard any of this at the time," Bessie said thoughtfully.

"Well, we didn't tell anyone," Bahey said. "We didn't want anyone to think that Karen was the type to run off with a man like that, did we?"

"And she never heard from him again?" Bessie checked.

"Oh, he wrote once or twice, but I destroyed the letters before she saw them," Bahey said.

"But if he wrote to her later, it can't be his body we've found," Bessie said in confusion.

"I took her with me in July," Bahey told Bessie. "He wrote to her in August, but he was still on the island until September, right?"

Bessie nodded. "So he was thinking of leaving in July, but didn't actually go until September. That's interesting, but I'm not sure why."

Joney and Bahey both laughed, and after a moment Bessie joined in. "I don't think we've solved anything," Bessie said after a bit.

"Karen was certain that the body is Jacob's," Bahey said. "She said the watch proves it."

"Did she have any idea who might have wanted to kill him?" Bessie asked.

"She said he'd had some trouble with a farmer in Douglas," Bahey reported. "Apparently, he'd offered to buy the man's farm, but then, after he'd had it surveyed, he decided he didn't want it. Jacob told Karen that the man was really angry about the deal falling through. That's why Jacob moved to Laxey, to get away from that farmer."

"I don't suppose Karen knew the farmer's name?" Bessie asked.

"She didn't," Bahey said. "At the time it wasn't important to her."

"It seems a fairly flimsy motive for murder," Bessie speculated.

"He also left a few angry women in Douglas," Bahey told her. "But Karen didn't know their names, either."

"I hope you don't mind if I tell John Rockwell everything you've told me," Bessie said.

"Of course not," Bahey assured her. "I talked to Inspector Corkill once, but I suppose I should ring him again now that I've talked to Karen."

"You should," Bessie agreed. "He'll be able to check out the Douglas connections to the case."

"I'd rather you didn't tell anyone else, though," Bahey added. "Karen would rather people didn't know anything about her relationship with Jacob. She's quite happy for everyone to think she was just one of his many female friends."

"I'll keep it to myself," Bessie promised.

"Karen wants to come over for whatever service they have for him over here," Bahey said as Bessie prepared to leave. "She said she still has a spot in her heart for Jacob. He was the first man she ever loved."

Bessie, who'd never really recovered from the loss of her first love, understood the sentiment perfectly. "I'd love to see her while she's here," she told Bahey.

"We'll have to have lunch or something," Bahey said.

"I shall have to knock on doors on my way out," Bessie told Bahey. "There are a few people here who haven't responded to my Thanksgiving invitation."

"I'm not sure why you invited them all," Bahey said. "You only lived here for a month, not even."

"I know, but I haven't had neighbours for many years," Bessie told her. "The cottages around mine have been holiday cottages for a very long time. One of the strangest part of staying here was having other people all around me. I just thought it would be nice to see them all again."

As Bessie reached the door, it suddenly swung open. "Ah, just in time to get a hug," Howard Mayer beamed at Bessie.

It took several minutes to hear all about his daughter and the baby before Bessie could finally get on her way. She quickly moved across the corridor and knocked. She got no answer from Ruth Ansel's flat, and it seemed that Muriel Kerry was out as well. She was luckier on her third attempt.

"Ah, Bessie, I did hope we'd see you again one day," Bertie Ayers said, his eyes twinkling at her. "You certainly livened up the place when you were here. I don't suppose you'd like to come back?"

"No, not even a little bit," Bessie said, surprising them both with her blunt honesty. She laughed. "Sorry, but I love my home too much," she explained. "I hope you're planning to come to my Thanksgiving dinner?"

"Oh, aye, I forgot to ring you and let you know, though, didn't I?"

Bertie shook his head. "I'll make it up to you by bringing my own gin, shall I?"

"Of course not," Bessie said. "You're not to bring anything but yourself."

"Oh," he said. He glanced around and then lowered his voice, even though the hallway was deserted. "I did wonder if I might bring a friend," he whispered.

"Of course you can," Bessie said in surprise. "Is it anyone I know?"

Bertie grinned. "Well, Muriel and I have been spending more time together, you see. I did think, that is, I thought she might like coming to your little gathering as a couple. I know you invited her as well, but, I well, anyway, it'll upset Ruth, no doubt, but well, maybe it's time I settled down a bit, don't you think?"

"I'm very happy for you both," Bessie said. "I'll look forward to seeing you a week on Saturday."

Bessie headed for the lift, mentally shaking her head at Bertie. Time to settle down? At sixty-something? Maybe it was, at that.

Bessie tried the flats on the first floor, but no one seemed to be at home. She'd just include them all in her count to the restaurant and see who turned up, she decided. In no particular hurry to get home, Bessie headed into the Douglas town centre for a wander around the shops. An hour later, she'd bought several things she hadn't realised she needed and was ready to ring Dave.

She was coming out of the chemist when she nearly fell over as a toddler cut across her path. "Oh, dear, are you okay?" she asked the little girl, who looked up at her and burst in tears.

"Kylie, you mustn't run away," the pretty blonde woman who was two steps behind the girl gasped. "I'm ever so sorry," she said to Bessie.

"Liz?" Bessie asked.

"Oh, goodness, Bessie? I'm even more sorry now," Liz Martin said with a laugh. She gave Bessie a hug and then picked up the still sniffling child.

"This is Kylie, in case you didn't realise," Liz said.

Bessie smiled at the beautiful child. "She looks just like you," she told Liz.

"Bill says so as well," Liz told her. "But I suppose that's only fair, as Jackson looks exactly like his father."

"That does seem very fair," Bessie agreed.

"I'm so glad I ran into you, actually," Liz said. "I know I rang and said we'd come for the dinner next week, but I'm ever so worried about bringing the children. As you've seen, Kylie isn't always the best-behaved child in the world. I'd hate for her to ruin your special event."

"Thanksgiving is for families," Bessie said insistently. "I'd love to have a whole room full of children, but I simply don't know any others. They can't do anything except run around and be noisy, and that's not a problem, that's part of what makes the holiday special."

Liz looked doubtful. "I suppose, if they don't behave, we can always leave early," she said.

"It will be fine," Bessie said. "It isn't fancy or formal, it's just a lot of food and a lot of good friends."

"Thank you so much for including us," Liz said.

"I so enjoyed taking Manx with you," Bessie told her. "I hope you're keeping it up."

"I'm trying, but I have the advantage of living next door to Marjorie, of course."

"And Marjorie will be there next week," Bessie told her. "And Henry and Joney Quirk from our class as well."

"Oh, it will be like a reunion," Liz said happily. "Maybe we'll have time to have a chat in Manx at some point."

"Oh, I do hope not," Bessie told her.

Liz laughed. "Maybe not, then."

Bessie rang for her taxi as Liz dashed off, chasing her energetic toddler again. Dave had Bessie back in Laxey in time for her evening meal.

After she'd eaten, she rang John and told him everything she'd learned from Bahey.

"We need to find more of the women who went out with Jacob," John said. "I want to know how many of them thought he was going to take them back across with him."

"I can ring a few people tomorrow," Bessie suggested. "Some of them might be happier talking to me than to the police."

"That's a great idea," John said. "Any background information you can gather would be greatly appreciated."

A short time later Bessie headed to bed. She felt restless, but she slept well.

CHAPTER 7

Another rainy morning meant that Bessie was back in her waterproofs and Wellington boots for her walk. She kept it short again, just going far enough to wave to Thomas before heading for home.

With the breakfast dishes washed, dried, and back in the cupboards, she sat down with her telephone and began to ring a few of her many friends and acquaintances around Laxey. After an hour, she'd updated her copy of the list she'd given John with quite a few additional notes. She took a break for tea, and just moments after she'd put the phone down, it rang.

"Bessie, it's John," the voice said. "I was just about to start ringing around to try to track down a few of the women who went out with Jacob, and I thought I'd check with you first and see how you're doing with them."

"I've spoken to three women who went out with him," Bessie reported. "All three said that they only went out with him two or three times and that it was just a bit of fun, nothing more."

John noted the names of the women Bessie had reached. "What's next on your agenda?" he asked Bessie.

"I've tracked down phone numbers for three of the women who

are across now," she said. "I was going to try ringing them, but maybe you'd prefer to do that?"

"Give me their details and leave them with me," John said. "If we get a positive identification on the body soon, we might have them questioned by someone from their local station, rather than talk to them by telephone."

"I'm still trying to find someone who might know what happened to Susan Black or Anna Long," Bessie said. "I'll keep working on them until after lunch. I have an appointment this afternoon to meet with one of the women on the list."

"Which one?" John asked.

"Mona Kelly, although technically she's Mona Smythe now," Bessie replied. "She just happens to live in the same building as Sarah and Mike Combe and I've been promising them a visit for weeks. When I spoke with Mona, she didn't want to talk on the telephone, so I suggested I should come and see her. After we talk, I'll drop in on Sarah and Mike and save myself a separate trip to Port Erin."

"I'm not sure I want you visiting suspects," John said.

"Surely Mona Kelly isn't a suspect," Bessie replied.

"At this point, everyone on the island is a suspect," John said. "We haven't even identified the remains. If they do turn out to be Jacob Conover's, the women he spent time with will have to be considered very seriously."

"Mona is a sweet lady who wouldn't hurt a fly," Bessie told him. "Anyway, even if she killed Jacob all those years ago, she has no reason to do anything to me. We're just going to have tea and a chat, that's all."

"Ring me when you arrive at her flat and then again when you leave," John demanded.

"Oh, good heavens," Bessie exclaimed. "I'm sure to forget. Please don't storm her flat with a dozen armed men or anything. Mona and I would probably both have heart attacks."

"Try not to forget," John said. "You know I worry about you."

"I know, but Mona is sixty-three, not even five feet tall and I'm sure she doesn't weigh more than eighty-five pounds. I'm certain I'm quite safe with her."

"I'm sure you're right," John said. "But after everything you've been through this year, you ought to know that murderers come in all shapes and sizes."

"You're right, of course," Bessie said. "I'll try to remember to ring you."

"Good. And good luck with finding our two missing women. I hope you can track them down. I'd like to talk to every woman he took out, and I don't have the time or resources to track them down myself, at least not until we're sure who we've found."

"Who else could it be?" Bessie asked.

"That's a very good question," John told her. "If I had any ideas on that score, I'd be digging into them as well. For now, we're working on the assumption that it's Jacob Conover, at least in part because we don't have any other possibilities."

Bessie spent another hour on the phone, talking to various people. She learned a lot of interesting news about her friends and neighbours, but none of it was relevant to the case. No one was able to help her with her search for the two missing women.

After a light lunch, Bessie took a taxi to Port Erin. The driver her service sent was new to the job and to the island, so Bessie found herself giving him directions as they went. When he pulled into the car park for Mona's building, Bessie gave him an encouraging smile.

"You will be able to find your way back to Douglas, won't you?" she asked.

"I think so," the man replied. "Although I'm tempted to take a long lunch break and simply wait here until you're ready to go back."

"I don't know how long I'll be," Bessie told him. "I'm going to visit some friends. It could be several hours."

He nodded. "I'm sure I'll be fine," he said cheerfully. "I'll just keep heading north with the sea on my right."

"That's it exactly," Bessie told him. "Thank you."

She walked into the building and pressed the lift button, quickly ringing John while she waited. A few minutes later she was knocking on Mona's door.

"Bessie, it's so good to see you," Mona said as she swung her door open.

Studying her friend in the doorway, Bessie thought she'd been just about right in her description to John. Mona was tiny, with grey hair in a tight bun and brown eyes that looked more lively than Bessie remembered.

"How are you?" Bessie asked, giving the woman a gentle hug.

"I'm very well," Mona replied. "I do think the south of the island agrees with me, after all those years up north." She led Bessie into a spacious sitting room with gorgeous views of the sea below.

"What a wonderful view," Bessie exclaimed.

"Yes, it's something special," Mona agreed. "Frank would have hated it."

Bessie laughed. Mona's husband, Frank Smythe, had worked for the island's ferry service for many years. He once told Bessie he couldn't understand why people were so interested in sea views. "I see the sea all the time," he'd grumbled. "When I'm at home, I like to see trees and grass."

Frank had died of a heart attack some years earlier, and Bessie had been surprised when Mona had almost immediately sold their small house in Laxey and bought this seaside flat in Port Erin. Bessie had only seen the woman a couple of times in the intervening years, but clearly Mona was happy with her choice.

"Do the children like it?" Bessie asked.

Mona shrugged. "They're both too busy with their lives to bother much with me," she said. "Paul is in London. He married a positively nasty woman who insists that they spend every holiday and special occasion with her horrid family. At least they don't have children to ruin. Mary and her husband, Jack, live in Derby. They have two adorable little ones and I'd love to see more of them, but Mary and Jack are both teachers and have no money to speak of. I'll go and spend Christmas with them; I usually do."

Mona took Bessie into the modern kitchen and put the kettle on. A plate full of biscuits and small cakes was already in the centre of the table in one corner of the room. They both sat down with tea and a few biscuits and quickly caught up on a few mutual acquaintances before Bessie brought the conversation around to the real reason for her visit.

"I was surprised you didn't want to talk about Jacob Conover when I rang," Bessie said, trying to keep her tone casual.

Mona shrugged. "It isn't that I don't want to talk about him, exactly. I just don't see the point."

"The police need all of the information they can get if they're going to track down his killer," Bessie said.

"Yes, I'm sure they do," Mona replied. "But I haven't any useful information, that's what I mean. I had dinner with the man a couple of times, but it was just a couple of times and it was a long time ago."

"I'm sorry, but I'm going to ask you some rude questions," Bessie told her. "You don't have to answer them if you don't want to."

"I didn't go to bed with him, if that's what you're wondering," Mona told her.

Bessie found herself blushing under the other woman's steady gaze. "That wasn't it at all," she said quickly. "I was wondering who decided to end the relationship, that's all."

Mona laughed. "I suppose that's a rude question in its own way," she said. "But I don't mind answering it. As far as I can remember, it was pretty much a mutual decision."

Bessie deliberately bit into a biscuit, hoping that her silence might get Mona to reveal more.

"I know," Mona said after a moment. "Everyone who has ever been tossed aside says that it was mutual." She laughed and took a drink of her tea. "In this case, though, it actually was. I liked Jacob and he was fun to spend time with, but we both knew it wasn't going to lead anywhere."

"Why not?" Bessie asked.

"I didn't want to be a farmer's wife," Mona said. "I had big dreams in those days and they didn't include the long hours and hard work that comes with owning a farm."

"I can certainly understand that," Bessie said.

"I didn't really want to get married at all," Mona continued. "I wanted to go to university and, well, never mind all of that." Mona stopped and drank some tea, her cheeks pink.

"What did you want to do?" Bessie asked.

Mona sighed. "I thought I was going to be a famous writer," she said sheepishly. "I read a lot of Agatha Christie's books and I thought I would write mysteries like hers and make a fortune."

"It's never too late to try," Bessie said.

"Oh, really, Bessie," Mona said. "I'm far too old to start now. Anyway, I was working as a secretary in one of the schools when I met Frank, and my parents thought I ought to marry him. I was already twenty-five when I met him and my mum was convinced I'd be an old maid if I let him get away."

"I'm serious," Bessie told her. "You're never too old to chase your dreams. You should try writing a book."

"I never travelled or did anything exciting," Mona replied. "I've nowhere exotic to set my murder."

"What wrong with the Isle of Man?" Bessie demanded.

Mona laughed. "No one would want to read murder mysteries set on the Isle of Man," she said emphatically. "But let's get back to Jacob, shall we? I didn't want to marry him and he didn't want to settle down, really. So we went out a few times and then he moved on to the next girl who caught his eye, and I didn't mind a bit."

"Some of the women involved must have minded a great deal," Bessie said.

"I don't know," Mona said. "Like I said, Jacob was a lot of fun, but he was very honest about his feelings. He liked keeping company with pretty young women, but he wasn't looking for a wife or even a steady girlfriend. I'm sure one or two women wanted more, but as far as I remember, no one got more than a few dinners from him before he moved on."

"What about Karen Corlett?" Bessie asked.

"Did he go out with Karen?" Mona replied. She sat back in her chair, a thoughtful look on her face. "I simply don't remember," she said after a minute. "I wouldn't be surprised, as Karen was beautiful and sweet, but I don't recall hearing about them as a couple. Then again, he went through women so quickly, I'm sure I didn't hear about most of them."

"Who can you remember him going out with?" Bessie asked.

Mona thought for another minute and then mentioned a few names. Everyone she could recall was already on Bessie's list.

"I don't think I'm much help," Mona said as she poured more tea for them both.

"Tell me about Jacob," Bessie invited her. "I only spoke to him once or twice and only for a moment. What was he like?"

Mona nibbled her way through a custard cream before she answered. "He seemed quite sophisticated to me, especially considering I'd never been off the island. I don't know where his money came from, but he certainly seemed to have plenty of it and he didn't mind spending it, either. He took me out for nice meals and brought me flowers, as well."

"Someone suggested that he tried to persuade one of the women he went out with to move across with him," Bessie said.

"When we were together, he made it clear that he wasn't looking for a serious relationship," Mona replied. "But maybe he found someone else that he did get serious about."

"Who might have killed him?" Bessie asked.

Mona shook her head. "I've been wondering that ever since I saw the photo in the paper," she said. "I was at the pub the night before he was meant to be going home. Everyone who was there seemed quite sad that he was going. But he was going, that was certain. I can't imagine why anyone would have killed him when he was leaving anyway."

"That's certainly one question the police have to answer."

"I said he had plenty of money," Mona said thoughtfully. "Maybe someone hit him over the head to steal his money and then found that they'd killed him by mistake."

"Surely, if that were the case, they'd have taken the watch as well?"

"Maybe they thought the watch was too distinctive," Mona

suggested. "Considering how many people recognised it even after all these years, they were probably right, if that's what happened."

"So what connects him to the Clague farm?" was Bessie's next question.

"I haven't a clue," Mona replied. "He may well have taken Fenella out, of course. She'd have been the right age. But beyond that, I can't think of anything to connect him to the farm."

"Did he make any male friends while he was here?" Bessie asked as the thought crossed her mind.

"I don't think he had time for other men," Mona told her. "Anyway, most of the local lads resented the fact that Jacob took out just about every single woman in the village."

"Did any of them resent it enough to start a fight about it?" Bessie asked.

"Not that I recall. Certainly not during the gathering at the pub. Jacob was buying the drinks, after all. Anyway, he was leaving. Even if some of the locals didn't like him, he was getting on the ferry the very next day."

"You never saw him spending any time with Niall Clague or Eoin Faragher?" Bessie asked.

"I'm sure they were both at the pub that last night," Mona replied. "Just about the entire village was there, at least for a few minutes. But I don't remember Jacob spending any time talking with either of them. While I was there, he was walking around talking to everyone for a few minutes and then moving on. Of course, I was only there for an hour or so. I remember hearing that Jacob and a few of the others didn't leave until last orders."

"I don't suppose you can remember hearing who was with Jacob at the end of the night?"

"It was so long ago," Mona protested. She sipped her tea, her eyes gazing into the distance. After a few minutes she shook her head. "I'm sorry," she told Bessie. "I don't remember. I'm sure it was a few of the men who drank at the pub on a regular basis, though. I think I'd recall if I'd heard anything unexpected or unusual about that night."

Bessie sighed. "I appreciate your help," she told the woman. "And the tea and biscuits."

"It was nice to see you again," Mona replied. "We should do this more often. I love living down here, but I do feel a bit isolated sometimes. I don't really know anyone here."

"Let's meet in the middle next time," Bessie suggested. "We can have lunch in Douglas or something."

"Oh, I'd like that," Mona agreed quickly. "Maybe one day next week?"

Bessie was surprised at the woman's enthusiasm, but she quickly checked her calendar. After a moment, the pair had agreed to meet for lunch at one of Bessie's favourite Douglas eateries in a fortnight's time.

"I do hope the police will have everything wrapped up with regard to Jacob Conover by then," Bessie said as Mona walked her to the door.

"Oh, me, too," Mona replied. "I hate thinking that someone I know might have had a hand in his death."

"Maybe by the time we meet again, you'll have a chapter or two written," Bessie said in the doorway. "I'd be happy to read it as you go along. I adore Agatha Christie."

Mona flushed. "I don't think, that is, well, we'll see," she muttered.

Bessie grinned and then turned and walked down the corridor. It was time to visit some other friends. While she was looking forward to seeing Mike and Sarah Combe, they wouldn't be able to help with the investigation into Jacob's death. Mike hadn't grown up in Laxey and Sarah was too young to have interested the man. Still, the last several times she'd seen Sarah had been under very sad circumstances. Today was just a friendly visit. She quickly rang John to reassure him of her safety just before she knocked.

"Ah, Bessie, you're looking wonderful," Mike said when he opened the door to their flat.

Bessie smiled and followed him into the kitchen, where Sarah was just filling the kettle.

"Bessie," she exclaimed. She put the kettle down on the counter and rushed over to hug Bessie. "I'm so pleased that you stopped in," she said. "Mike and I have been talking about trying to arrange a chance to see you, but we've both been so busy."

"You're looking well," she told the woman, pleased that her words were truthful. In July, Sarah had lost her mother, and not long after that she'd found out that her brother, long believed to have emigrated to Australia, was dead. The events had taken a toll on the woman, but today she looked as if she was sleeping and eating properly again.

"I'm feeling better," Sarah told her. "Mike's been wonderful. He's really looked after me and spoiled me. I think I'm starting to get back to normal now, although I still miss mum more than I should, considering how difficult our relationship was."

Bessie nodded. "I know what you mean," she said. "I find that I'm missing a great many old friends, especially this time of year."

"Did my mum used to go to your Thanksgiving dinners?" Sarah asked.

"No," Bessie replied. "When they first started, I kept them very small, and if I had invited your mother, I would have had to invite all of the Raspberry Jam Ladies. It's only in the last few years that I've started having larger gatherings, but I never felt as if I should include the Jam Ladies."

"I'm really looking forward to it," Mike told her as Sarah poured the tea. "Even if I'm unlikely to know anyone else."

Bessie ran through her guest list in her head. "You might not know anyone at that," she said after a moment. "Although I have invited Spencer. I'm sure you've met him." Spencer Cannon was another child of one of the Raspberry Jam Ladies. He and Sarah had grown up together, although he'd moved off the island in adulthood. He was back now after Bessie had helped him locate a job on the island, and he was hugely grateful to her.

"I did meet Spencer at, um, well, Adam's service," Mike said. "He and Sarah are trying to get together at least once a month, just to chat about old times, so I've seen him once or twice since as well."

"I didn't care for him when we were younger," Sarah said. "But then, I didn't care much for boys in general. But he's turned into a really nice man and his girlfriend, Beverly, is great fun."

The trio sipped tea and ate biscuits while they chatted. It was over an hour later when Bessie glanced at her watch.

"Oh, goodness," she exclaimed. "I really must be going. I do hope I won't have too much trouble getting a taxi."

"Let us run you home," Sarah suggested. "Mike's been promising me dinner at *La Terrazza* for months."

"I don't want to inconvenience you," Bessie said.

"It's no problem," Mike told her. "I keep making excuses not to drive to Laxey. This way, we're already there, so we may as well have dinner."

Bessie laughed. "The food is excellent there," she told the couple. "You won't be sorry."

"Would you like to join us?" Sarah asked.

"Oh, no, but thank you very much," Bessie said. "I'm far too full of biscuits and tea to enjoy myself. Besides, you two should have a romantic dinner together. I'm told it helps keep marriages strong."

Sarah and Mike exchanged glances. "After everything we've been through lately, a nice romantic dinner together is probably just what we need," Sarah said.

"And I enjoy treating the woman I love to something special," Mike said, taking Sarah's hand in his.

Bessie smiled at the pair, happy that they were coming through their rough times together.

"I do hope you aren't too involved in what's going on at the Clague farm," Sarah said she they made their way to Mike's car.

"I'm trying to help the police gather some background, but that's all," Bessie told her. "I don't suppose you remember anything about Jacob Conover?"

Sarah shook her head. "I have a vague recollection of his being talked about by my parents," she told Bessie. "But he was an adult, so not at all interesting to me at the time."

"That sounds about right," Bessie laughed.

The journey back to Laxey felt short to Bessie as the trio chatted about everything and nothing. At Bessie's cottage, Mike insisted on walking Bessie to her door and escorting her inside.

"It gets dark so early now," he commented as he helped Bessie from the car.

"It does," Bessie agreed. "But I'm quite capable of getting myself inside anyway."

"Thank you again for taking the time to visit," he said at her door. "We'll see you at Thanksgiving dinner."

Bessie locked the door behind him and sighed. It was time for her evening meal, but she felt completely full after having tea with cakes and biscuits twice. Nothing sounded good, so she decided to read for a little while before making herself something. She'd just found her place in her book when her phone rang. As long as she'd been interrupted, she decided to answer the call.

"Hello?"

"Bessie, it's Doona. I've just finished with my solicitor from across and, well, I just needed someone to talk to."

"Why don't you come over?" Bessie suggested. "I've had two lots of tea and biscuits already today. Maybe you could bring something a little bit healthier than that with you?"

Doona laughed. "I'll bring fish and chips," she said. "At least that's what sounds good to me. Would you rather have something else?"

"Fish and chips is fine," Bessie said, even though she wasn't sure that they were much healthier than biscuits.

"I'll see you in a few minutes," Doona promised before she disconnected.

Bessie used the time to wipe down her kitchen counters and check that her small downstairs loo was clean. Doona's car was pulling to the small parking area outside Bessie's cottage as Bessie finished.

As Doona climbed out of her car, Bessie saw that her friend was upset. She opened the cottage door and rushed outside to greet Doona with a huge hug.

"It's nice to see you, too," Doona said with a laugh as Bessie released her.

"You looked upset," Bessie replied.

"I am, a bit," Doona admitted. "But I'm also hungry." Doona opened her boot and handed Bessie a large bag, the contents of which smelled delicious.

"You put the food in your boot?" Bessie questioned.

"If I hadn't, there wouldn't be any chips left to go with the fish," Doona told her.

Inside the cottage, Bessie got down plates and the pair quickly filled them with the battered fish and thick and salty chips. Bessie handed Doona a fizzy drink and then sat down with one for herself. They ate in silence for several minutes.

"That was gorgeous," Bessie said when her plate was empty.

"It was very nice," Doona agreed. "But I didn't bring a pudding."

"How about an apple?" Bessie suggested. "After that meal, we should have something healthy."

Doona made a face and then laughed. "You're right, and I agree, as long as I can have a few biscuits with it."

Bessie handed her friend an apple and then put chocolate biscuits on a plate. She switched the kettle on and then sat back down with her own piece of fruit.

"So I met with my solicitor," Doona said after a moment. "Things are still in a state of confusion, really. The accounts of the company that Charles was a partner in are being very closely examined. It's clear that Lawrence Jenkins was manipulating the books, but no one is certain who knew about it. Charles isn't around to defend himself, of course. Anyway, there is a lot of money tied up in the company, but no one can touch it until the police and the inland revenue finish their investigation."

"What a mess," Bessie said, shaking her head. "Do you have enough money to pay the solicitor? I can always help you out..." she trailed off when Doona held up a hand.

"I'm fine," she told Bessie. "In fact, I'm more than fine. Charles had several life insurance policies and he had me listed as the beneficiary on all of them. Only one has paid out so far, but the solicitor brought me a cheque for almost fifty thousand pounds."

"Well, my goodness," Bessie exclaimed.

"Exactly," Doona said. "I don't really feel as if I should accept the money, as we were only together for such a short time."

"Of course you should take the money," Bessie said firmly. "If you don't take it, where would it go?"

"I suppose to his relatives in New Zealand that he'd never met," Doona said.

"Well, there you are. You knew him and even loved him, if only for a short time."

"I loved for a long time," Doona said sadly. "It was only recently that I started feeling like I wasn't still in love with him."

"So the money is yours. What will you do with your sudden windfall?"

"I think I'll pay down my mortgage, at least a little bit," Doona said. "And maybe do up the house some, as well. I don't really know. It isn't enough that I can quit my job and just go travelling or anything, although if the solicitor is to be believed, I might be in line for considerably more once everything is settled."

"That would be wonderful," Bessie said. "But I think you're sensible to not count on it."

"I'm definitely not counting on it," Doona replied. "But I will admit to indulging in the odd fantasy about it now and then."

Bessie laughed. Doona was looking better and sounding happier than she had in some time. "Nothing wrong with a good fantasy or two," she said.

The pair tidied up the kitchen and then took a long walk on the beach. It was chilly and dark, but they each took a torch and enjoyed the peacefulness as they walked along listening to the waves splashing onto the shore.

"There are lights on in Thie yn Traie," Bessie said when they'd reached the stairs to the mansion above them.

"When Doncan and I were chatting tonight before the solicitor arrived, he mentioned that someone was seriously considering purchasing the place," Doona told her. "He said something about them staying there for the weekend to see how they liked it."

"That's interesting," Bessie said thoughtfully. "I do hope they like it enough to buy it."

"I'd better get home," Doona said when they returned to the cottage. "Are you going to the auction tomorrow?"

"I don't think so," Bessie said. "I've given the auction company my maximum bid for the painting. I'm not sure I could stand it, sitting there and watching it get sold. If my bid is the highest, I'll be thrilled, but if it isn't, I'll just have to be happy with having the view."

Doona nodded. "I might go," she told her friend. "I understand there are a lot of different items going under the hammer, including televisions, jewellery, furniture and appliances. Now I have some unexpected money to spend, maybe I can get something special."

Bessie bit back all the words of caution and warning that sprang to her lips. "I hope you find something perfect," she told her friend.

"Me, too," Doona said.

Bessie locked the door behind her and then did a final check of the kitchen. She was just about to switch off the ringer on her phone when the phone rang.

"Hello?" she said, curious who would be ringing so late and hoping it wasn't an insurance salesman.

"Bessie? It's Fenella Faragher. We've been so busy with the police and everything that Eoin and I forgot all about your turkeys. Or rather, we forgot to have you back to see them. I don't suppose you'd be free tomorrow? Only we need to get them ready, you understand, so tomorrow is about the deadline if you want to see them, well, while they're still alive."

"I can come up tomorrow," Bessie agreed. "What time?"

They settled on two o'clock and Bessie headed up to bed with her mind racing. She hoped she would get to see both Eoin and Fenella; she had a great many questions for both of them.

CHAPTER 8

Bessie woke up at six as normal. She took a shower and then, once dressed, headed out for her usual walk. Thie yn Traie was dark as she walked towards it. On the way back home, she saw Thomas Shimmin unpacking his car for another day of painting.

"How is it all coming along?" she asked, having walked up the beach to greet him in the small car park for the holiday cottages.

"It's fine," he replied. "I've finished a couple of the cottages, but it seems to be taking longer this year than it has in the past. I suppose I'm just getting slower as I get older."

"Maybe you should get someone in to help you out," Bessie suggested.

Thomas shrugged. "It isn't like I'm in a hurry," he said. "I'd like to have them all done before Christmas, but really, as long as they're ready for our first bookings in the spring, I'll be good."

"Just giving them all a coat of beige?" Bessie asked.

"It isn't beige," he protested. "It's 'Soft Ivory Mist,' or that's what is says on the tins, anyway."

"So beige," Bessie said with a laugh.

"Yep, and don't you start, too," he told her.

Bessie gave him a questioning look.

"Oh, Maggie has been saying that we ought to paint the cottages with brighter and more interesting colours. She's been watching some show on the telly where they change rooms all around and make them hideous, and now she wants to give each cottage a theme, whatever that means."

"Oh, my," Bessie said. "Yet again, I don't think I'm missing anything by not having a telly."

"I'd miss watching the football," Thomas said. "But everything else just seems to put ideas in Maggie's head. Fancy having one of the cottages all decorated in animal prints. It doesn't bear thinking about."

"Beige is lovely," Bessie said with a laugh. "And you don't have to worry about anyone complaining about it, either."

"Exactly," Thomas replied. "Now if you could just convince Maggie of that, I'd be a happy man."

"I can try to have a chat with her at Thanksgiving," Bessie suggested. "Although it's going to be an awfully busy day."

"Don't you worry about it," Thomas assured her. "Maggie can have all the crazy ideas she likes; it isn't as if she's going to actually do any of the work around here. Maybe, if I get the painting done early enough, I'll let her redecorate one cottage and we'll see how it goes. But I can promise you it won't be filled with animal prints, that's for sure."

"It will be interesting to see what Maggie comes up with," Bessie said.

"I'm not sure interesting is the right word," Thomas replied.

He headed into one of the cottages while Bessie continued on her way home. Once inside, she looked around her overcrowded kitchen. Every room in the cottage was the same, full of things she'd accumulated over an entire life lived within the same space. It would feel much more spacious if she'd cleared out most of the books, but that was something Bessie wasn't prepared to even consider. She looked around again and then sighed. Her heirs would have quite a job to do to clear the place out after she'd gone.

Her morning post brought a few photocopied sheets from

Marjorie Stevens at the Manx Museum library. Bessie read the note that accompanied them.

Bessie, I thought you might like to see what you could make of these copies of some of the oldest wills we have at the museum now that you've taken the course in reading old handwriting. There are four here and hundreds more at the museum if you enjoy the work. Let me know. Marjorie.

Sitting down at her desk, Bessie looked over the copied sheets. At first glance they were completely indecipherable, but when she started to focus on one page, she began to pick out a few words here and there. Of course wills generally follow a standard format, which meant the first words of the documents should all be the same. Feeling as if she was working on a particularly complex puzzle, Bessie worked her way through the document, word by word, sometimes letter by letter, until she had a very rough transcription. She sat back with a happy sigh. When she glanced at the clock, she was shocked to find that it was past midday.

"I haven't had lunch," she exclaimed. Her tummy rumbled back at her, and laughing to herself, she headed to the kitchen to remedy the situation. By the time she'd eaten and tidied up, she needed to get ready to go the Clague farm. Her taxi arrived right on time for the journey and she chatted easily with Dave as they made their way north.

"I'll have to ring when I've finished," she told him when he dropped her off at the farmhouse. "I've no idea how long this will take."

Bessie walked to the door and knocked loudly. She was conscious that Dave was watching her, waiting until he was certain that someone was home before he drove away. That was just one of the reasons he was her favourite driver. After a few moments, the door swung open.

"Fenella, how are you?" Bessie asked as she waved to Dave and entered the house.

"Oh, fine," Fenella muttered.

Bessie looked hard at the woman. It didn't look as if Fenella had slept since the last time Bessie had seen her. Her hair was pulled back into a messy plait and Bessie could see half a dozen pins sticking out of it at various angles. Bessie couldn't resist giving the woman a quick hug. Fenella went rigid under the contact.

"I'm sorry," she muttered as Bessie pulled back quickly. "I'm just not dealing very well with any of this."

"I'm sure finding the body was upsetting," Bessie said in a soothing tone. "I do hope nothing else is bothering you."

Fenella shrugged. "I just hate not knowing what happened," she said. Bessie could hear tears in the woman's voice.

"Did you know Jacob Conover?" Bessie asked.

"Ah, Bessie, there you are," Eoin's voice boomed through the small entryway where they were still standing. "Sorry that you've had to come back. That dead man is causing no end of trouble."

Bessie smiled at the man as he joined them. "Hello, Eoin," she said. He, too, looked tired, but Bessie wondered if he had more serious health problems than she'd realised. He was tall and he'd always been a somewhat imposing figure as he strode around the farm, but now he seemed to have shrunk somehow. His grey hair had thinned dramatically as well since Bessie had seen him last, only a year earlier.

"I know," he barked at her. "I look awful. Oh, you're too polite to say it to my face, but I have a mirror, not that I spend any time looking in it, you know. Still, the doctors keep giving me medicines and saying they'll fix me. I'm sure I felt better before they got their hands on me, but now I'm stuck with them." He shook his head. "I know I can't live forever, no matter what them doctors say."

"I hope you haven't been too upset by the discovery of the body," Bessie said.

"Oh, I have enough of my own things to worry about without fretting over that," Eoin told her. "But let's go and see the birds, shall we?"

"I'd love a quick chat with Fenella when we're done," Bessie said, glancing at the woman, even though she'd addressed the comment to Eoin.

"Come on back up and we'll have a cuppa," Fenella offered. "It's chilly out in the barns. You'll want a hot drink anyway."

"Let's get moving," Eoin said. "I have to see to the cows next. Nothing gets done when I'm not there."

Bessie followed the man out the front door and down the short path to the road. He opened the door to the car that was parked there, and then when Bessie was safely tucked up inside, he walked around and climbed in the driver's side.

"Is this a new car?" Bessie asked as they drove slowly towards one of the barns.

"Aye, it's new for us, anyway," Eoin replied. "I wanted something that would get me around in a bit more comfort. I'm getting too old for riding tractors everywhere."

Bessie nodded, remembering previous visits where Eoin, and before him Niall, would boost Bessie into a tractor for a scary and bumpy ride across the farm. In the last few years, Eoin had taken to driving small cars that struggled to get around the unpaved farm roads. This vehicle was much larger and far more comfortable, at least as far as Bessie was concerned.

"Is Fenella very upset about the dead man?" Bessie asked as they waited for several sheep to move across the road.

Eoin shrugged. "I don't reckon either of us knew the man they think it was," he told her. "I suppose that the body has been there for so long it feels sort of unreal or something."

"You don't remember Jacob Conover?" Bessie asked.

"Nope," he replied. "I was working on the farm in those days, just as an assistant farmhand. I was far too busy up here working to socialise. I didn't get into Laxey village more than once a month, and that was usually when I took things to the market. Really, I don't remember much from those days. It was a long time ago, of course."

"I understand he was looking to buy a farm in the area," Bessie said. "I thought maybe you met him when he came to look at the farm."

Eoin chuckled. "If he did have any idea of buying the farm, Niall would have set him straight pretty quick. There was no way Niall was ever going to sell the Clague farm to any one from across, that's for sure."

"I wonder if Niall would remember him," Bessie said thoughtfully.

"He doesn't remember his own name, most days," Eoin told her. "As much as I hate being sick, I'd rather deal with my problems than his. His body is holding out much better than his mind. He can't even remember how to feed himself some days. It's a shame, really."

"It is," Bessie agreed. "Perhaps I should pay him a visit. I haven't seen him in a long time."

"Don't expect him to remember you," Eoin warned her. "Although, you never know, he might. Or he might think you are your mother, if you look like her. He gets confused a lot."

Bessie pressed her lips together and sat back in her seat. She knew she did resemble her mother, but the thought wasn't a pleasant one. Bessie had never forgiven her parents, blaming them for Matthew's untimely death. When first her father and then her mother had died many years later, Bessie hadn't spoken to either of them since the day she'd been told of Matthew's passing. Now, after many more years had flown by, Bessie deeply regretted her behaviour, but, of course, she could do nothing to change the past.

The last sheep finally decided to meander out of the way and Eoin pressed the accelerator. "Maybe we can get through before any of the others decide to take a walk," he muttered as they crossed the large field.

After another minute, he stopped in front of a large barn. "Careful of the mud," he warned Bessie as he helped her from the car.

Bessie took his arm and let him lead her into the barn. Inside, what looked like dozens or even hundreds of turkeys were busily eating and chasing one another around large pens.

"I have your lot down here," Eoin told Bessie. He led to the corner of the barn where five large birds were on their own in a small enclosure.

"I thought I only asked for four," Bessie said.

"Aye, but I had a fifth that I thought would be ready early as well," Eoin told her. "If you don't want it, I'll keep it for myself."

"I probably could use five," Bessie replied. "There seem to be an awful lot of people coming to my dinner."

"And you're happy with them all?" he asked.

Bessie looked at the five birds and wondered what she was meant to be considering. They all looked fine to her, but then they always did. "I'm sure they'll be delicious," she said after a moment.

Eoin nodded. "I'll get you back up to the house, then, so you can have some tea with Fen."

They were nearly back to the farmhouse before Eoin spoke again. "I hope you won't be talking to Fen about the body," he said.

Bessie opened her mouth and then closed it again. She had no idea how she wanted to respond. After a moment, Eoin continued.

"She's pretty upset, you see," he told her. "I think she's worried that her father, well, I suppose he had to know about it, didn't he?"

Bessie nodded slowly. "I suppose Niall may have known something about it," she said. "But it's also possible that he didn't. Maybe Jacob, if that is who it is, got into a fight with one of the farmhands or something. He could have been killed accidently and the farmhand might have buried the body in the back of the barn."

"I like that idea," Eoin said. "We've had dozens of temporary workers over the years and some of them were quite capable of killing a man, I reckon."

"I don't suppose you remember any of their names or know where they are now?" Bessie asked.

"I don't suppose I do," Eoin said. "Fen might have kept track of a few of them, but once they left here, I didn't really care where they went or what they did."

"What about any that were here when Jacob Conover was on the island?"

Eoin shrugged. "Like I said, I didn't really keep track. In those days Niall was in charge, anyway. I was just one of the hired help."

"Until you and Fenella fell in love," Bessie said.

"Best thing that ever happened to me," the man replied.

Bessie smiled to herself as she saw the look that came over the man's face. He was clearly still deeply in love with his wife, even after all of their years together.

He pulled up in front of the farmhouse and turned to Bessie. "I really hope you don't upset Fen," he said anxiously. "She hasn't slept properly since that body turned up. I'm hoping, given enough time, she'll forget all about it."

"I should think she'll sleep better once the police work out what happened to the man," Bessie replied. "And the only way they're going to do that is if everyone answers all their questions with as much information as they can provide."

"I've told them everything I know and so has Fen," Eoin said angrily. "Anyway, you aren't the police, so you don't need to bother my wife."

"I'll just have a cup of tea and chat about the weather," Bessie said in her most reassuring voice. "Thank you for letting me see the turkeys. I'm really looking forward to the feast."

"I'll have them delivered to The Swing Bridge in plenty of time," Eoin told her.

Bessie got out of the car and walked up the path to the house. If Eoin felt that strongly about it, she wouldn't ask Fenella any questions, no matter how difficult that might be. She knocked and then turned and smiled at Eoin, who was still sitting in the car watching her. When Fenella opened the door, Bessie gave Eoin a quick wave and then quickly entered the house.

"Did he tell you not to talk about the body?" Fenella asked as she led Bessie into the spacious kitchen.

"I promised him I won't ask any questions," Bessie told her.

Fenella sighed deeply. "That man," she said tiredly. She waved Bessie into a chair at the small wooden table in one corner of the kitchen. Bessie watched as the other woman switched on the kettle and piled a few biscuits on a plate.

"Sorry they aren't my own," she said as she put the plate on the table. "I don't bake very often these days. Eoin doesn't care if they're shop-bought; he doesn't eat much anyway, with his health."

"I'm certainly not going to complain," Bessie told her. "You're being kind enough to provide tea and biscuits, after all."

Fenella smiled. "I know you only want to talk to me about the body, no matter what you promised my husband."

Bessie shook her head. "I'm happy to talk about whatever you'd like," she told the woman. "But I am curious about the body and I would like to know who it was and what happened to him."

Fenella nodded. "It is a strange thing, isn't it? I can't believe the body has been there all this time and we never knew about it. But it worries me as well."

"I suppose you must worry that your father was involved," Bessie replied, carefully making her remark a statement, not a question.

Fenella got up from the table and began to make the tea. She didn't reply until after it was poured and served. Then she sat back down and looked at Bessie. "He doesn't remember me," she said sadly. "And it's harder and harder for me to remember what he was like before, when he was younger and his mind was sharp."

"He was a very hard-working man," Bessie said. "He loved this farm and he loved you. He was so proud of you, and of everything that you did."

"I remember I came third in a race on sports day when I was in year three or four. You might have thought I'd won an Olympic medal the way he carried on when I told him."

Bessie reached out to pat Fenella's hand as the woman's eyes filled with tears. "It's so hard," she told Bessie. "Sometimes he has moments where he remembers something from long ago, and we laugh and reminisce together and it's almost magical, and then suddenly he's lost again."

"I'm so sorry," Bessie said.

Fenella took a deep breath and then straightened in her chair. "Still, mustn't complain. He's happy where he is, even if he gets confused a great deal. I visit when I can, but the farm takes up a lot of my time. If he did know what was happening, he'd understand."

Bessie nodded. "He would at that," she said. "Perhaps I'll go and see him one day soon. I'd like to do that."

"I'm sure he'd like that as well," Fenella said. "He loves visitors, even though he rarely recognises anyone. If you take him some chocolate biscuits, he'll like you even more."

Bessie laughed. "I think I can manage that," she said.

"Please don't ask him about the body," Fenella said. "He's so confused anyway, there's no telling what he'd say."

"I won't," Bessie promised.

"That police woman, she's going to interview him, she said," Fenella told her. "Like you can interview someone in that state."

"Inspector Lambert?" Bessie asked.

"That's the one," Fenella agreed. "She talked to me for hours, and then asked Eoin the same questions. I'm sure she's going to ask my father all manner of things he can't possibly answer."

"She has a job to do," Bessie said.

"I know, but my father might say anything," Fenella complained. "He might confess to murder or even blame Eoin for it. He's not in his right mind."

"I'm sure they'll take that into account," Bessie assured her. "And it's just possible he might remember something that's relevant."

"Except you can never be sure with him, whether he's actually remembering something or just making things up."

"But with the body found here, she has to talk to him," Bessie said. "It was his farm in those days. If anyone ought to know what happened, it's him."

Fenella nodded. "But whatever he knows is now trapped inside a very fragmented brain," she said sadly.

A dozen questions popped into Bessie's head, but mindful of her promise to Eoin, she washed them all down with a sip of tea. Fenella was watching her closely and after a minute she chuckled.

"You did say you'd promised Eoin not to ask anything," she said. "But I can't stand seeing you biting your tongue so hard. For what it's worth, I don't really remember Jacob Conover at all. I was eighteen the summer he was here and I was busy learning all about running the farm."

She looked down at the table and blushed. "Eoin was just starting to court me that summer as well," she said quietly. "But I didn't really notice until later. I'd never really had a boyfriend so I just thought he was being nice for the longest time."

"It's a good thing he was persistent," Bessie said with a laugh.

"He told me once that he very nearly gave up on me. I gather there were one or two other young ladies who were not quite as stupid about men as I was. Eoin didn't go to the pub very often, but I don't think he was short of company when he did stop in for a drink."

Bessie smiled. "He was a good-looking young man," she remembered. "I think there were a few young women who were quite disappointed when he married you."

Fenella nodded. "Of course, there were a few men who were disappointed as well," she pointed out. "But that was mostly because I was the heir to the Clague farm."

"You were a lovely young woman," Bessie said stoutly. "I'm sure more than one man in the village would have taken you out, given the opportunity."

"But my father wasn't about to let that happen," Fenella told her. "He didn't want me to get married until I was older. Eoin only managed to court me because he was here on the farm. My father didn't really notice our relationship was developing until it was too late and Eoin was asking for my hand. If it had been anyone else, my father would have chased him away for sure."

"You don't remember the man, but his body was found on your farm," Bessie mused.

"Which isn't a question, but I will answer what you want to know," Fenella said with a grin. "Unfortunately, it isn't much of an answer, though. I haven't the slightest idea why he was on our farm. I suppose it's possible he was killed somewhere else, though, and the body was just hidden here."

"Yes, I suppose you're right," Bessie said. "Although that does rather complicate things. I'd much rather think that he came up here to talk to one of the farmhands after the pub and that person accidently killed him and hid the body."

Fenella nodded. "I quite like that solution," she said. "We've had a huge number of farmhands over the years. Most of them didn't last long, though. Farming is hard work and many of them decided to move across and try to find something that was easier and paid better."

"Farming is hard work," Bessie agreed. "I'm not sure how you've managed to keep it up for all these years."

"It's my farm," Fenella told her. "I can't imagine doing anything else."

"I don't suppose you've kept in touch with any of the farmhands you've hired over the years," Bessie said.

"Only a few," Fenella told her. "Eoin isn't the least bit sentimental, but some of them, the ones who stay for a year or more, become almost like family. I usually insist on getting a forwarding address for them and I usually write, at least once or twice. If they write back, I keep up the correspondence."

"So what's the longest you've kept in touch with anyone?" Bessie asked.

"Oh, I have one man I write to who worked here in the forties," Fenella told her. "He got married and ended up going down the pits in Yorkshire. He and my father were friends and he used to write every year about how much he missed the island and hated it in the mine. I still get a card every Christmas from him. His wife died about twenty years ago, but his children are all over there, so he's never come back."

"I wonder if anyone you're still in touch with would remember Jacob," Bessie said thoughtfully.

"I didn't think of that," Fenella exclaimed. "I'll have to go through my book and see who might have been here at the right time."

"I don't know, if I'd killed someone and hidden the body, if I'd keep in touch or not," Bessie mused.

"I think I'd simply disappear," Fenella said. "You could do that in those days."

Bessie didn't get to reply. A loud buzzing noise interrupted their talk.

"Someone's at the door," Fenella said. "You stay here and I'll go see who it is."

Fenella was back a moment later, with Inspector Anna Lambert following close behind her.

"Would you like a cuppa?" Fenella asked the woman.

"No, thank you," Anna answered coolly. "I just have a few quick questions. I can wait until Miss Cubbon leaves. I don't want to interrupt your visit."

"I just came to see my turkeys," Bessie told her. "And then Fenella was kind enough to make me some tea."

"Indeed," the woman said, frowning.

Bessie got to her feet. "I'll just ring for a taxi," she said, feeling flustered. She dug out her mobile. After a short conversation, she smiled sheepishly at the other women. "It's going to be a few minutes," she said apologetically. "I can wait in another room or outside, if you'd like."

"Don't be silly," Fenella said. "Sit back down and have another biscuit. The inspector can ask her questions in front of you. I haven't anything to hide."

For a moment Bessie thought the policewoman was going to argue, but after a long pause she smiled tightly.

"If you prefer," she said. Anna sat down on the edge of one of the chairs and looked from Fenella to Bessie and back again. "How many farmhands do you have working here at any given time?" she asked.

"Oh, it varies depending on the time of year," Fenella answered. "At harvest time we have more, but this time of year we only have one or two. Eoin and I do most of the work."

"So you don't employ most of them all year around?" Anna asked.

"No. We only have one or two men that are here all year. They have quarters on the east end of the farm."

"And have either of them been here since the nineteen-fifties?"

Fenella laughed. She sobered quickly under Anna's icy stare. "Sorry, but I don't think either of them were born in the nineteen-fifties," she replied. "We hire men who are young and strong. It's a tough job and most of them don't do it for more than a year or two before they move on. The ones that really love it, they start saving up and buy their own little plots as soon as they can so that all of their hard labour goes to their own profits, not someone else's."

"Do you still keep in touch with any of your former farmhands, then?" was Anna's next question.

Fenella nodded. "That's just what Bessie and I were discussing when you arrived," she exclaimed.

"Really?" Anna said, giving Bessie a hard look.

"Yes, she was wondering if anyone who used to work here might remember Jacob," Fenella said, apparently oblivious to Anna's darkening mood.

"Yes, I was just wondering the same thing myself," Anna said. "I'd appreciate it if you could make me a list of everyone who was here in the fifties, with their contact information."

"Of course I can," Fenella agreed.

When she didn't move, Anna spoke again. "Now," she said in a commanding voice.

"Oh, I didn't, that is, of course." Fenella got up from the table. "I'll just go and get my book," she said.

Bessie grabbed a biscuit and took a huge bite, focussing all of her attention on the crumbly treat. She could feel Anna's eyes on her, but she wasn't brave enough to look up. After only a moment, Fenella was back.

"Here we are," she said brightly. "Now, let me see."

The doorbell sounded, and Bessie sighed with relief. Her taxi had arrived. She said a quick good-bye to Fenella who was now busily turning pages in her address book. She gave Bessie a distracted wave as Bessie rushed from the room. At the front door, Bessie picked up her handbag.

"I know John is rather fond of you." Anna's icy voice stopped Bessie as she reached for the door handle. "But I'll thank you to stay out of my investigation."

Bessie glanced over at the woman and nodded. "Of course," she muttered. She pulled the door open and nearly tripped over her own feet in her eagerness to get out of the house.

"Steady on," Dave laughed, taking her arm. "I do hope you haven't seen a ghost."

"Oh, no," Bessie told him. "Although I think that might have been less scary."

CHAPTER 9

Dave drove Bessie home, and she immediately made herself a cup of tea to calm her nerves. It took two cups of tea and a fancy chocolate biscuit to finally make her feel better.

"And I haven't even done anything wrong," Bessie said to her mirror image as she washed the chocolate off her fingers. "I might have been snooping a little bit, but I didn't ask Fenella any questions about the body. It's only natural that she wanted to talk about it, anyway."

She made a face at herself. "That woman has me talking to myself," she muttered as she walked back into the kitchen. "This will never do." She looked out the window at the beach. A bit of sea air and exercise were exactly what she needed.

November was always cool and there was a light wind blowing in across the sea, so Bessie put on a warm coat before she ventured out. She put her head down and marched steadily across the sand, trying to clear her mind. She'd reached Thie yn Traie before she began to feel soothed by the sounds of the sea. Stopping at the bottom of the stairs, she looked up the cliff at the house perched above her. There were lights on inside and she found herself wanting to climb the stairs to see what was going on. She shook her head and forced herself to turn away from temptation.

After walking a short distance farther, Bessie decided to head for home. She turned around and then gasped. There were two people descending the stairs from Thie yn Traie to the beach. Bessie stopped and watched as they made their way down the steep steps. There was something familiar about the couple, but Bessie was too far away to be certain who they were. When they reached the ground, they turned and began to walk towards Bessie.

"Mary?" Bessie called as she watched their approach. "George? What are you two doing down here?"

George and Mary Quayle were both smiling brightly when they reached Bessie's side. Everyone exchanged hugs.

George had been partners with Grant Robertson and had been questioned by the police for many weeks as they investigated Grant's businesses. He'd never been formally arrested, and eventually the police had determined that he hadn't been involved in Grant's illegal activities. While George had been busy with the police, Mary had gone across to stay with family and friends. Bessie hadn't realised that the woman had returned to the island.

"I was going to ring you later," Mary said. "I just got back to the island last night."

"I'm so glad you're back," Bessie replied. "I wanted to invite you and George to my Thanksgiving feast, but I wasn't sure if you would be here."

"I'm back now and not thinking of going away again anytime soon," Mary said emphatically.

"I don't plan on letting her go away again," George added in his booming voice.

Bessie smiled at the pair. George looked exactly the same. He was a large man with a loud voice who always sounded like he was selling something, a relic of his years working in sales. Mary was tiny, and after the stresses of the previous weeks, she looked even thinner and more fragile than ever. Bessie knew that the woman's delicate exterior hid a steel core, but she worried about her friend nevertheless.

"We'd love to come," Mary told Bessie.

"But what brings you to Laxey Beach on a cold November afternoon?" Bessie asked.

"We're looking at Thie yn Traie," Mary replied.

"You are?" Bessie exclaimed.

"The house in Douglas is too large for just us," Mary told her. "Thie yn Traie is huge, too, of course, but it's smaller than our current home. George is ready to retire properly now and we thought maybe we should downsize a bit."

Only someone very rich would consider Thie yn Traie, with its many sprawling wings, downsizing, Bessie mused. She had to admit that the mansion on the beach above them was somewhat smaller than the huge estate the couple owned on the outskirts of Douglas, though.

"We could be neighbours," Bessie said.

"I have to say, that's one of the reasons I wanted to look at the place," Mary told her.

"I've only seen a few rooms inside; is it nice?" Bessie asked.

Mary looked at George. He laughed. "I'm not sure I'd describe it that way," he said. "The previous owners are selling it fully furnished, but their taste isn't anything like ours, which complicates things. The first thing we'd need to do, if we do buy the house, is clear it all out."

"It's very cold," Mary said. "It doesn't feel like home at all."

"The previous owners only used it as a summer home," Bessie said. "It never was a proper family house."

"Well, it will be if we buy it," Mary said firmly. "We've had my favourite designer through twice now and she has many good ideas that will help warm up the spaces. Once we get our own furniture in there and paint and decorate, it won't be the same house at all."

"I do hope you'll invite me over to have a look," Bessie said.

"We haven't bought it yet," George said. "And I'm not convinced it's our best move."

"I still have to talk him into it," Mary told Bessie with a wink. "He loves that monstrosity we live in now."

"It's a wonderful house," George said defensively.

"It is, dear," Mary said, patting his arm. "But the children are all grown up and on their own, well, except for Elizabeth. We don't need all that space and we don't need to be in Douglas, either, since you won't be working anymore."

"I'm still going to have a few little investments to manage," George grumbled.

"But you can manage them from Laxey just as well," Mary said.

"Yes, I know, but we worked so hard to get the Douglas house done just the way we want it," George argued.

"And it still isn't done," Mary reminded him. "You've redone our suite three times and you still aren't happy with it because the spaces just aren't right. You have to admit that the master suite here is pretty perfect."

"I love the layout of the suite and the views from the windows," George admitted.

"If it gets a fresh coat of paint, some new carpets, and we change out the furniture, it will be perfect," Mary said happily.

"We'll see," George said.

Mary smiled at Bessie. "I think it will be perfect," she told her. "And there's a huge wing for Elizabeth on the opposite side of the house that will be just right for her until she works out what she wants to do next."

Bessie wondered to herself if the girl might make up her mind a bit faster if her parents stopped letting her live at home without any responsibilities.

"Are you looking at any other properties?" Bessie asked.

"There's a small estate in the middle of the island, near the Wildlife Park, that's just come on the market," Mary told her. "But I really want to be near the sea."

"We did see a gorgeous home, right on the beach, in Port Erin," George interjected.

"It was lovely," Mary agreed. "But Port Erin feels so far away, and there wasn't a separate wing for Elizabeth, either."

"Yes, dear," George said. He'd obviously lost interest in the conversation and now he stared out at the sea.

"Well, I hope we buy Thie yn Traie," Mary told Bessie. "Once we redecorate, I think it will be perfect for us. I'm so looking forward to getting out of Douglas."

"I'm going to go back up and look at the master suite again," George told Mary. "You take your time with Bessie, though."

The women watched as George made his way back to the stairs. As he began his ascent, Mary sighed deeply.

"All of this has been very hard on him," she said quietly.

"I'm sure it's been difficult for both of you," Bessie replied.

"Oh, I just went and stayed with some friends across. It was almost like an extended holiday for me. George had to stay here and deal with all the questions and suspicions."

"I understand he's been cleared of any wrongdoing," Bessie said.

"He has," Mary nodded. "But many people still seem to think he's guilty of something, even if the police don't."

"That's awful," Bessie said.

"What's worse is that many of the men and women that run the businesses that George and Grant have invested in over the years have been the first to want to cut all of their ties with George."

"I imagine they don't want any connections with Grant," Bessie mused.

"But George had nothing to do with Grant's schemes, not the illegal ones, anyway." She shook her head. "I'm glad that George is working less, as the various projects get cancelled or taken over by other investors, but George is devastated."

Bessie gave Mary a hug. "If I can do anything, please let me know," she murmured.

"I don't suppose you'd like to start a small company and would like George to invest in it?" Mary said teasingly.

"Not really," Bessie laughed. "But if I hear of anyone else who might be, I will let you know."

"I was almost afraid to talk to you," Mary told her, confidingly. "So many of our friends are no longer speaking to us."

"Really? That's horrible as well."

"In a way, it feels worse," Mary said. "With the businesses, we can tell ourselves that it's just good business practice for them to distance themselves from Grant, which means from George by association. But with friends, it's simply personal."

"Well, I don't abandon my friends when they find themselves having difficulties," Bessie said stoutly. She could see tears in Mary's eyes.

"Thank you," Mary said. "That's just one more reason why I hope we buy Thie yn Traie. I'd love to have you close by. I could come and visit you when George starts complaining about how bored he is being home all the time. He thrives on social contact and he hasn't been invited anywhere in weeks."

Bessie knew that Mary was shy and preferred to stay home; she was always surprised at how often opposites really did attract. Still, the pair seemed to have a successful marriage, in spite of their differences.

"Well, I've invited you to Thanksgiving," Bessie said.

"And I didn't even have to check our availability," Mary said sadly. "We're always available at the moment."

"I can't believe this little bit of bother is going to defeat George," Bessie said. "Given a bit of time, I'm sure he'll bounce back."

"I think so, too," Mary agreed. "He's very resilient, really. And he still has plenty of money to throw around. It won't be long before people start asking for his help again, I think. As for our friends, well, I'm happy to make new ones. Most of the old ones were only interested in George's money, anyway."

"I hope you can enjoy some time together before he gets busy again," Bessie told her friend.

"I've only been back a day and he's already making me crazy," Mary said with a laugh. "I used to complain because he never had time for me, but now I'm miserable because he's constantly underfoot."

"Maybe you'll be able to find a better balance, once he starts to get busy again," Bessie said.

"I do hope so," Mary told her. "I must say I'm feeling as if I'm awfully hard to please."

Bessie laughed. "We all are," she said. "We think we want something, but then we get it and it isn't at all what we were expecting. Anyway, you know where I am whenever you need a break from George."

"I might just take you up on that," Mary said. "But for today I'd better get back up to the house and see what he's doing. If I'm not there to point out all of the wonderful things about the house, he might decide he doesn't want to move after all."

Bessie watched her friend climb back up the steep steps. She returned the gesture as Mary waved to her from the top of the stairs. A few minutes later, she found herself waving at Thomas Shimmin as she walked past the cottages. Back at her cottage, she felt as if she'd been out for hours. The light on her answering machine was blinking frantically.

"Bessie, we were just talking here at the station and we thought maybe it was time for a group chat about things," Doona's voice said. "John's offered to host at his new house so we can all have a look. I'll pick you up at six, unless you ring me back. Hugh's offered to bring dinner, so you don't have to worry about that, either."

As it was already half five, Bessie didn't have time to do much of anything. She sat down with a book, but found that she couldn't concentrate on the plot. Instead, she found herself thinking about the dead man and wondering about his connection with the Clague farm. Doona was at her door a short time later.

"I can't wait to see what John's done with the house," Bessie told Doona as Doona drove the short distance.

"I never saw it before he bought it, but the layout was similar to mine when it was first built. I don't know how much they changed when they updated it, though."

"They changed a lot," Bessie told her. "You'll love his kitchen."

"I was thinking I might redo mine, now that I have a little bit of spare money," Doona said thoughtfully. "Or maybe I'll just pay down my mortgage and be sensible," she added with a sigh. "It isn't like I cook all that often, anyway."

"I think, if you're going to spend money on your house, that you should renovate your bathroom," Bessie told her. "You've always wanted a fancy bathtub. You enjoyed the one on our holiday, didn't you?"

"I suppose," Doona replied. "There was a lot on my mind at the time. I'm sure I'd have enjoyed it a lot more under more normal circumstances."

"Think how nice it would be to have one of those tubs in your own bathroom," Bessie said.

"What would you do if you suddenly inherited a bunch of money?" Doona asked.

"I'd add a library to my cottage," Bessie told her. "Although I probably wouldn't get planning permission. I had enough trouble getting permission for the changes I've made over the years."

Doona pulled to a stop in a parking space in front of John's house.

"I still don't like the exterior," Bessie grumbled as she climbed out of the car.

"It is a bit, well, different," Doona said. "It makes the house stand out a bit in our neighbourhood."

Doona's home was just a short distance away. Bessie glanced up the street towards the house that had belonged to Nancy King, Sarah's mother. After her mother's death and the discovery of a body behind a false wall, Sarah and her brothers had taken the property off the market while they discussed what to do next. The house was too far away from John's for Bessie to see if they'd been working on it, though.

The pair made their way up the walk to John's front door. Doona knocked and they waited patiently.

"Ah, good evening," John said as he pulled the door open. He glanced back into the house, obviously distracted by something.

"We did say half six, didn't we?" Doona asked as she and Bessie entered the house.

"Yes, of course," John said. "It's just, I was trying, that is," he shook his head. "I was just trying to get some last-minute cleaning done and I've left the can of furniture polish somewhere," he told them both. "I can't for the life of me remember where I had it last, so when you trip over it or knock it over, I'm awfully sorry."

Bessie and Doona both laughed. "You shouldn't worry about cleaning for us," Bessie told him. "I couldn't care less if there's a bit of dust around the place."

"But your cottage is always spotless," John replied. "I couldn't have welcomed you to a mess."

Bessie glanced around the large sitting room that the door opened into. "This space looks wonderful," she said, changing the subject slightly. "I love the colour you've used in here."

John looked around at the room. "It isn't bad," he said after a moment. "It looks darker on the walls than it did in the can, but I think the room is large enough that it works anyway."

"So show us the rest," Bessie demanded. "And we'll see if we can find your furniture polish on the way."

"So the dining room is just..." he was interrupted by a knock on the door.

"That'll be Hugh," he said.

But when John pulled the door open, there was a young blonde woman standing there. She smiled brightly at John and then frowned at Bessie and Doona.

"I didn't realise you had company," she said, her voice light and airy. "I was hoping I might be able to borrow some sugar."

"Of course," John said. He looked over at his guests and then back at the new arrival. "Ah, Doona and Bessie, this is Holly. She's just moved in next door."

Bessie smiled at the woman. "Nice to meet you," she said politely. "What do you need the sugar for?"

The woman blinked at her. "The sugar? Why, that is, I'm baking biscuits," she said after an awkward pause."

"I love to bake," Bessie said. "What sort of biscuits are you making?"

The girl frowned and then looked at the ground. "Um, just digestives," she muttered.

"Really?" Bessie asked. "You must share your recipe. I find digestives ever so difficult to get right myself. It's so much easier to buy them than make them."

The girl shrugged. Before she could reply, Hugh came up behind her on the walkway carrying several large boxes of food.

"Oh, more company," she said. "You know what, never mind about the sugar. I'll just get out of your way."

"I can get your sugar if you want to wait a minute," John protested.

"No, I'm not really in the mood for baking any more," Holly replied. "Thanks anyway."

Bessie and the others watched her as she quickly crossed the grass back to the small house next door.

"If she wanted sugar, I want my head examined," Doona exclaimed as Holly disappeared inside.

Bessie laughed, but John looked at them with a confused frown. "What do you mean?" he asked.

"Doona is suggesting that your lovely neighbour was, perhaps, just making an excuse to visit you," Bessie told him gently.

"Why would she do that?" John asked, sounding genuinely baffled.

Bessie smiled. "She's new to the island, right? I reckon she's single, and you're an attractive single man. I would imagine she's looking to make friends."

John blushed. "But I'm not really single, not yet. And even if I were single, I'm certainly not looking. Anyway, she's far too young for me, don't you think?"

"Let's not worry about that right now," Bessie suggested. "We were going to take a tour, but maybe we should eat first, since the food is here."

"The kitchen is straight ahead," John told them.

Hugh and Doona headed in the right direction, while Bessie stopped John. "The lovely Holly could be a problem, if you aren't careful," she said quietly.

"I hope not," John replied. "I have quite enough problems right now."

"Just make sure you don't encourage her," Bessie suggested. "Be polite, but don't invite her in, don't accept any invitations to her place and try not to be alone with her if you can help it."

John nodded. "I should have realised," he said. "But I never expect women to be interested in me."

Bessie laughed. "You're a very attractive man," she told him. "If I were a few years younger, I'd be giving Holly a run for her money."

Now John chuckled. "If you were a few years younger, I think I'd be chasing you," he told Bessie.

The pair linked arms and John escorted her into his shiny new kitchen. Doona and Hugh were laying out the food and John quickly found plates for them.

"We can sit in the formal dining room if you'd like," John said as everyone filled their plates. "Or we can just sit in here."

"Let's just stay here," Bessie said. "It's warm and cosy."

They all took seats around the small round table in one corner of the room. John got everyone drinks and then they all turned their attention to eating. After several minutes of silence, Bessie spoke.

"This is delicious," she said. "Thank you, Hugh."

"You're welcome," he said. "I've been wanting to try this place. It just opened near the station, but they're only open in the evening; they don't do lunches. Grace has been too busy to go out much lately, so tonight was a good excuse to try it."

"Well, it's very good," Bessie said.

"I brought a cake from the bakery next to it as well," Hugh told her.

"Cake? You are spoiling us," Bessie said with a laugh.

"I decided we needed a treat, since we have to talk about murder," Hugh told her.

"Or at least unexplained death," John interjected. "We have no real evidence that our dead man was murdered, at least not yet."

"But someone hid the body," Hugh said. "That seems like murder to me."

John nodded. "We're investigating it as murder, at least until we hear otherwise," he said.

"Have you made any progress on identifying the body?" Bessie asked.

John shook his head. "We're still waiting on the DNA tests.

Because of the very distinctive watch, we suspect that the body is Jacob Conover's, but we can't be sure, of course."

"He still hasn't turned up alive anywhere, then?" Bessie wondered.

"No. He's been listed as a missing person in Liverpool and London for forty-odd years," John replied. "His sister is pretty certain it must be him."

"That poor woman," Doona said. "Imagine not knowing where your brother was for all that time."

"She's coming over to the island if it does turn out to be him," John said. "She's mentioned wanting to meet anyone who might remember him."

Bessie nodded. "I'd be happy to talk to her," she said. "I didn't know him well, but I do remember him."

"I'm sure she'd appreciate that," John told her.

"So where are we with means and motive and opportunity?" Hugh asked.

"Nowhere," John said glumly. "It was such a long time ago, we're struggling to come up with any of those things for anyone."

"I'm sure several young ladies were quite upset with how they were treated, but I can't see any of them resorting to murder," Bessie said. "And I can't get past the fact that the man was leaving. Why would anyone kill him if he was leaving anyway?"

"That's a very good question," John said. "Anna has suggested that maybe he was just telling people he was leaving, but he was really just moving to another part of the island or something."

"To do what?" Bessie demanded. "He was supposed to be looking for a farm to buy. If he wanted to look elsewhere in the island, surely he wouldn't be doing it in secret?"

"What about jealous boyfriends?" Hugh asked. "If he went out with just about every single young woman in Laxey, that must have upset a few of the young men."

"We're checking on that as much as we can," John said. "But it was a long time ago. Many of the men and women we've spoken to don't seem to remember much from that summer."

"I think we should focus on finding his connection with the Clague farm," Bessie said thoughtfully. "Why was he buried there?"

"No one I've talked to can give me any reason why he was there," John said, sounding frustrated. "If only we could talk to Niall."

"I thought Anna was going to try," Bessie said.

"She did," John said. "He told her all about Christmas in the nineteen-thirties, but couldn't remember her name from one minute to the next."

Bessie sighed. "I was thinking about going to see him," she said.

John looked at her for a minute and then sighed. Before he could speak, Doona started collecting the dishes.

"We should have cake," she said brightly.

Hugh got up and opened the bakery box. The cake inside was beautifully decorated.

"It seems a shame to eat it," Bessie said as she stared at the treat.

"It would be a bigger shame to throw it away," Hugh said logically.

John handed him a stack of small plates and a knife and Hugh cut very generous slices from the cake. The group fell silent again as they enjoyed their pudding.

"That was fabulous," Doona said as she scraped up her last bite.

"It was really good," Bessie agreed.

"At least now I know where to get the cakes for my kids' birthdays," John said with a grin.

"Where were we?" Bessie asked as she helped Doona tidy up.

"We were talking about Niall," Doona told her. "And how frustrating it is that he's, um, not able to help more."

"Could he have murdered Jacob Conover?" Hugh asked the question that everyone else was thinking.

Bessie sighed. "I'd like to be able to say no," she said sadly. "But I simply don't know. I can't say I ever knew him especially well. He kept to himself, and the farm and raising Fenella kept him very busy, anyway. I think he'd have needed a very strong motive, but he may have had one; I just don't know what it was."

"Maybe Jacob was annoying Fenella," Doona suggested.

Bessie frowned. "Both she and Eoin claim they don't remember him," she said. "But I don't believe them. Fenella must have met him, at least once or twice. She used to come into town to the market every week and he used to spend a lot of time there, talking with all of the girls."

"Why would she lie?" Doona asked.

"The only thing I can think is that she suspects that her father had something to do with the man's death," Bessie replied. "Maybe she's trying to protect him."

"Him or Eoin?" Hugh asked.

Bessie shrugged. "I suspect she'd lie for both of them," she said.

"They have to be close to the top of the suspect list," Hugh said. "If only because the body was found on their farm."

"Is there anyone else on the list at all?" Bessie asked. "I mean, I can't imagine anyone else being able to hide the body there without getting caught."

"We're trying to track down as many of the farm's former farmhands as we can," John said. "Many of them were just casual labour who only worked on the farm for a season or so and then moved on. It's possible, maybe even probable, that one of them had a fight with Jacob Conover and killed him. Whether he could have hidden the body in that barn without Niall knowing about it is another question, but for now we're focussing on one thing at a time."

"Anna was at the farm asking Fenella for any information she had for anyone who'd ever worked for them," Bessie said. "I got the feeling Fenella hadn't kept track of many of them."

"No, when I spoke to Anna this afternoon she said she'd only been able to get about a dozen names from Fenella," John said.

"Were any of them on the island in the right year?" Bessie asked.

John shrugged. "Anna's going through the list. Fenella couldn't be sure of exactly when any of them were here, apparently."

"I suppose it's a waste of time talking about means," Hugh said.

"From what I understand, he must have died the night of his leaving party," Bessie said. "He was supposed to take the ferry the next morning. It never crossed my mind to question whether he made it on board or not."

"The killer was lucky there," John said. "I've spoken to several people who were at that party, and no one seems to recall who Jacob left with or where he said he was going. The woman he was rooming with passed away many years ago, so we can't ask her if he ever came back for his belongings."

"That's a point," Bessie said. "Someone must have gone and taken them or Margaret would have said something."

"We're trying to track his things down and also find out what happened to his car," John said.

"I'd forgotten about that car," Bessie exclaimed. "It was a nice one. Much nicer than most of the people around here could afford. I wonder what ever happened to it."

"So do we," John said.

"I seem to remember him selling it to someone in Douglas a short time before he was supposed to leave," Bessie said, struggling to remember. "I'm not sure, though."

They talked in circles for several more minutes, but no one seemed to be able to add anything useful to the discussion. Bessie found herself yawning for the third time.

"I think it's time to call it a night," she said reluctantly. "As much as I'm enjoying the company and the conversation."

"Doona, I'll take Bessie home. I know you have to be in early tomorrow," John said.

"Are you sure?" Doona asked.

"I don't have to be in until ten," he told her. "But I saw you were on the schedule at seven."

Doona nodded. "That's because Anna hates me," she said.

John shook his head. "She doesn't hate you," he said. "She just likes to rotate the shifts around. That way no one has to be in at seven every day."

"But Karen likes working at seven," Doona protested. "And now Anna has us all bouncing around and we can never remember when we're meant to be working."

"We're going to have a staff meeting next week," John said. "Everyone will be able to raise their concerns at that time."

Doona looked like she wanted to say something, but she snapped her mouth shut and got up from the table.

"Thank you for hosting us tonight," she said to John. "And thank you for dinner," she told Hugh. She gave Bessie a hug and then all four of them walked towards the front door.

"We never got our tour," Bessie exclaimed.

"Go and have a quick look, then," John told her. "I'll wait here."

Bessie and Doona walked through the house quickly, opening and closing doors as they went. Bessie felt quite self-conscious as she peeked into the bedrooms and bathrooms.

"It's lovely," she told John a few minutes later, handing him the can of furniture polish she'd found on the dining room table.

"The colours all work very well together," Doona said. "And it looks as if it will be a comfortable home for you and your children."

John held the door for Doona and Hugh and then he and Bessie followed them out. John's car was behind Doona's and he helped Bessie into the passenger seat. The pair was silent on the short drive back to Bessie's cottage.

"Thank you for the ride," Bessie said as John pulled to a stop outside her door.

"I'll just come in and check that everything is okay," John told her.

Bessie bit back a frustrated sigh. She hated when her friends fussed over her, but she knew they were only doing it because they cared. After she unlocked her door, she let John take the lead. She checked her answering machine and did a few little jobs around the kitchen while she listened to John stomping around the cottage.

"It was good to see you," he said to Bessie when he returned to the kitchen.

"It was wonderful to see you," Bessie replied, giving him a hug. "Your new house is just about perfect. I'm sure the children will love it."

John smiled and headed for the door. Before he opened it he stopped and turned to Bessie, a frown on his face. "Anna isn't happy with you," he said hesitatingly. "She thinks you're interfering with her investigation."

"I am not," Bessie replied angrily.

"I know," John told her. "And I told her you can be a hugely valuable resource as well, but she doesn't work that way. I think you'd be wise to try to stay out of her way."

"I'm not quite sure how I'm meant to do that," Bessie said tartly. "It isn't as if she tells me what she's going to do next."

John flushed. "I just, that is, well, maybe you should stay away from the Clague farm for a while, and from anyone connected to it."

"You don't want me to go and see Niall," Bessie said.

"I don't mind if you go and see Niall," John countered. "But Anna doesn't think you should."

"Are you telling me I can't go and see him?" Bessie demanded.

"No," John said in a tired voice. "You can do whatever you like, just be prepared for Anna to dislike it."

"I'm not sure I care what Anna thinks," Bessie said.

John nodded. "I just don't want you to make an enemy of her," he said.

CHAPTER 10

John's words seemed to stay in Bessie's head all through the night. As she walked on the beach the next morning, she tried to think. She didn't want to anger Anna Lambert, but she wanted to see Niall and ask him about Jacob. As far as she could tell, there was no way to visit him without upsetting Anna.

Back at her cottage, she paced in circles around her sitting room. What she needed was a very good reason to visit Niall, one that had nothing to do with the dead man. Her phone interrupted her thoughts.

"Bessie, it's Doncan," Bessie's advocate's voice came down the line. "I was just ringing to tell you how sorry I am, but the painting went for more than your top bid."

Bessie sighed. "I didn't really think I'd win it," she replied, swallowing her disappointment. "It really is a beautiful painting. I hope it's going to a good home."

"I'm not sure where it's going," Doncan told her. "The winner had submitted a sealed bid, like you did, and chose to remain anonymous."

"Well, never mind," Bessie said. "Maybe I'll see it somewhere one day."

"Maybe," Doncan laughed.

"Anyway, I'll see you on Saturday," Bessie told him.

"You will indeed," Doncan replied.

Bessie sat down and thought for a moment. She'd invited Niall to her Thanksgiving feast once, many years earlier. He'd laughed and told her that farming was a full-time job and that he couldn't take a whole afternoon out to sit around eating and drinking. Bessie could remember the conversation like it had been yesterday.

"Ask me again when I've retired," he'd laughed.

"I will," Bessie had promised.

"And now I shall keep that promise," Bessie said loudly. Anna Lambert probably wouldn't think that was a very good excuse for visiting the man, but Bessie decided she didn't care. Now that she'd thought of it, she was eager to invite Niall to her dinner. There was no way he'd be able to attend, given his health, but she owed him the invitation.

She rang her taxi service and booked a car to take her to Douglas in the afternoon. Her morning was spent with a good book. After a light lunch, she waited impatiently for her taxi. Seeing Mark Stone, her least favourite driver, driving the car that came to collect her made her frown.

Mark leaned on the car's horn as Bessie grabbed her handbag and locked up the cottage. She could see impatience on his face as she crossed to the car.

"Douglas?" he asked as he turned the car around while she was fastening her seatbelt. "I don't suppose you'd rather go to Ramsey?"

"No, I would not," Bessie said firmly.

"Only I told a friend I'd give him a ride somewhere," Mark explained. "But he's in Ramsey. I'd hate to make him wait while I take you all the way to Douglas."

Bessie looked at him, sure that her astonishment would be obvious from her expression. "You'd like me to change my plans for the day to accommodate your friend?" Bessie asked.

"Well, I mean, maybe we could just swing by Ramsey and collect him," Mark suggested. "It isn't that much out of the way."

Bessie stared at him for a moment. "If you really must," she said. "But obviously I don't expect to be charged for that portion of the trip. And I assume your friend, as he's sharing the ride, will share the cost of the journey from Ramsey to Douglas with me."

Mark frowned. "Well, I'm sort of taking him as a favour, you see," he told Bessie. "I can't make him pay, not really."

"Well, I won't be paying full fare if I'm sharing the ride," Bessie said sharply. "Especially as the journey will take a good deal longer as we will be going in the wrong direction for much of it."

Mark sighed deeply. "Never mind," he said grumpily. "I'll just take you to Douglas and make Joe wait."

"As you're doing him a favour, he shouldn't mind," Bessie said.

"Aye, but he will," Mark muttered. That was the last thing that he said to Bessie during the journey, and Bessie wasn't feeling inclined to make polite conversation.

"So, Douglas Gardens, are you thinking it's time to look into nursing homes?" he asked as he pulled up in front of Bessie's destination.

"I'm visiting a friend," Bessie told him.

"I reckon most of your friends are in homes now, aren't they?" Mark asked. "I mean, they all must be getting on a bit, mustn't they? If they're still around, that is."

Bessie counted to ten slowly and then counted again, backwards this time. She wasn't feeling much calmer as she bit her lip and climbed out of the taxi. "Bill me," she said curtly, turning and walking briskly away from the car before she said something she might regret later.

"What a horrible man," she muttered to herself as she made her way through the glass doors at the entrance to the nursing home.

"I do hope you aren't talking about me," a familiar voice spoke from right inside the door.

Bessie looked over and smiled brightly. "Inspector Corkill, what a pleasant surprise."

"You really must call me Pete," he replied, looking Bessie up and down. "You're looking very well," he added.

"You are as well," Bessie replied. The Douglas area police inspector had taken some time to warm up to Bessie following their unfortunate meeting after Bessie had found a murdered man, but now their relationship had developed into something like friendship. As Bessie studied him now, she realised that he was smiling, something she wasn't sure she'd seen him do before. He looked fitter and healthier than he had the last time she's seen him, as well.

"Ah, Bessie, what brings you to Douglas?" Helen Baxter, a pretty blonde nurse that Bessie knew from the woman's interest in the medical history of the island, had joined them. Now she linked arms with Pete and rested her head on his shoulder.

Bessie smiled. Perhaps the changes in Pete had a simple explanation. "I came to visit an old friend," she told the woman. "I've never actually been here before, but it's meant to be a very nice facility."

Helen nodded. "I stopped by to visit a former patient," she told Bessie. "She was telling me how much she loves it here, and from everything I've seen, it's a very nice place."

"Yes, well, I can't imagine moving out of my little cottage, but I do have to say it is nice to know there are good alternatives," Bessie replied.

"We should get going," Pete broke in. "You have a lot of shopping you want to get done before dinner."

Helen laughed. "We have a booking somewhere posh," she told Bessie. "It's a rare treat and I thought I ought to have a new dress and shoes."

"Well, have a wonderful time," Bessie said, wondering if they were celebrating something special, but not wanting to pry.

"I'm sure we will," Helen told her. "And we're both really looking forward to your party next weekend as well."

"I'm glad," Bessie said with a smile. "It's going to be my biggest ever Thanksgiving feast."

"We'll see you then," Pete said.

Helen gave Bessie a big hug and then the couple disappeared out the doors Bessie had just come in. She smiled to herself as she crossed the reception area. Helen and Pete made a very attractive couple and Bessie was really happy to see them together.

"How may I help you?" the young woman behind the reception desk asked Bessie.

"I'd like to visit Niall Clague," Bessie told her. "We're old friends."

The girl tapped something into her computer and then gave Bessie a well-practiced smile. "He's in room 127," she said. "I'll just buzz one of the girls to take you back."

"Thank you," Bessie replied.

"I'm sure he'll be glad to have a visitor," the girl said. "But I feel I should warn you that he isn't always, well, he has problems with his memory. He often forgets who people are and he can get very confused when he talks about the past."

Bessie nodded. "I know his daughter, Fenella," she said. "She's told me that her father isn't doing very well."

"That's sadly true," the girl said, nodding. "But I know he'll be happy that someone has come to see him, anyway."

Bessie wasn't so sure about that, but she smiled and nodded as she waited for someone to escort her to Niall's room. It was only a moment later that a young girl came out through the door to the left of the reception desk.

"Hi," she said brightly to Bessie. "I'm Noreen, and I'm one of the nursing assistants here."

"Hey, Noreen, can you show our guest to Niall Clague's room, please?" the girl behind the desk asked. "Maybe you can stay with them for a few minutes. You know how Mr. Clague can be when something unexpected happens."

Noreen nodded. "If you'd like to follow me," she said to Bessie. She led the way to the door she'd just come out of and tapped in a code on the panel next to it. Bessie heard the click as it unlocked. Noreen pulled the door open and then motioned for Bessie to go through first.

"How does Niall get when something unexpected happens?" Bessie asked nervously as they made their way down the corridor.

"Oh, he can get a bit upset, that's all," the girl replied in the same cheery tone that was starting to annoy Bessie. "He likes his routine, does our Niall." She glanced over at Bessie. "Which isn't to say he doesn't like visitors," she added quickly. "Just that he can find visitors a bit overwhelming, that's all."

"Well, if I upset him, I'll go," Bessie replied. "I didn't come to see him to upset him."

"I'm sure it will be fine," Noreen assured her. "He's a favourite of mine, so I'm pretty good at dealing with him."

Noreen paused outside the open door to room 127 and knocked gently. When there was no reply, she knocked again, with more force.

"Niall? It's Noreen. Can we come in?" she called.

"I suppose," a low voice called back.

Noreen led Bessie into the spacious room. Bessie looked around approvingly at the solid wooden furniture and spotlessly clean room. Noreen had gone straight to the chair that had been placed in front of the television, even though the telly was dark.

"Niall, do you remember I told you that you were going to have a visitor today?" Noreen asked. She glanced up at Bessie and winked at her. "Here she is."

The man in the chair looked up slowly. Bessie was shocked at how old and frail he looked. His many years of hard physical labour on the farm had given him broad shoulders and strong arms. Now he appeared to have shrunk in much the same way his son-in-law had. Fenella had told Bessie that her father was still physically strong, but Bessie wondered if the woman was seeing what she wanted to see rather than reality. The man staring up at her looked incredibly fragile.

"Bessie?" he said now. "Bessie Cubbon? Is that you? My goodness, woman, you've grown old."

Bessie laughed and sat down in the chair opposite him, after passing him the box of chocolate biscuits she'd brought. "We both have, Niall," she replied. "Growing old isn't so bad."

"I don't know," Niall said. "I think I'd rather be young again, if I had a choice."

Bessie nodded. "Unfortunately, we don't get that choice," she said.

"I'll just leave you two for a short visit," Noreen said, her tone still perky. "I'll be back to check on you in a little while."

Niall watched her go. "She's too bloody perky," he told Bessie after she'd disappeared from view. "I think she's helping herself to something from the drugs cabinet when no one is looking. It's not possible for someone to be that happy all the time."

"She seems like a very nice girl," Bessie replied. "But how are you?"

"Eh, I'm old and my mind has gone," he told her. He set the box of biscuits on the table next to him and sighed. "I miss my farm and the animals and I don't know why Marion never visits. Can you tell her to come and see me, please?"

Bessie felt her smile falter. She'd been thinking that Niall seemed perfectly normal up until then. "I was just at the farm yesterday," she said, choosing her words carefully. "Eoin showed me the birds he's put aside for my Thanksgiving feast."

"Ah, is it that time again?" Niall asked.

"It is, and I'd love for you to come this year," Bessie told him.

"They don't let me out," Niall replied. "I can't go anywhere. They're afraid I'll get lost, you see."

Bessie wasn't sure how to respond to that. "I'm sure, if you'd like to come, we can work something out," she said after an awkward pause.

Niall seemed to think for a moment. "No, that's okay," he said eventually. "I'm hoping Marion will come and live with me here soon. If I go away for a day, I might miss her."

Bessie nodded, her mind racing. She wanted to bring the conversation around to Jacob Conover, but she didn't want to upset the man who was clearly struggling with reality.

"I hope Eoin is taking good care of my farm," Niall said now. "Once I'm well again, I'll be taking it back over and he'll have to go, of course."

"That would be difficult for Fenella, wouldn't it?" Bessie asked, wondering where the man's mind was wandering.

"Difficult for Fen? Why?" Niall demanded.

"Well, since she's married to Eoin," Bessie explained.

"She is?" Niall asked. "When did that happen?"

"Oh, some time back," Bessie said vaguely.

"The police were here, you know," Niall said suddenly.

"Were they?" Bessie asked.

"They wanted to talk to me about some man who disappeared a long time ago," he replied. "I said I couldn't remember him. My memory isn't very good, you see."

"Never mind, I'm sure it doesn't matter," Bessie said soothingly.

"I do remember him, though," Niall told her in a whisper. "He wasn't a nice man. He chased after all the girls. I wasn't going to have him chasing after Fen, though. I told her to stay away from him. She was a good girl."

"You did a good job bringing her up," Bessie told the man.

"It was hard," he replied. "She never liked farming. She wanted to be a nurse."

"She did?" Bessie asked in surprise.

"She did what?"

"Fenella wanted to be a nurse?"

"Did she?" the man replied. "I didn't know that."

Bessie shook her head. She could only hope that Anna Lambert had had a similarly odd conversation with the man and had realised that she couldn't rely on anything he'd said.

"What was that man's name?" Niall asked Bessie.

"What man?"

"The one that police lady kept asking me about. I can't seem to remember his name."

Bessie took a deep breath. "Maybe it was Jacob Conover," she said.

Niall frowned. "That doesn't sound right," he replied. "I remember Jacob Conover. He said he wanted to buy my farm, but I didn't want to sell it to him. He didn't care, though. He was going home, back across, where he'd come from." Niall stopped talking and looked out the window.

Bessie sat back in her chair and wondered how much of what Niall had said was true. The man was clearly confused about many things, but other times he seemed lucid. His comments on Jacob matched what Bessie already knew about the man.

"Ah, Bessie Cubbon? What brings you here?" he said suddenly, looking at Bessie as if he'd just noticed her.

"I came to invite you to my Thanksgiving dinner," she told him.

"Ah, you know I have a farm to run," he replied, shaking his head. "Maybe in another twenty years, when I'm retired and have nothing else to do." Before Bessie could reply, he went back to looking out the window. Within minutes, he fell asleep, leaving Bessie wondering what to do with herself.

"How's the visit going?" Noreen asked from the doorway.

"Niall's fallen asleep," Bessie told her.

"He does that," Noreen replied, her voice still relentlessly cheerful. "When he wakes up, he's sometimes quite disoriented."

"Oh, dear," Bessie exclaimed. "He's been rather confused anyway. I'm not sure how much he really remembers and how much is muddled."

"On good days, he's about fifty-fifty," the girl told her. "On bad days he doesn't even remember his own name."

Bessie sighed. "It's such a shame," she said. "At least he's getting good care here."

"We do our best," the girl replied. "He's a sweet man and we all enjoy looking after him, at least most of the time."

Niall made a sudden noise and then sat up in his chair. "Who's that?" he demanded.

"It's just me," Noreen said soothingly. "It's Noreen. I was just talking to your guest."

"My guest?" Niall looked at Bessie. "Who are you?"

Bessie smiled and got to her feet. "I'm an old friend," she said. "But I really must be going. It was lovely to see you."

"I'm awfully tired," Niall said to Noreen. "Could I take a nap?"

"Of course you can," Noreen told him.

Bessie walked towards the door.

"If you'll just wait a minute, I'll show you out," Noreen told her.

Bessie watched as the girl helped Niall climb into bed. She fussed over him for a minute, adjusting his blankets and pillows until he was satisfied.

"Sleep well," she whispered as she straightened and turned to go.

"Will there be ice cream at dinner?" Niall asked.

"I'm sure we can find some for you," Noreen told him, patting his hand where it rested on top of the blankets.

"Oh, good," Niall muttered. He closed his eyes and seemed to fall asleep almost instantly.

"I doubt that he'll remember you were here when he wakes up," Noreen told Bessie. "But you never know. He certainly remembers that policewoman who was here a few days ago, but that's probably because she upset him so much."

"Did she? How sad," Bessie murmured.

"Yes, we actually had to ring the doctor to come and check on Niall. He was so upset by her visit," Noreen told her. "I understand she's investigating a murder, but even if Niall did it, he certainly doesn't remember it now, at least not reliably."

"I can't believe that Niall ever killed anyone," Bessie said.

"You should have seen him when the police were here," Noreen said. "He was furiously angry. I saw a side of him I didn't know existed, and it was a little bit scary. Anyway, I do think just about anyone can kill someone else if they feel they have enough of a reason."

"Sadly, you may be right," Bessie said.

Noreen held open the door to the reception area and Bessie walked through it. "Thank you," she told the girl.

"It was my pleasure," the girl replied. "It's always nice to have a bit of variety in our day."

Bessie turned to leave, but stopped as Fenella came in through the building's front door.

"Bessie? You did say you were going to visit my father. How is he?"

"He'd just settled in for a nap as I was leaving," Bessie told her.

"I might as well get tea and a cake, then," Fenella said with a sigh. "He won't thank me for waking him up."

"Is there a café here?" Bessie asked.

"In that corner," Fenella replied, waving towards the opposite corner of the room.

Bessie glanced over and saw a glass door with a sign that read "Garden Café." "Let me buy you a cuppa and a slice of cake," she told Fenella.

"I can buy my own drink," Fenella said crossly.

"But why not let me treat?" Bessie said persuasively. "I'm simply returning the favour after our visit together yesterday."

Fenella looked as if she might argue, but after a moment she shrugged and headed towards the door to the café. Bessie followed. The room only had a dozen or so tables, but most were empty. In one corner, a woman in a bathrobe and slippers was sipping a drink, and at another table two women in nurses' uniforms were eating sandwiches. Fenella chose a table in the centre of the room and dropped into a chair. Bessie joined her.

"The food here is edible, but not spectacular," Fenella told Bessie in a soft voice. "But the cakes are excellent."

Bessie glanced at her watch. It was nearly time for dinner, so she really shouldn't have cake. She looked over the menu and sighed. There was no way she was going to be able to resist the sticky toffee pudding, no matter how indulgent it was. The waitress was efficient, but not friendly. Both women ordered tea and cake.

"Do you visit your father often?" Bessie asked after the waitress had delivered their tea.

"When I can," the other woman replied. "The farm is a lot of work, of course, but I like to see him at least once or twice a week."

"He seemed to remember me, at least at first," Bessie told her.

"He has good days and bad days, and some days he has good and bad hours or even minutes," Fenella replied. "The doctors aren't sure if he truly has dementia or if he's simply having problems with his memory due to all the different medications he's on."

"I didn't realise he needed medication," Bessie said.

"He has high blood pressure and heart problems as well as liver issues and partial kidney failure," she sighed. "Actually, I should probably just tell you what is working in his body rather than what isn't. The simple answer is nothing."

Bessie patted her hand. "I'm sorry," she said. "He was always so much larger than life when he was younger. It must be hard to see him this way."

"The doctors keep telling me that he's going to go any time now. They've been saying that for two years. When that policewoman was here, questioning him, they were worried he'd have a heart attack, but he just keeps hanging on. I hate seeing him so ill, but I can't imagine how awful it will be to lose him."

"I'm sure Inspector Lambert didn't mean to upset your father," Bessie said.

"I don't know about that," Fenella said bitterly. "He told me she accused him of murder."

Bessie gasped. "That's shocking."

Fenella shrugged. "Of course, it might not be true," she sighed. "That's just how my father remembered it. He couldn't remember who she thought he'd killed, though. He was all mixed up and for a while he thought that she'd said he'd killed Eoin."

"No wonder he was upset," Bessie said.

"Did he mention anything to you about the body or the police?" Fenella asked.

"He said they'd been to see him," Bessie told her. "And he said that Jacob Conover wasn't a nice man. He also told me that you wanted to be a nurse."

Fenella stared at her for a moment and then gave a shout of laughter. The waitress delivered their cakes then, looking nervously at Fenella as she put them on the table.

"Sorry," Fenella said after she'd taken a bite and washed it down with some tea. "My father doesn't remember his name or my name half the time, but he remembered that?" She shook her head. "I tried for years to persuade him to let me go to nursing school as soon as I was old enough, but he wanted me to stay and help with the farm. He thought I ought to get married and have lots of children who could carry on with the family farm, no matter what I wanted to do."

Bessie patted her hand. "I'm sorry," she said. "It was such a different time, wasn't it? Children today don't realise how much more influence our parents had in our lives than today's parents do."

Fenella nodded. "I ended up marrying Eoin to make my father happy," she told Bessie. "Oh, don't get me wrong, I fell in love with him and we've had a good life together, but marrying him was never my first choice."

"I'm sorry," Bessie said.

"It surprises me that my father remembered that," Fenella said thoughtfully. "At the time I didn't think he took my plans at all seriously. Maybe he was listening, even as he was saying no."

"Maybe he regrets saying no," Bessie suggested.

"How different my life would be if I could do it all over again," Fenella said with a sigh.

"I think we'd all make different choices if we could go back," Bessie said quietly. "But as soon as you start doing things differently, everything changes."

"I'm not sure that would be a bad thing," Fenella said.

Bessie noticed the tears in the other woman's eyes. "But you do love Eoin," she reminded her gently.

"And he loves me," Fenella said. "I've never had any reason to doubt that."

Bessie couldn't think of a suitable reply for that, so she sipped her tea and ate her pudding. The other woman did the same.

"I'd better go and see my father," Fenella said after a few minutes.

"It was nice to talk with you," Bessie said. "You and Eoin should come for Thanksgiving dinner on Saturday."

Fenella shook her head. "Thank you, but we're going to have company," she told Bessie. "Nicholas and Sarah are coming across to see us."

"How nice," Bessie exclaimed. "Eoin must be delighted."

Fenella shrugged. "He reckons they've heard he isn't well and are coming over to make sure of their inheritance," she said.

"Surely not," Bessie said.

"I don't know. We'll see when they get here, I suppose."

"Nicholas hasn't been on the island for years, has he?" Bessie asked.

"Not since he turned eighteen," Fenella told her. "He couldn't wait to get off the island, of course, but he settled down eventually."

"I wonder if he remembers Jacob Conover," Bessie said thoughtfully.

"I shouldn't think so," Fenella said quickly. "He would have still been in his teens when the man was here. I'm sure he didn't pay any attention to him."

Bessie nodded. "Teenagers can be incredibly self-absorbed, can't they?" she laughed.

"Anyway, they arrive on Wednesday. I just hope they don't stay for too long."

"Didn't you tell me that they had children? Are they bringing any of them across?"

Fenella shook her head. "Their oldest, Ned, is staying behind to run the farm. The others are scattered around the country and apparently don't have any interest in visiting, at least not at the moment."

While she was answering Bessie, Fenella rose to her feet. "Must go," she muttered. She walked off, pausing at the door to wave to Bessie before leaving the small café. Bessie paid the bill and then headed out into the reception area again. She dug out her mobile phone and rang her taxi service.

"We'll send Dave," the dispatcher told her. "He's just dropping someone at the Sea Terminal."

Bessie disconnected and smiled. Dave would make up for her having to put with Mark on the drive down. He was at the nursing home only a few minutes later and the pair chatted happily all the way back to Laxey.

CHAPTER 11

The next day, Monday, Bessie took a shorter than normal walk along the beach. She needed a few things from a grocery shop and she didn't really fancy taking a taxi to the nearest one. At breakfast, when she realised she was out of bread, she'd decided that she'd simply walk up the hill to the small corner shop at the top. The girl who worked there was rude and difficult, but the location was convenient.

She waved to Thomas, who was still working hard on the cottages, and then returned home to collect her handbag. The walk up the hill was somewhat challenging, but the walk home would be easier. A buzzer announced her arrival as she pushed the door open.

She smiled when she spotted the woman behind the till. "Anne? But I thought you were done with working here," she said, happy to see her friend there, rather than the grumpy young woman whose father owned the shop.

"I thought I was as well," Anne Caine replied. "But I'm bored sitting at home and they were short-handed, so I said I'd come in for a short time to help out."

Bessie smiled. "You worked too hard for too many years to be able to just sit home and relax, I think."

Anne nodded. "I've read dozens of books and magazines, cleaned the whole house from top to bottom at least three times and completely reorganised every drawer and wardrobe. I'm not used to not having to work."

"But I'm so happy for you that you don't," Bessie replied.

Anne had worked for all of her adult life to support her son and her husband, who was much better at holding down a seat at the pub than a job. Not long after her husband left her, an unexpected inheritance had transformed her and her son's fortunes.

"How's Andy doing?" Bessie asked. She was very fond of Anne's son, who had gone across in September to start studying at a culinary college.

"He's good," Anne told her. "He's already learned a lot, and he's very excited about everything they teach. He isn't just learning about cooking and food prep, he's also learning how to run a business and how to find good staff and all sorts of useful things. When he finishes, in two or three years, he'll be ready to open his own restaurant."

"And I'm sure it will be a huge success," Bessie said happily.

"I am, too," Anne said. "Actually, Andy rang me last night. He said you'd invited him to your Thanksgiving feast."

"I did," Bessie agreed. "I don't know if he can get the time off to come, but I'd really love to see him."

"He's coming," Anne told her. "He said he was going to ring you today to let you know for sure."

"That is good news," Bessie exclaimed. "And you're coming as well, aren't you?"

"Oh yes, thank you again for asking me," Anne replied.

"You're both welcome to bring a friend, if you'd like," Bessie said. "I don't know if you or Andy are seeing anyone at the moment."

Anne laughed. "I'm not," she said emphatically. "Jack is doing his best to hold up the divorce. He thinks he can get some money out of me, but as it's all in Andy's name, that isn't likely. Anyway, I won't be considering a new relationship until the divorce is final."

"I'm sorry Jack is giving you trouble," Bessie said.

"It's hardly surprising," Anne replied with a shrug. "He was never anything but trouble. When I think back now..." she trailed off and shook her head. "Never mind, Andy's doing great and he's happy," she said. "That's what matters most to me."

"I'll have to ask him, when he rings, if he'll be bringing a guest," Bessie said.

"He might be," Anne told her. "There is a girl at school that he seems to be quite taken with. He said something about trying to persuade her to come across with him."

"That's interesting," Bessie said.

Another customer walked into the shop, interrupting the conversation. Bessie grabbed a basket and made her way around, gathering what she needed. By the time she was finished, the other woman was gone.

"Are you going to be here regularly again?" she asked as Anne rang up her purchases.

"For the next few weeks, I will," Anne answered. "The owner's daughter has exams at college. Apparently she needs time off to study and then time off to take them. I'll be working weekdays here until she returns."

"That's excellent news," Bessie said. "I can start shopping here for bread and milk again."

Anne smiled. "Just about everyone who has come in has seemed happy to see me back," she told Bessie. "I'm pretty sure it has less to do with me and more to do with how miserable the owner's daughter is, but it still makes me feel appreciated."

"You were a fixture here for so many years," Bessie said. "The shop never felt quite right when you were gone."

"It's much nicer now, knowing I don't have to be here," Anne confided. "After all those years of struggling to pay the bills and keep food on the table, it's nice to know that if I get tired of being here, I can quit and go back to sitting at home with a good book."

"And if you run out of books, you can come and see me," Bessie told her. "I have shelves full of excellent books and I'd be happy to lend you as many as you'd like."

"I might just take you up on that," Anne said. "In January, when the holidays are over, maybe."

"I'll see you Saturday," Bessie said cheerfully. "Or maybe even sooner," she added as she headed out the door.

Having her friend back behind the counter in the corner shop improved Bessie's mood immeasurably. She'd always appreciated being able to pop up the hill to pick up things she needed, and now she could do so again for a few weeks without having to deal with the surly girl who had replaced Anne.

Back in her cottage, Bessie put her shopping away and then listened to her answering machine messages. A couple of friends had rung to double-check the arrangements for Saturday and John Rockwell had left a message asking her to ring him back.

Bessie took care of the easy calls first, giving one friend directions to the restaurant and confirming the time with another. Then she rang John at police headquarters.

"Laxey Neighbourhood Policing, this is Doona, how may I help you?" the familiar voice came down the line.

"Hello, Doona. It's Bessie. John asked me to ring him back."

"I'll connect you," Doona said.

Bessie decided that someone must have been nearby or else Doona would have taken the time to chat for a bit before putting her through. Although she couldn't prove it, Bessie suspected that Anna Lambert was within earshot.

"Good morning, Bessie," John's voice came down the line. "I was hoping I might buy you lunch today," he said.

"I'd like that," Bessie replied. "Where and when?"

"How about if I collect you at half eleven?" John suggested. "I thought we might drive over to Lonan so I can try out that little place you were so fond of."

"Oh, that does sound good," Bessie said with enthusiasm. The small café had only been open for a few months, but it had already developed a reputation for excellence. They specialised in creating sampler plates with small portions of a variety of dishes. Bessie's favourite part was that they did the same for pudding.

"I'll see you around half eleven, then," John told her.

Bessie spent the rest of her morning going through the papers from the Manx Museum. She worked carefully on transcribing each document, leaving spaces in her transcription for words she couldn't quite work out. She found that after going through the whole of the first document once, that when she started it over again, she could read more than she'd originally thought. Marjorie had called it "getting your eye in," so that you began to pick out the distinct way the letters were formed in each document. At eleven, she put her work away, satisfied that she'd accomplished more than she'd expected.

After changing into a brightly coloured jumper and a long skirt, Bessie combed her hair and added a bit of makeup to her face. She powdered her nose and added a swipe of lipstick, sticking her tongue out at herself when she'd finished."

"You'll never be beautiful," she told her reflection. "But you've managed with what you have for this long."

She knew that, in her youth, she had been considered rather pretty, if not exactly beautiful, but she'd never really worried about her looks. There was little point in fussing over them now, she thought.

John was right on time. Bessie was watching for him, and as he pulled into the parking area for her cottage, she let herself out and locked the door behind her. She crossed to the car as he emerged.

"How are you today?" he asked as he gave her a quick hug.

"I'm well," Bessie replied as John took her arm and escorted her to the passenger side of the car. "How are you?"

"I'm well, also," John assured her. He opened her door and then helped her into the vehicle. When she was safely inside, he pushed the door shut and then climbed back into the driver's seat.

"I've heard so many good things about this place," John told her as he drove. "But I haven't had a chance to try it yet."

"I've only been there once," Bessie replied. "But it was excellent and I keep meaning to go back."

"It isn't in the most convenient of locations," John said.

"No, Lonan wouldn't be my first choice if I wanted to open a restaurant," Bessie said. "I'm not sure why they chose it."

"Who are they?" John asked.

"Oh, let me see if I can remember," Bessie said. She thought for a minute. "George and Mary Quayle invested in the business," she told John. "It's owned by a young couple from across who were looking for a small town where they could have their own restaurant and maybe start a family. The names will come to me in a minute." She sat silently, trying to get herself to remember.

A few minutes later, John pulled into the small car park for the café. As he slid his car into the last available space, Bessie clapped her hands.

"Dan and Carol Jenkins," she said triumphantly. "He's the genius in the kitchen and she handles the front of the house."

"I really should have come by and introduced myself before now," John told her. "Lonan is my responsibility as much as Laxey is, but there are two excellent constables here who do a great job keeping everything under control."

"I'm sure they'll be delighted to meet you today," Bessie said. "That is, if we can get a table."

She and John were approaching the café and Bessie was surprised to find a short queue in the doorway. She smiled politely at a few people she recognised as she and John joined the end of the line.

"It looks as if they aren't having any trouble with their out-of-the-way location," John remarked.

"No, clearly not," Bessie agreed.

A moment later Carol Jenkins appeared in the doorway. She looked tired but happy as she surveyed the small crowd.

"My goodness, where have you all come from?" she exclaimed. "You must have heard that Dan is doing a pie special today, haven't you?"

An appreciative murmur went through the group as Carol ushered the first four people in the queue into the café.

"What is a pie special?" John asked Bessie in a whisper.

"I've no idea," Bessie replied quietly.

A few minutes later, Carol had found tables for everyone in front of them and turned her attention to Bessie and John.

"Ah, it's Bessie, isn't it?" she asked, smiling brightly at the pair.

"It is, yes," Bessie replied.

"You came in with Mary when we were first open," Carol said. "That was only a few months ago, but it seems forever."

"You're much busier now than you were then," Bessie said. "And deservedly so, if the food is half as good as I remember."

"We're doing almost too well," Carol said with a laugh. "I'm quite run off my feet. We're looking to hire some more help and we've been able to pay back a large portion of what George and Mary invested with us, as well. It's been a crazy few months."

"I'm so happy for you," Bessie told the girl.

"But you want a table," Carol said. She looked back into the restaurant and then smiled. "Give me one minute," she told Bessie and John.

Bessie watched from the doorway as the girl cleared away plates from a small table for two in a quiet corner. The couple at the table paid their bill and then collected their things. Bessie moved out of the way to let them exit the café. A moment later, Carol was back.

"Here we go," she said, leading John and Bessie to the table. "As I said, today's special is all about dishes with pie in the name. Our main course special is a sampler plate with shepherd's pie, cottage pie, steak and kidney pie, and fish pie. Our pudding sampler is a slice of American-style apple pie, a small mince pie, and a piece of lemon tart pie."

"Lemon tart pie?" Bessie asked.

Carol laughed "Okay, it's a lemon tart. We ran out of puddings with pie in the name, so we cheated, just a little bit. It's really too early for mince pies as well, but no one has complained."

"I won't complain, either," Bessie told her. "I'll have both of the sampler plates, although I might need my sweet course packed up to go."

Carol nodded. "We can do full-sized servings of any of the specialty items, if you'd rather not have the sampler," she told John. "Or we have our regular menu." She gestured towards the printed menus on the table.

"Oh, no, I'll try the sampler as well," John told here. "Just the main course one for now. I'm not sure I'll have room for pudding."

Carol smiled. "As Bessie said, you can always take it home," she told him. "What about drinks?"

They both asked for tea before Carol rushed away. Bessie sat back and watched for a few minutes as the girl raced around the room, delivering drinks and food and taking orders. The small queue at the door grew again as people lingered over their meals and the delicious sweets.

"It certainly is a lot busier now than it was the last time I was here," Bessie told John.

"They could use at least one more person out here," John replied.

A moment later a tall and muscular man emerged from the kitchen, carrying a tray. He headed straight for Bessie.

"Tea for two?" he asked, grinning at them.

"Yes, but aren't you meant to be cooking?" Bessie asked.

"Everything is ticking over nicely in the kitchen," he assured her. "And Carol is run off her feet out here."

"John, this is Dan, Carol's husband, and the wonderful chef here," Bessie performed the introductions.

"It's a pleasure," Dan said, shaking hands with John. "But I better get back to it or Carol might start to realise how much easier I have it than she does."

"I don't believe that," Bessie laughed.

"Now, what can I do for you?" Bessie asked John after her first sip of tea.

"What makes you think I want something?" John asked.

Bessie smiled at him. "I'm sure you'd love to take me to lunch on a regular basis, just for the pleasure of my company, but I know you're too busy to do that, especially in the middle of a murder investigation. So what's going on?"

John laughed. "I'm going to have to start taking you to lunch for no reason just so you stop being so suspicious of me," he said.

Bessie smiled. "But..." she said suggestively.

"But you're right, I did want to talk to you about the case," John admitted with a sigh. "And I wanted to get away from the station for a little while as well."

"I gather Inspector Lambert wouldn't approve of your talking to me," Bessie said.

John shrugged. "She has her own way of doing things," he replied. "And she doesn't believe in involving civilians in murder investigations. I have to say that I tend to agree with her, as well. But when it comes to Laxey, well, you're my very best source of information. Sometimes some civilians can be incredibly useful."

Bessie nodded. "I'm always happy to help," she said.

"Yes, well, that's why we're here," John told her. "It will be in the papers tonight, so I'm not giving anything away, but the body at the Clague farm has been positively identified."

"Jacob Conover?" Bessie asked.

"Yes," John said.

Before Bessie could answer, Carol was there, delivering plates full of steaming hot food.

"Everything looks wonderful," Bessie exclaimed as she looked over the plate.

"Enjoy, and let me know if you need anything," Carol told them.

For several minutes the pair focussed on their meals. "The shepherd's pie is my favourite," Bessie said after a while.

"I like the steak and kidney," John told her. "I never do that at home."

"Even the fish pie is good, and I'm not a huge fan of fish," Bessie replied.

"The crust is very flaky, which gives it a wonderful texture," John said.

Bessie laughed. "We sound like food critics," she said.

"I hope that doesn't mean you don't like it," Dan's voice surprised Bessie.

"It's all wonderful," Bessie told him. "It's just way too much food."

"We can box up whatever you can't finish," Dan offered.

"Oh, I think I'll probably finish it all," Bessie replied. "But I won't have room for anything else."

"We'll box up your puddings," Dan said. "And I'll add a sheet with instructions for how best to serve them."

Bessie grinned. "If you were within walking distance of my cottage, I'd eat here every day," she told the man.

"We were actually talking about relocating into Laxey," Dan said. "We're kind of out of the way here."

"That doesn't seem to be hurting your business," Bessie said, glancing around the still full restaurant.

"No," Dan agreed. "So maybe we'll stay where we are, at least for now."

When Carol came to clear their empty plates, John agreed that he'd take a pudding sampler home with him as well.

"So now that you know who you've found, does that change anything?" Bessie asked.

"It certainly narrows down the possibilities," John said. "Jacob's sister is coming over on the late ferry tonight. It will be interesting to see what she has to say, although I don't expect her to be much help."

"Didn't you say that she didn't even know he was on the island?" Bessie checked.

"That's what she said when I spoke to her on the telephone," John replied.

"It would be better if he'd sent lots of long letters back to her all about his stay here," Bessie said.

"It would indeed," John agreed. "But at least we can get more background from her."

"You said she might like to meet me," Bessie recalled.

"I told her I'd try to set up meetings for her with a few people who remember her brother," John said. "I've included you on the list of people we're going to visit."

"Who else is she going to meet?" Bessie asked.

"Mona Kelly Smythe has agreed to meet with her," John told her. "She said she has nothing but fond memories of the man and she's a widow, so there's no one to get jealous or upset if she talks about him."

"I hadn't thought of that," Bessie said. "I suppose some of the women he spent time with would rather their husbands didn't know about it."

"That's what we keep running into," John replied. "Some women simply don't want to talk about their youthful flirtations."

"I wonder if Fenella is keeping quiet so as not to upset Eoin," Bessie mused. "I can't help but think she must have known the man. At the time it seemed like he went with every girl around her age."

"Jacob's sister would like to meet them and also Niall," John said. "Since their farm is where the body was found."

"I wouldn't recommend letting her meet Niall," Bessie said. "He's very easily confused and upset."

John nodded. "Fenella told me the same thing," he said. "I'm going to take Jane to meet with Fenella and Eoin and to see where the body was found, but I've told her she can't meet Niall."

"So what time should I expect you tomorrow?" Bessie asked.

"I think probably some time after two," John said, flipping through his notebook as he spoke. "She arrives tonight and we're visiting the farm in the morning. I thought I'd take her to lunch somewhere before we come to see you."

"That sounds good," Bessie agreed. "I'll bake some biscuits or something and we can have tea."

John nodded. Carol arrived then with two small boxes. "Here you are," she said brightly. "Your sweet course, all ready to go. Dan's included heating instructions for the items that are best warm."

After John paid the bill, the pair headed back out into the autumn sunshine. He helped Bessie into the car and then drove her back to her cottage.

"Thank you for a lovely lunch," she told her at her door.

"Thank you for joining me."

"I don't feel as if I helped at all," Bessie said. "We hardly even discussed the case and I didn't tell you anything new."

"But we've sorted a meeting tomorrow with Jacob's sister," John reminded her. "I'm sure she'll tell you more than she'll tell me. You can chat with her about her brother while I take a walk on the beach or something."

Bessie nodded. "I just hope I can find out something useful," she said. "It sort of feels as if this is an impossible case."

"It was a long time ago and our most important witness isn't capable of helping," John said. "This one might end up in the cold case file for a very long time."

Bessie frowned as she let herself into her cottage. She hated the thought that someone might get away with murder, even if the killer was poor old Niall Clague, who certainly could never be tried, even if John found evidence of his guilt. For once Bessie's answering machine light was steady.

"Ha, no one even missed me," she said as she put her pudding box on the counter. Before she could move, however, the phone rang. She laughed at herself as she picked up the receiver.

"Ah, Aunt Bessie, one of my most favourite people ever, how are you?" Andy Caine's voice boomed down the wire.

"Andy, it's so good to hear your voice. I feel as if you've been gone forever," Bessie replied.

"It's only been a few months," Andy said. "And I'm coming home this weekend just for you."

"I saw your mother at the corner shop today and she mentioned that. I'm ever so glad."

"Don't tell me mum is working again?" Andy said, sighing deeply. "There's more than enough money now. She doesn't have to work. She can just relax and enjoy life."

"She said she was bored at home," Bessie replied. "She's worked hard her entire life. Working now and then is probably good for her."

"Once I finish my course, she can come and work for me," Andy said. "I'm going to need all the help I can get."

"Are you enjoying the course?" Bessie asked.

"It's super. Some of it is hard work, like the classes in keeping accounts and things, but the cooking and baking courses are great and I've made a bunch of new friends."

"Your mother said you might want to bring a friend for Thanksgiving," Bessie said.

"Ah, yes, well, if it's okay with you."

Bessie felt as if she could almost hear the young man blushing. "Of course you may bring a friend," she replied. "Is it someone from your course?"

"Yes, she's, well, she's just a friend, really."

"But you're hoping for more."

"You know me too well," Andy complained.

"Tell me about her," Bessie invited.

"Her name is Sue and she twenty-three," Andy began. "She went to university for a year to do maths, but she didn't really like it. She ended up getting a job as a waitress and discovered that she likes that sort of work. After a while, she decided she should go to culinary school so she can have her own restaurant instead of working for someone else."

"Good for her," Bessie said.

"Yeah, she's really good at the math and the account-keeping stuff, so I thought maybe, when we're done here, she might be a good partner for me. I could do the cooking and she could handle the business end of things."

"What does she think of that idea?"

"Oh, I haven't, that is, it's just a vague thought for now," Andy told her. "The first thing I have to do is get her over to the island. She's never been and if she doesn't like it, well, that will be the end of that, won't it?"

"I suppose so. I do hope she likes it here. Your mother has her heart set on you coming back when you've finished your course."

"I do as well," he said emphatically. "The island is home. I never felt settled when I lived over here, I just didn't want to be anywhere near my father, or rather the man I thought was my father."

"But you're happy enough at school?"

"Oh, school's great, but it's only temporary. The island will always be home."

"I'm really looking forward to seeing you on Saturday," Bessie said.

"Do you need any help with the food? I'd be happy to help out, if you'd like."

"I'm letting the restaurant handle everything," Bessie told him. "Of course once your restaurant is open, I'll have to have Thanksgiving there."

"My first banquet booking," Andy laughed. "I'm going to hold you to that."

"I hope you do," Bessie replied.

When the young man disconnected, Bessie sat for a moment thinking about how much his life had changed in just a short while. Sometimes good things happened to good people, she mused. Before she got back up, the phone rang again.

"Bessie, I just got off the phone with Jane Harris, Jacob's sister. She should be at your cottage around two tomorrow," John Rockwell told her.

"Wasn't that what we said earlier?" Bessie asked.

"It was, but I was going to bring her to see you. Mrs. Harris would prefer to come on her own."

"Oh, I see," Bessie said. "I suppose it doesn't really matter."

"No, Mrs. Harris isn't a suspect or anything," John said. "But I am very curious to hear what she has to say. She's meeting with me in the morning, but I'll still want to know what you discuss with her."

"Of course," Bessie replied. "Shall I ring you when she leaves?"

"No, don't ring," John said quickly. "I'll come over and see you some time in the evening."

"That works for me," Bessie agreed. "I don't expect to do much more than tell her how sorry I am for her loss, though."

"I'm hoping she might be able to shed some light on why her brother was on the island," John told her. "She might know what sort of farm he was looking for and how much money he had to spend. I'd like to know which farmers he approached. At the moment no one will admit to having spoken to him about their property."

"And I don't remember anything specific," Bessie said. "I probably didn't pay that much attention, really. He wasn't here for that long and I don't think any of the area farmers were at all interested in selling to him."

"Well, the more you can find out from Mrs. Harris, the better,"

John told her. "I'm not sure she's going to be terribly forthcoming with me."

"Why not? Surely she wants her brother's killer found."

"I got the impression that she isn't fond of the police," John said. "I may have misinterpreted her, though."

"I doubt it. You're usually an excellent judge of character," Bessie said. "I won't tell Mrs. Harris that we're friends."

"That's probably wise."

Bessie made herself a light evening meal to go with her delicious puddings. Once she'd eaten every last bite, she searched through a box that had recently arrived from the bookshop in Ramsey. She had a long list of favourite authors and the shop sent her anything new by any of them on a monthly basis. Sometimes they added a book or two that one of the booksellers thought might interest her. Now Bessie dug out a paperback thriller by an author she'd never tried.

"How bad can it be?" she said to no one.

She sank down in her most comfortable chair with a cup of tea and a plate with a few biscuits on it, prepared to get lost in the story. Two hours later, she was tired, but her heart was racing and she knew she'd never sleep if she didn't finish the book. It was much later than her normal bedtime when the hero and heroine finally escaped from the killer's lair and saved the world, or at least their little corner of it.

Bessie sat back in her chair and sighed with relief. Everything had worked out in the end. She laughed when she noticed her teacup; it was still full with tea that was now quite cold. Clearly she'd been more absorbed in her story than she'd realised. She quite forgotten to drink her tea or eat her biscuits.

After tidying up her forgotten snack, Bessie headed to bed hoping she might sleep a little bit later than normal the next morning. Her meeting with Jane Harris could be an interesting one and Bessie wanted to be at her best when the woman arrived.

CHAPTER 12

Tuesday didn't start well for Bessie. She woke at her normal time of six o'clock, feeling tired and out of sorts. After trying unsuccessfully for several minutes to get back to sleep, she finally rolled out of bed and took her shower. Tea and toast did little to wake her up, so she set a pot of coffee brewing before heading out for a walk. She opened her door and gasped. The wind was blowing strongly and rain was pouring down. She pushed the door shut and leaned against it, sighing deeply. The weather seemed to match her mood.

After pulling on her Wellington boots and her waterproofs, she tried again, this time making it out the door and into the storm. She marched through the rain to the very first of the holiday cottages and then turned and stomped home again as quickly as she could. That would have to do for a walk for the morning, she decided as she stood dripping in her kitchen. The smell of coffee made her smile and she poured herself a cup and took a sip before stripping off her wet things.

With company due that afternoon, Bessie spent her morning cleaning and tidying the cottage. She made herself a light lunch and then got out the ingredients for her favourite shortbread recipe. She'd only just measured the flour when someone knocked on her door.

"You must be Elizabeth Cubbon," the woman in the doorway said when Bessie opened the door.

"I am," Bessie admitted. "Jane Harris?"

"Yes, that's right," the woman nodded and then frowned. "The weather's beastly, isn't it?"

"Oh, do come in," Bessie exclaimed, stepping backwards to let the woman get out of the wind and rain.

Bessie studied the new arrival as the woman removed her sodden trench coat. She could have been anywhere between forty and seventy, Bessie thought, though she knew the woman must be around sixty. Her hair was dark brown, with only a few grey streaks that were almost like highlights. Her makeup, in spite of the rain, was impeccable, and her clothes were obviously expensive. She was slender and as Bessie took the dripping coat from her, she seemed to be looking down her nose at Bessie. As she was several inches taller than Bessie and she was wearing black boots with four-inch heels, that wasn't difficult for her.

"Please sit down," Bessie said, gesturing towards the kitchen table.

"In here?" the woman sniffed.

"I was just going to make some shortbread," Bessie told her. "I didn't think you'd be here for another hour."

"My earlier visit didn't take long," the woman replied. "I don't suppose you can wait and do your baking after I've gone?"

"I was only baking for your benefit," Bessie said. "But I'm sure I have some digestives or something in the cupboard, if you would rather."

"Oh, goodness, I don't eat such things," the woman replied. "Anyway, I don't want to take up much of your time. The policeman I spoke to said that you remembered my brother. Otherwise, I wouldn't bother you at all."

"Why don't we move into the sitting room, then," Bessie suggested. "It will be more comfortable."

The woman nodded her approval and then followed Bessie into

the next room. Bessie sat down in her favourite chair and motioned towards the couch across from it. "Have a seat," she suggested.

"How long have you lived here?" the woman demanded as she perched herself on the edge of the couch.

"A great many years," Bessie replied.

"Yes, it does rather show, doesn't it?" Jane glanced around the room and Bessie supposed, from the look on her face, that she wasn't impressed with what she was seeing.

"It's small and cosy," Bessie told her. "But I love it."

"I'm sure you do," the woman said in a patronising tone.

Bessie bit her tongue. The woman was in mourning for her brother; Bessie needed to make allowances, she told herself.

"So, what do you remember about Jacob?" Jane demanded.

"Not much," Bessie said. "I remember he made quite an impression on the young ladies in the village, though. He seemed to go out with nearly every single woman living here."

"I'm assuming that doesn't include you," Jane said. "You're far too old."

Bessie flushed. "He wasn't my type," she answered curtly.

"Well, that's just as well, isn't it? I've tried to get that policeman to give me a list of women Jacob spent time with, but he won't. I'd appreciate it if you'd share some names and contact information with me. I'd very much like to talk to some of the women who were involved with him."

"I'm afraid I don't really have that information," Bessie said. "Who have you been able to speak with so far?"

"Oh, some woman called Mona who went out with Jacob once or twice. I'm more interested in who he was seeing more seriously."

"From what I saw, he wasn't seeing anyone seriously," Bessie told her. "He seemed to go out with a different woman every other day."

"But he was looking for a wife," Jane said.

"He was?" Bessie asked, surprised.

Jane nodded. "When he left home, he told our father that he was going to find himself a nice hard-working farmer's daughter to bring back and help run the farm. He was lazy, my brother. He thought if he found a farmer's daughter who was used to hard work, she could take over a lot of the difficult work and he could sit around and drink whiskey all day."

"What makes you think he'd found someone here?" Bessie asked.

Jane shrugged. "When Jacob set his mind to something, he generally managed to accomplish it," she replied.

"He wanted to buy a farm here, but he didn't manage that," Bessie said.

"No, he didn't," Jane asserted. "He may have told people that was why he was here, but the last thing he wanted was to stay on the Isle of Man. He was using that as an excuse to meet farmers and their daughters, that's all."

"I thought someone told me that you didn't even know he was on the island," Bessie said.

"I didn't," Jane agreed.

"So maybe he came over here and fell in love with the place," Bessie suggested. "Maybe he decided to buy a farm here, rather than go back home."

"He didn't have any money," Jane replied. "Father gave him enough for a short holiday, but he certainly couldn't have bought any property over here, or anywhere else for that matter."

Bessie pressed her lips together, her mind racing. "So when did you last hear from him?" she asked after a moment.

"From what I can determine, he sent us a letter just before he left Liverpool for the island," Jane replied. "He'd been courting a young woman there, but her father didn't like the idea of her moving away. The father wanted her to stay and work on their farm. From what Jacob said in his letters, there was an ugly scene. Anyway, Jacob wrote that he'd decided to head south and see what he could find."

"But he came across to the island instead," Bessie said.

"Yes," Jane nodded. "I've no idea why."

"He was getting ready to leave the island when he died, though," Bessie said after a moment.

"Which is another reason why I think he'd found a bride," Jane said. "If he'd come and taken a look around and not found anyone suitable, he'd have moved on quickly, but he stayed for several months. That suggests to me that he'd found someone and was courting her."

"Maybe she turned him down when he asked her to move across with him," Bessie said, thinking about Bahey removing Karen from the island to get her away from Jacob.

"I'm assuming that's what happened," Jane said. "But I'd really like to speak to her. If things had been different, we might have been sisters-in-law, and I'd like to hear what she remembers about my brother."

"I'm afraid I can't suggest any likely candidates," Bessie told her, remembering her promise to Bahey that she wouldn't tell anyone about Karen's relationship with the man. "I can tell you that at the time he simply seemed to be going out with everyone for a very short time and not getting serious about anyone," Bessie added.

"That's what Mona told me as well," she replied. "But I don't believe it."

"Do you think the woman he was seeing, if there was one, might have had something to do with his death?" Bessie asked.

"Maybe," Jane said. "I keep thinking he probably just got into a bar fight that ended up coming to blows. Jacob had a temper and he got thrown out of our local pub at least twice a year for getting into fights with other customers. I'd like to believe that there was a fight and his death was accidental. That's less painful to think about than the possibility that he was murdered."

Bessie nodded. "I'm sorry," she said. "I can't imagine how difficult this must be for you."

Jane dug a tissue out of her handbag and touched it to her eyes, which looked quite dry to Bessie. "Thank you," the woman said softly. "The years of not knowing were very difficult as well."

"Yes, I'm sure they were," Bessie said. "Perhaps you'd like a cup of tea?"

"Oh, no," Jane exclaimed. "I don't drink tea."

"Can I get you anything?"

"No, thank you. I'd rather hear more about Jacob, if you remember any more?"

"I really wish I did," Bessie told her. "I only met him a couple of times. He seemed intelligent and full of confidence. I was under the impression that he was here to buy property, and I think that's pretty much all we ever discussed. I recall suggesting a farm a few miles outside the village to him and his asking me about the owner and his family."

"Did the owner have any available daughters?" Jane asked.

"Now that you mention it, no," Bessie said.

"And do you know if my brother ever took your advice?"

"He didn't," Bessie replied. "The owner was actually considering selling at that time and I remember asking him about Jacob a short time later. Your brother never did go to see him."

"As I said, he wasn't looking to buy anything," Jane said. "But the story gave him a good excuse to visit all of the area farms."

"I wish I could help you more," Bessie said.

"Yes, well, I'm off to see where they found the body next," Jane told her. "I understand the people who have the farm now don't remember Jacob."

"I'm sure they must have some vague memories of him," Bessie said. "But it was a very long time ago, after all."

"I wish I could say that you've been very helpful, but you really haven't," the woman said, getting to her feet. "I appreciate your being willing to see me, even if it has been rather a waste of time."

Bessie stared at her, unable to think of a polite way to reply. She got to her feet and followed the woman back into the kitchen.

"I do think that your police could try a bit harder," Jane said as she pulled her coat back on. "The don't seem to be doing much of anything."

"It's difficult for them to find anyone who remembers your brother," Bessie said, eager to defend John and his hard work. "He was only here for a short time and that was a long time ago," she added. "They're doing their best to track down as many people as they can, though."

"Yes, well, I'm not impressed with their work thus far. Apparently, the man who used to own the farm where Jacob was found is not right in the head. I gather the police have interviewed him, but they couldn't get any sense out of him. Perhaps I should insist that they try harder."

"I'm not sure there's much anyone can do with poor Niall Clague," Bessie said. "He's very ill and his memory is completely unreliable."

"Or so he says," Jane retorted. "I'm sure that must be the easiest thing in the world to fake. If I'd murdered someone, I'd probably pretend to be crazy in order to avoid answering questions."

"He's been having trouble with his memory for many years," Bessie said, keeping her voice steady. "It isn't like he suddenly started pretending to forget when the body was found."

Jane shrugged. "I still think it's suspicious," she said. "And I've said that repeatedly to the two policeman with whom I've spoken. Well, one is a policewoman, actually, but I've told her many times that I think that Nigel Clague needs to be pushed harder."

"It's Niall," Bessie said tightly. "And I'm sure the police have done their best with him."

"I wish I had your confidence in their efforts," the woman said sharply. "But then, it isn't your brother's body that's been found, is it? It's all so distressing."

The tissue came out again and Bessie found herself peering at it, looking for any signs of wetness. It looked completely dry as the woman dabbed at her eyes and then slid the tissue back into her pocket.

"Do let me know if you think of any more questions for me," Bessie said as she showed the woman to the door. "I wish I could remember more."

"I'm going home later today," the woman replied. "Perhaps you'd be good enough to give me your number? If I think of any further questions, I'll ring you."

Bessie found a scrap of paper and a pencil in a drawer and wrote down her number. "Please do ring, if you think I can help," she said, confident that she'd never hear from the unpleasant woman again.

"Yes, well, we can but hope," Jane said.

Bessie opened the door for the woman and watched as she climbed into the expensive-looking car that was parked outside. As it pulled away, Bessie noted that it was from one of the island's hire car firms. Pushing the door shut, Bessie turned the lock and then sighed. The ingredients for shortbread were still spread across the counter, so she decided to go ahead and bake, even if her guest had already come and gone. Once the shortbread was in the oven, she reached for the phone. She'd might as well just ring John and save him a trip later in the day. A knock on the door stopped her hand in midair.

"I'm earlier than I thought I would be," John said from her doorstep. "I hope that isn't a problem."

"Of course not," Bessie assured him. She stepped back to let him in and then smiled. "The sun is trying to peek out," she said as she shut the door behind him.

"The wind seems to be keeping the clouds moving along," John told her. "It rained pretty much all morning, so I imagine we're due a few hours of sunshine before sunset."

"Maybe I'll get another walk in," Bessie said. "It wasn't exactly walking weather this morning."

The oven timer buzzed, interrupting their chat.

"Is that shortbread?" John asked as Bessie pulled the tray from the oven.

"It is; would you like some?"

John smiled. "I feel like a small child who's just been given an unexpected treat. I'd love some, if you don't mind."

"Of course I don't mind," Bessie told him. "I was planning to make it for my guest, but she turned up before I'd finished. After she left I felt as if I needed a treat."

John chuckled. "Does that mean you didn't get along well with Mrs. Harris?" he asked.

"We got along fine," Bessie replied as she switched on the kettle. "But I didn't like her."

"She didn't seem to be the most likable person," John said. "But she's not happy with our investigation. I thought that might why she was, um, unfriendly at the station."

"I think she's pretty unfriendly everywhere," Bessie said. "I told her I was certain you were doing your best, but she didn't seem to believe me."

"I'm sure it's difficult, finding out your brother was murdered many years ago, but we really are doing everything we can."

"She seems to think you should be pushing Niall more."

"Yes, she said that to me and Anna when we met," John replied. "I don't think she believes that he's really unwell." He shrugged. "She also suggested that we should have found the body at some point in the last forty years. She seems to think we were negligent in not locating it at some point."

"Pardon?" Bessie said. "How were you supposed to find the body of a man who was never even reported as missing?" she demanded.

John shook his head. "She's upset," he said. "I don't think she even knows what she's saying half of the time."

"I'm sorry you have to deal with her," Bessie said. She made them each a cup of tea and then put generous servings of the warm shortbread onto plates.

"It's all part of the job," John said, sipping his tea. "Ah, this helps more than you can know," he told Bessie.

"So what did you and Jane Harris talk about?" John asked after he'd finished half of his shortbread.

"She thinks Jacob was here looking for a wife, rather than a farm," Bessie told him.

"And what did you think of that idea?"

Bessie shrugged. "I was just turning it over in my head while I was baking," she said. "What she said made sense, and it ties in with what Bahey told me, but it doesn't fit well with what I remember of the man. He certainly didn't act like a man who was looking to settle down."

"None of the women I've spoken to about the man have said that he suggested marriage or anything other than a few casual evenings out," John told her. "I haven't talked to Karen yet, although I've read Pete's report on what Bahey told him."

Bessie nodded. "From what I saw of him, he was all about having a bit of fun. Maybe his sister is remembering what she wants to remember, rather than the truth."

John shrugged. "I wouldn't suggest any such thing to her," he told Bessie.

"No, I wouldn't, either," Bessie agreed with a laugh. "Would you like more shortbread?"

"Oh, I shouldn't," John said. He flushed. "But I'd love some."

Bessie cut him another generous piece, taking a much smaller helping for herself. She told herself that she was just having more so that John didn't feel self-conscious about eating in front of her, but she knew that wasn't strictly true.

"I'm going to tell you something else," John said, after Bessie had refilled his teacup. "It's going to be in the papers tomorrow, so I expect it's probably all over the island already."

"If it is, I haven't heard it," Bessie said. "I haven't heard anything new about the case since the body was positively identified."

"When we began to clear out the space around where the body was found, we discovered that it wasn't simply packed with Fenella's mother's things," John told her. "At the very back of the space we found Jacob's suitcases."

"I suppose that explains what happened to them," Bessie said thoughtfully. "It's also another connection between Jacob and the Clague farm."

"Maybe," John said. "Or maybe, having found a good spot to hide the body, the killer just dumped the suitcases there as well."

"But that would have taken time," Bessie said. "And the longer he was there, the greater the chances that Niall or Eoin would find him."

"Unless Niall or Eoin, or both, were involved," John added the obvious conclusion.

Bessie nodded. "Poor Fenella. She must be worried sick about her father."

"Anna's going back down to question him again tomorrow," John told her. "She's having his doctor meet her there to help out."

"Jane suggested that he might be faking his confusion," Bessie said. "Anna doesn't really think that's the case, does she?"

"I couldn't possibly tell you what Anna thinks," John replied. "Having a doctor there will help protect both Anna and Niall, though. Fenella wants to be there as well. I'm not sure if Anna has agreed to that or not, though."

Bessie sighed. "It's all very sad," she said. "How is Eoin holding up through all of this?"

"It seems to be taking a toll," John told her. "He doesn't look well, but he insisted that he's fine when I asked."

"Do you have any suspects, other than Eoin and Niall?" Bessie had to ask.

"We're in the process of tracking down as many of the former farmhands as we can," John replied. "In cold cases like this, the whole process can be rather long and drawn-out. Many of the people we're looking for have passed away. Many of those who are still around have little or no recollection of the man, even if there were here at the right time."

"He was only on the island for a short time," Bessie said. "I suspect he made much more of an impression on the young women in Laxey than on the young men."

"That definitely seems to be have been the case," John agreed. "We're also looking at the time he spent in Douglas, but it seems that barely anyone remembers him from the short time he was there, aside from one woman who went to dinner with him a couple of times. She's still a little bit angry at him for dropping her after that, or at least that's the impression that Pete got from her."

"Inspector Corkill is also an excellent judge of character," Bessie said. "I suspect he's right about the woman, whoever she is."

"I believe I told you that there was an angry farmer who'd hoped to sell his land to Jacob as well," John said. "He died many years ago, though, so I only heard the story second-hand. The disagreement happened some months before Jacob's death, so I find it hard to believe that it's relevant to his murder, but we are trying to look into it as much as we can."

"Did the farmer in question have a daughter about the right age for Jacob?" Bessie asked, thinking about her conversation with Jane Harris.

"He did," John confirmed. "But from what she's said, her father never let the man get near her. Apparently, the man was very protective. She didn't marry until after her father died, when she was nearly forty."

"Interesting," Bessie remarked. "Fenella said that her father didn't want her to marry young, either. She said Eoin only managed to court her because he was already on the farm and could do so without her father really noticing."

"Do you think Niall was happy with Eoin as his son-in-law?" John asked.

Bessie nodded. "Eoin has always been a very hard worker," she replied. "He started on the farm as seasonal help, but he quickly became indispensible to Niall. For a while it looked as if his brother was going to do the same, but then Nicholas made some unfortunate friends and ended up leaving the island."

John nodded. "I understand he's a farmer now," he said.

"It's funny, isn't it? I reckon he ended up doing what he knew, once he'd calmed down a bit."

"Fenella said something about him visiting soon."

"Yes, I think she said he and his wife are arriving tomorrow," Bessie confirmed.

"Are you going to see him?"

"I wasn't really planning on it," Bessie said in surprise. "Why?"

"I just wondered," John said, waving a hand. "It doesn't matter. Anna or I will be interviewing him, but I thought you might have a chance to chat with him as well."

"I'll have to see if I can find an excuse to visit the farm," Bessie mused. "I was just there to see my turkeys, so I'll have to think of another reason."

"You should probably stay away from the farm," John said. "Anna won't welcome the interference, and you know I don't like it when you're caught up in murder investigations. Whatever happened on that farm all those years ago, I have to believe that at least one of the people who lives there knew about it."

"You mentioned Eoin and Niall as suspects; what about Fenella?" Bessie asked.

"She's on the list," John said. "She was only eighteen that summer, and she claims she doesn't remember the man, but she might be lying."

"I suppose, if she did kill him, she would lie, wouldn't she?" Bessie speculated.

John shrugged. "I think, if it were me, that I'd admit to having met the man once or twice, but nothing more. Lying is dangerous. We only have to find one witness who remembers seeing her with Jacob on some occasion and we'll know she was lying. Then we'll want to know why she was lying."

"But you haven't found anyone who ever saw them together yet, right?"

"No, but we still have a lot of people we need to find and question," John said. He sighed deeply. "I think this might be my least favourite case ever," he told Bessie. "After forty years, most of the possible witnesses have died, moved away or forgotten what happened back then. I'm not sure we'll ever know who killed Jacob Conover."

"I do hope Anna doesn't push poor Niall too hard," Bessie said.

"Poor Niall might be a murderer," John pointed out.

Bessie thought for a moment. "I can't come up with a motive for him," she said. "Unless it was just an accident and all he did was hide the body."

"That's still a crime," John said.

"But not nearly as bad as murder."

The pair talked in circles for another half hour until John suddenly noticed the time. "You'll be wanting to get some dinner," he said to Bessie as he stood up. "I didn't mean to stay so long."

"No worries," Bessie laughed. "I've eaten so much shortbread that I'm not really hungry."

"I'd better get home. I have a few things left to finish before the kids get here on Friday afternoon," John said.

"I can't wait to see them again," Bessie said. "I hope they aren't too bored at the Thanksgiving feast. It is going to be mostly adults, after all."

"I'm sure they'll be fine. It will do them good to spend some time working on their social skills, and if they get too bored, we can always leave right after the meal."

"Don't rush off before pudding," Bessie exclaimed. "Have you ever tried pumpkin pie?"

"No," John shook his head. "And I'm not sure I want to."

Bessie laughed. "I will insist that you have a very thin slice," she said. "If you don't like it, you don't have to eat more than a single bite, but I do like everyone to try it. It's one of the mainstays of an American Thanksgiving."

"I'll try it, if you want me to," John told her.

"There will be apple pie as well," Bessie said. "If you don't like the pumpkin, you can switch to apple."

"I love apple pie," John said. "And I don't have it very often."

"I make one now and again," Bessie said. "But never in November. That way it's truly special on Thanksgiving."

"Thank you for the tea, the biscuits and the conversation," John said at the door. "Let me know if you run into Nicholas Faragher while he's here. I don't expect you to quiz him about the murder, but I'd be interested to hear his thoughts on the subject if it comes up."

Bessie let him out and then sat down to think. She needed to find an excuse to visit the Clague farm so that she could talk to Nicholas. The matter was on her mind as she made herself a light meal. After she'd mindlessly eaten it, she took a short, moonlit walk along the beach. The wind had died down and the rain had stopped, but it was quite cold. She inhaled the salty sea air and smiled to herself. Whatever the weather, she loved her island. She'd just let herself back in when the phone rang.

"Bessie, it's Fenella up at the Clague farm. Nicholas is arriving tomorrow and I was wondering if you'd like to come for tea? I'm afraid we'll have nothing to say to the man and his wife, and Eoin and I thought that you might be able to help keep the conversation flowing. You did know him when he was younger, after all."

"I'd be happy to," Bessie said, trying to keep her voice as neutral as possible. She didn't want Fenella to know how eager she was to see Nicholas.

"I'll have Eoin come and collect you," Fenella told her. "He'll be at your cottage around half two, if that's okay?"

"That's fine," Bessie replied.

After a final tidying up of the kitchen, Bessie found a book that promised to be far less interesting than the one from the previous night. She was determined to get some much-needed sleep tonight. Tomorrow seemed like it might be a quite interesting day.

CHAPTER 13

The rain hadn't returned when Bessie got up on Wednesday morning. She took that as a good omen and headed out for a longer walk. She walked past the holiday cottages, which were still dark, and on past Thie yn Traie, which was also unlit, at least as far as Bessie could tell from the beach. Half an hour later, she finally turned around and headed for home. Thie yn Traie was still dark, but there were lights on in some of the holiday cottages as Bessie strolled past them. She waved to Thomas, who was hard at work in one of them, before she finally made her way home.

In her kitchen, she slipped off her shoes and sank into the closest chair. She was tired from the long walk, but she felt better than she had in a long while. The physical exertions had helped to clear her head, although she wasn't sure she was very happy with some of the ideas that had entered into it.

Feeling as if she needed to chat with a friend, Bessie rang the police station.

"Laxey Neighbourhood Policing, this is Doona. How can I help you?"

"Ah, Doona, I just wanted to hear a friendly voice," Bessie said. "This whole business with Jacob Conover is upsetting me."

"Why don't I bring you some lunch in a little while," Doona suggested. "I'm only doing a short shift today, so I have the afternoon off."

"Are you sure you don't mind?" Bessie asked. She hated feeling as if she was a burden to her friends.

"Of course I don't mind," Doona said firmly. "I've been wanting to visit anyway, I just haven't had the time. I'll be there right around midday with sandwiches from the new shop that just opened over the road."

Bessie disconnected and smiled. She was ever so grateful for her friends. Transcriptions for the museum easily filled the rest of the morning. Shortly before Doona was meant to arrive, Bessie sat back and grinned.

"I think I might just be getting the hang of this," she said to herself. "And it's much more interesting than I thought it might be, as well."

In the kitchen, she refilled the kettle and switched it on while she waited for her friend. Doona's car pulled up next to the cottage only a few minutes later.

"Hello, dear," Doona said as she hugged Bessie. "I'm sorry you're feeling upset."

Bessie squeezed her friend tightly. "You would think, after everything that's happened in the last year or so, that I would be getting used to such things, wouldn't you?"

"I do hope none of us ever get used to murder," Doona replied.

Bessie pulled out plates as Doona unpacked sandwiches, crisps, and other goodies. Once Bessie made tea, the pair sat down to eat.

"Is there something specific bothering you about the case?" Doona asked.

"I just can't help feeling that Niall was involved in some way," Bessie replied. "I feel bad for Fenella. She has enough problems with both her father and Eoin being ill. It can't be easy for her."

"Do you think she suspects her father?"

"She must," Bessie said. "I can't see how anyone else could have hidden the body and the suitcases there, at least not without Niall noticing."

"What about Eoin?"

"That would be even worse for Fenella," Bessie said with a sigh. "But I have to believe that one or both of them had to be involved in hiding the body, even if they didn't have anything to do with the murder."

"Maybe it wasn't murder," Doona suggested. "The coroner hasn't determined a cause of death yet and isn't likely to, from what I've heard. It was too long ago and the body is badly damaged from its years underground. Maybe the poor man just slipped and fell and hit his head on something."

"Then why hide the body?"

"Maybe everyone was quite drunk and they were worried they'd be blamed for his death?" Doona said. She shrugged. "There could be any number of possible explanations, all much nicer to consider than murder."

"Yes, that's true," Bessie said. She took a bite of a sandwich and then smiled at Doona. "This is really good."

"The place is new, but the young constables have all been saying good things. We seem to have something new in there every month. I don't know why nothing lasts very long. It seems like the guys eat there, whatever they're serving, just about every day."

"I understand restaurants are very hard work and that some huge percentage of them fail every year," Bessie said. "Although that little corner of Laxey does seem to have worse luck than most."

"And luck is probably at least part of the equation," Doona said.

When the sandwiches were all gone, Bessie pulled out the last of the shortbread.

"Oh, goodness, you know I love this," Doona exclaimed as Bessie handed her a serving.

"I'm ever so grateful for you coming over," Bessie said after a while.

"I don't think I helped at all," Doona replied. "Do you want to talk about anything?"

"Not really. It's just nice to have pleasant company. I'm going up the Clague farm this afternoon to see Nicholas and meet his wife."

"Does John know?"

"I don't think so. I was going to ring him once I got home."

"Make sure that you do," Doona said. "He's keeping a close eye on the farm and its residents at the moment."

"He has the same suspicions about Niall or Eoin as I do, doesn't he?"

"I'm not sure who he suspects," Doona replied. "But I know he's interested in everything that happens on the farm."

"I talked to John yesterday and he suggested that I should try to chat with Nicholas," Bessie told her friend.

"It would be interesting to see if he remembers Jacob, especially considering his brother claims not to," Doona replied.

"I'm kind of dreading the visit," Bessie admitted. "I think that's why I was so unhappy this morning. I'd rather leave the whole matter to the police."

"If it's left to Anna, Niall will get the blame," Doona said. "She really doesn't like him for some reason, and she seems to be convinced that he's faking his illness."

"Well, he's had his doctors fooled for many years, then," Bessie retorted. "I'm really struggling to like Anna Lambert."

"I think you'd struggle to find anyone at the station that likes her, even a little bit," Doona said. "She's all sorts of difficult."

Bessie laughed. "That's an interesting description, and one that seems accurate."

"Do you need a ride up to the farm?" Doona asked as she and Bessie began to tidy up from their lunch.

"No, Eoin is collecting me."

"Please ring me if you need a ride home," Doona said. "I'm not doing much of anything this afternoon."

"We'll see how it goes," Bessie told her. "Fenella didn't mention having Eoin bring me home, actually."

After Doona left, Bessie paced around her kitchen for a few minutes. She was feeling very anxious about the meeting ahead. Finally, she took a deep breath and gave herself a stern lecture.

"You're going to see Nicholas and meet his wife. If you can find out anything to help John wrap up a forty-year-old murder, that's good too, but it isn't really very likely. Just relax and enjoy catching up with an old friend."

When she'd finished her little pep talk, a voice in her head just had to argue. "You weren't exactly friends with Nicholas Faragher," the voice reminded her. "In fact, you barely knew him."

Bessie ran a comb through her hair and added a touch of lipstick to her lips. It seemed best, all things considered, to simply ignore the voice in her head, so that's what she did. She was standing at the door watching when Eoin arrived. Bessie was struck again by how unwell he looked.

"How are you?" she asked, trying to sound casual, but feeling concerned.

"I'm fine," he said brusquely. "Are you ready? Fenella was sorry she said I'd collect you, as now she's been left alone with Nicholas and Sarah."

Bessie quickly locked her cottage and followed the man to his car. She'd barely shut the door when he started the engine and pulled away.

"Is Fenella finding it awkward talking to them, then?" Bessie asked after a moment.

Eoin shrugged. "I don't know," he said. "I've nothing much to say to them, though."

"Surely it's nice to see your brother again?"

"I suppose so."

Bessie waited for Eoin to continue, but he remained silent on the rest of the journey. For once they weren't held up by livestock, and Bessie felt as if the drive had been a very quick one as Eoin parked next to the farmhouse.

"You go on in," he told Bessie. "The door won't be locked. I need to check on a few things at, um, with the sheep. Tell Fenella I'll be less than an hour."

"Thank you for the ride," she said as she climbed out of the car. She'd only just shut the door before Eoin was pulling away. Shaking her head, she climbed up the steps to the house. She knocked once and then pushed the door open.

"Hello? Eoin said I should just let myself in," she called. "Hello?"

"Bessie? We're in the kitchen; come on back," Fenella's voice reached her.

Bessie walked through the house, practicing how she might smile when she reached the kitchen. Before she got there, though, Fenella met her.

"There you are," Fenella said. "You're right on time. The kettle has just boiled. But where is Eoin?"

"He said he had to check on something to do with the sheep," Bessie told her. "He said to tell you that he will be here in less than an hour."

Fenella frowned. "I'll bet," she muttered under her breath. "Come and see Nicholas then," she said to Bessie, giving her a bright smile.

Bessie could tell the smile was fake, but since she'd just forced a similar expression onto her own face, she didn't comment. In the kitchen, the guests were sitting at the table. They both got to their feet as Bessie and Fenella entered.

"Aunt Bessie," the man said, "you haven't changed a bit."

"I can't say the same about you," Bessie replied, looking him up and down.

Nicholas laughed. "I was skinny as a rail and full of the devil when you last saw me. I imagine I've changed a great deal."

Bessie nodded as she took in the man's altered appearance. He'd gained weight, but most of it appeared to be muscle. Nicholas was clearly a man who worked hard at some physical labour. He was mostly bald and his green eyes twinkled as he watched Bessie studying him.

"I hope I've turned out okay," he said now. "I got myself in with the wrong sort of friends for a few years there, but Sarah soon sorted me out." He gestured towards the woman standing next to him.

Bessie smiled at her. She looked to be around the same age as her husband. She was solidly built, with dimples and rosy cheeks. Bessie thought she looked like a kindly grandmother.

"It's ever so nice to meet you," Sarah said to Bessie. "Nick never talked much about his childhood on the island, but whenever he did, he always had fond memories of you."

"Did he?" Bessie blurted out without thinking.

The couple laughed. "I started working on the farm, at least part-time, when I was fifteen," Nicholas told her. "And I pretty much hated it. I didn't want to have to work so hard when other people were just sitting around all day doing what I thought were easier things. Anyway, you used to come up to see your Thanksgiving birds and you used to bring cakes or biscuits with you. It was always such a treat, those homemade goodies. It was about the only thing I liked about the farm for those years I was working here."

Bessie shook her head. "I don't remember doing that," she said.

"I remember," Fenella told her. "When I was little, your visit seemed to mark the start of Christmas for me. You used to bring me little presents as well, when I was a child."

"I do remember that," Bessie said after a moment. "I used to tell Niall to keep whatever I brought you for Christmas day."

"But he never did," Fenella said. "He used to give my the gifts the same day you were here. As he never did a lot for Christmas itself, sometimes your visit was even better than Christmas day."

"I wish I'd known," Bessie said. "I would have bought you better presents."

Fenella laughed. "I don't really remember anything you brought," she confessed. "But I know I was awfully excited at the time."

"Well, I'm glad you both have such fond memories of me," Bessie said, laughing.

"Christmas is always more fun when you have children to buy for, isn't it?" Sarah asked. "I loved the holidays when our five were small."

"Maybe one day one of them will get around to giving us a grandchild or two," Nicholas said. "Although none of them seem eager to settle down."

"You took your time," Sarah reminded him gently.

"I surely did," he admitted.

"So tell me about your children," Bessie suggested.

"Do sit down," Fenella said. "I'll just get the tea."

"Please let me help," Sarah said.

"Oh, no, you sit down and chat with Bessie," Fenella replied.

"Did you say you have five children?" Bessie asked once they were all seated.

"We did," Sarah said. "Unfortunately, our second son, Teddy, passed away when he was still quite young."

"I'm sorry," Bessie said.

"I was lucky to have the others," Sarah told her. "Between looking after them and running the farm, I was too busy to fall apart, even though I wanted to."

"It was a difficult time," Nicholas said. "But we got through it, at least as much as you ever can."

Bessie nodded. "I'm sure Fenella told me that your oldest helps run your farm now," she said as Fenella passed around cups of tea.

"Oh, yes. Ned's wonderful," Sarah said. "He's taken over ninety per cent of the work, and he's doing so much to make the farm more efficient and profitable as well; it's amazing."

"He went to university and studied farming," Nicholas said. Bessie could hear the pride in his voice. "He's a really smart kid."

"It's nice that you have someone to take on the farm work as you get older," Fenella said quietly as she joined them at the table. Sarah put her hand over Fenella's and gave it a pat.

Before anyone spoke, Fenella jumped back up again. "There are biscuits and sandwiches and scones," she told them all. "Everything is laid out. Please help yourselves."

Nicholas stood up and then held Sarah's chair for her as she rose. "Guests first," Sarah said, smiling at Bessie.

Bessie selected a few biscuits and a scone and then sat back down while the others filled their plates. There were so many questions she wanted to ask Nicholas, but she didn't want to be rude.

"Fenella tells me you were on the farm the day the body was found," Nicholas said as everyone began to enjoy their tea.

Bessie nearly choked on a biscuit at the unexpected turn in the conversation. "I was," she agreed after a moment. "Do you remember Jacob Conover?"

Nicholas looked at Fenella and then back at Bessie. "Not really," he said. "I have some vague recollection of the man, but I was pretty busy causing trouble and chasing after girls in those days."

"I thought you might remember him since he did quite a bit of girl chasing himself," Bessie commented.

"If I recall correctly, I spent most of that summer running after Anna Long. She wasn't interested, but I was sure that she'd come around eventually. I wonder what ever happened to her."

"I don't think anyone knows for sure," Bessie told him. "She left the island and as far as I know, no one knows for certain where she went."

"Really? How very strange," Nicholas said. "Maybe she came looking for me," he laughed.

"I think the police were the only ones looking for you after you left," Fenella said dryly.

Nicholas laughed again. "You could be right about that," he agreed.

"So how long are you planning to stay?" Bessie asked after a short lull in the conversation.

"About a week," Sarah replied. "We've left our return open for the moment. We came over because we want to help out, with Eoin's health being so fragile. We might stay a bit longer if Fenella and Eoin will actually let us do a few things around here."

"We're managing," Fenella said shortly.

"But why struggle?" Nicholas asked. "We're here and we're both quite used to farm work. Take advantage of us."

"You needn't worry about your inheritance," Fenella said coolly. "Even if we don't manage to keep up with the farm, the land will be worth a fortune when we go."

"We aren't the least bit interested in inheriting anything," Nicholas said, flushing. "If you've no one to leave things to, choose a useful charity and leave the farm to them. We're here because we care, not for any other reason."

"You haven't been back to the island in nearly forty years," Fenella said.

"No, and I'm sorry about that," Nicholas said. "I can't even offer any real excuse except we've been busy with our farm and our children. You and Eoin never came to see us, either, though."

"Eoin came to the wedding," Fenella said.

Sarah held up a hand. "Let's not argue," she said firmly. "None of us have done what we should have over the last forty years. Let's not spend the next forty pointing fingers and blaming one another. We really are here to help, if you want help. If you don't, we'll stay and visit for a few days and then go home. As for inheriting the farm, that's your choice, but I can promise you we have no expectations in that area."

"There isn't anyone else," Fenella told her.

"As Nicholas said, there are charities," Sarah replied. "It's your farm and you may do what you like with it. Our farm is quite successful in its own small way and our children are all settled and happy. Please do what you'd like with your money."

"Maybe we'll spend it all on alternative medicine," Eoin said from the doorway. "Conventional medicine doesn't seem to be helping me."

As he walked into the room and began to fill his own plate of food, Bessie couldn't help but compare his appearance with his brother's. Nicholas looked healthy and fit. Next to him, Eoin looked even more unwell than Bessie had previously believed.

"There are some very good options in alternative medicine," she said now.

"Not for what I have," Eoin told her. "I've actually seen every specialist out there. The only ones that have offered me a cure have been the dishonest ones." He chuckled. "I told the last one that I'd pay him in monthly installments over the next three years. After he'd promised me a cure, he struggled to justify why I had to pay for the whole treatment in advance."

Bessie smiled. "You'd think he would have at least pretended to believe his own sales pitch," she said.

"He was more worried about getting paid," Eoin replied. He sat down at the table and sipped his tea.

"We should have visited more often," Nicholas said quietly.

"You were busy and so were we," Eoin countered. "Farmers don't have time for socialising."

"I'd love it if you'd come and see our farm," Sarah said. "And it would be nice if you could meet our children."

"We'll have to see," Eoin said. "We'd have to find someone to take over here."

"Maybe you should go for a few days," Fenella said. "I could keep things going over here."

Eoin shrugged. "Let's see what the doctor says next week," he said. "And see how your father is doing. You don't want me gone if, well, you know what I mean."

Fenella nodded. "Does anyone need more tea?" she asked, getting up and bustling around the kitchen.

Bessie shook her head. "I really should be heading for home," she said. "Although it's been lovely seeing Nicholas again and meeting Sarah."

"It's been a real treat, seeing you," Nicholas said.

"You all should come to the Thanksgiving feast," Bessie said. "You'd be very welcome."

"I'm afraid we have other things to do on Saturday," Fenella said. "We've arranged to take my father out for a few hours that afternoon. They don't let me take him very often, because they have to send a nurse with us."

"I'm sure Niall will appreciate that," Bessie said.

"Last time we did it, he fell asleep in the car and didn't wake up until we got back to the home," Eoin said.

"It was still worthwhile," Fenella said softly.

"Yes, dear," Eoin replied, patting her hand.

"Thank you for a lovely afternoon," Bessie said. "I'll just ring for a taxi and be on my way."

"I can take you home," Fenella said. "Nicholas can help Eoin with the chores while I'm out."

"I'll stay and help the men," Sarah said. "I'm feeling as if I've been very lazy since we arrived."

Bessie gathered up her handbag and followed Fenella back

through the house. As they walked, she argued with herself about what she was going to say to Fenella in the car.

"Thank you for joining us," Fenella said after she'd pulled away from the house.

"It was nice to see Nicholas again," Bessie told her. "I was surprised he had such fond memories of me. Sarah seems very nice."

"She is," Fenella agreed. "I think the family farm will be in good hands with them when Eoin and I are gone."

"You have a good many years left, though," Bessie pointed out.

"I might, but Eoin doesn't," Fenella said.

"I'm sorry," Bessie said.

"He hasn't been well for a long time and the whole Jacob Conover thing isn't helping," Fenella told her. "It's added a lot of stress to our lives."

"I'm surprised you don't remember the man," Bessie said, choosing her words carefully.

"It was a long time ago," Fenella replied.

They'd reached the last pasture and several sheep were standing in the centre of the road. Fenella sighed as she rolled to a stop.

"It was a long time ago," Bessie agreed. "I had an interesting conversation with Jacob's sister yesterday, though."

"Did you? She came up to the farm, but I didn't really speak to her. Eoin showed her around a little bit and answered her questions."

"She has her own theory on why Jacob was here," Bessie said, keeping her tone casual. "She thinks he was looking for a farmer's daughter. Someone he could marry that would help him run his farm back home."

"As I said, I didn't speak to her," Fenella said.

Bessie stared hard at the woman, but Fenella wouldn't meet her eyes.

"He wanted to marry you, didn't he?" Bessie asked quietly.

Fenella looked over at her and then burst into tears. "No one knows that," she said through her tears. "No one except my father ever knew that."

Bessie put her arms around Fenella as she sobbed. She patted her back and whispered meaningless nothings as the sheep wandered off and the car idled. Eventually, Fenella lifted her head.

"I'm sorry," she said. "I never cry."

"Then you were long overdue," Bessie told her. "I didn't mean to upset you, though."

"I've been upset since the body was found," Fenella replied. "As soon as I saw the watch, I knew who it was, but I couldn't talk about it. Eoin never knew that Jacob and I had had a relationship. It would break his heart to find out now, and his health is so fragile as it is, I couldn't possibly say anything."

"So Jane Harris was right?" Bessie asked. "Jacob was looking for a wife?"

"I don't know if he was looking for one, exactly, but we fell in love," Fenella told her. "He was, well, special. He was different from any other man I'd ever met. He swept me off my feet, but I didn't want my father to know. He went out with all those other women so no one would know about me."

"It was very effective," Bessie remarked.

"He was supposed to come and get me after he left the pub that night," she continued. "I was all packed and ready to go. I'd told my father I was going and we'd had a huge row. I sat outside, with my suitcase, waiting all night."

Bessie hugged her again. "I'm so sorry," she murmured.

"When he never came for me, I assumed he'd changed his mind and gone back alone," Fenella said after a moment. "My father never said another word about it. A short time later Eoin started taking me out and I decided I might as well marry him and try to be happy. It worked reasonably well, I suppose."

Bessie shook her head. "You poor thing," she said.

"You can see why I'm feeling so much stress," Fenella said. "My father was the only person who knew about Jacob and me. I can't believe my father would kill him to stop me leaving, but I can't imagine why anyone else would have killed him, either."

"How angry was your father?" Bessie had to ask.

"He was furious at first," Fenella replied. "But after a while, he just went really quiet. I was young and stupid and too wrapped up in my own happiness to think about how much my leaving would hurt him, of course. I was all he had and he needed me to help keep the farm running. But all I could think about was how much I loved Jacob."

"You were eighteen," Bessie pointed out. "You had every right to chase your own happiness."

"I should have tried to persuade Jacob to stay here," the woman said sadly. "I was so excited about leaving that I didn't even consider the idea."

"From what Jane Harris said, Jacob wouldn't have agreed," Bessie said, not sure if she was helping the situation or not. "He needed to go back and run his family farm."

"I can't help but wish I'd tried. Maybe Jacob would still be alive. Things might have been very different."

"You need to talk to John Rockwell," Bessie said. "What you've told me might be relevant to the murder investigation."

"I can't," Fenella said. "If I tell him everything, it will get back to Eoin. I don't want to upset him. Not now."

"But John needs to know," Bessie argued.

"That Anna Lambert already thinks my father killed Jacob," Fenella argued. "This would just give her more ammunition."

"I can't keep what you've told me a secret," Bessie said, feeling miserable.

"Please, please, please, if you have to tell him, beg him not to tell Eoin," she said, sobbing again. "I think finding out might kill him, even before the cancer can."

Bessie sighed. "I'll do my best," she promised.

"And please don't tell Anna Lambert anything," Fenella added. "That woman already hates me and my father."

"I don't have any intention of speaking to her," Bessie said emphatically. "But I can't promise that John won't talk to her."

Fenella sighed. "I'm hoping to persuade Eoin to go back across with Nicholas and Sarah," she said. "Maybe you could wait to talk to the police until he's off the island?"

"I don't think this should wait," Bessie said. "Hasn't Jacob waited long enough for justice?"

Fenella laughed bitterly. "If I thought the killer was anyone other than my father, I'd agree with that sentiment," she said.

Before Bessie could reply, Fenella held up a hand. "Never mind," she said. "You do what you have to do. I'll deal with Eoin and my father. That's what I've done my whole life."

The pair was silent as Fenella drove Bessie home. At the cottage, Bessie turned to her.

"I'm really sorry," she said, "but John needs to know."

A sudden burst of noise interrupted Fenella's reply. "My mobile," Fenella said. She reached into her bag and found the phone. Bessie watched the woman's face as she spoke.

"Hello?"

"What's wrong?"

"I'll be right there."

Fenella disconnected the call and then stared at the phone in her hand.

"What's wrong?" Bessie asked after a minute.

"That was Eoin," Fenella said. "Douglas Gardens just rang the house. My father's gone."

CHAPTER 14

"What can I do to help?" Bessie asked quickly.

Fenella shook her head. "There's nothing," she said softly. "We made all of the arrangements a few years ago, while my father still had some good days. He wanted to be buried next to my mother and he wanted..." she trailed off and began to cry.

"Come inside," Bessie said as she hugged the woman again. "I'll make tea."

"I have to go home," Fenella said. "Eoin needs me. He'll be more upset than I am. My father was like a father to him, you know."

"I do know," Bessie said. "But I don't think you should be driving."

"I'm fine," Fenella said. "It isn't that far."

Bessie wanted to argue, but she couldn't think of any easy solution to the problem. If she rang for a taxi for Fenella, the woman would have to leave her car at Bessie's cottage. For the first time in a long while, Bessie was sorry she'd never learned to drive.

"It's okay," Fenella said now, her voice stronger. "It isn't exactly a shock. And with everything that could be coming, it might be a blessing."

"Please drive carefully," Bessie told her. "And ring me if you think of anything I can do. I'll ring you tomorrow morning to see what help you need."

"Thank you, Bessie," Fenella said. She gave Bessie another hug. Bessie walked to her cottage door, conscious that the woman was watching her. After she opened the door, she turned and waved. Fenella nodded and then drove slowly away.

Inside her home, Bessie paced around the kitchen. She knew she needed to ring John and tell him what she'd learned, but she didn't want to add to Fenella's troubles. Before she'd made up her mind what to do, her phone rang.

"John was wondering if we could all come over tonight," Doona said when Bessie answered. "He wants to discuss the case with you in light of today's sad news."

"That's fine," Bessie said. "But I haven't any food."

Doona laughed. "We'll bring something with us," she assured her friend. "John and I will be there at six. I'm not sure if Hugh's coming as well or not. He might already have plans."

"I hope he does," Bessie said. "I'd love to see him, but he needs to be spending time with Grace. She's going to give up on him if he doesn't get around to proposing before too much longer."

"I'm keeping my mouth shut on that matter," Doona said firmly. "I've made such a mess of my own personal life, I don't feel as if I should comment on anyone else's."

Bessie laughed. "As a middle-aged spinster, I probably shouldn't comment, either. But they do seem so very well-suited."

"They do," Doona agreed.

The conversation and the plans made Bessie feel better. John was coming over, but she hadn't actually invited him. Of course, she'd have to share what she'd learned with him, but at least Doona, and maybe Hugh, would be there as well.

With nothing to do but wait, Bessie took a short stroll down the beach. It was cold and growing dark, but it was dry, which was about all you could hope for on the island in late November. Very occasionally Bessie thought back to the long, cold, and snowy winters of her childhood in Ohio. Somehow it always made Christmas feel more special when there was a fluffy white layer of sparkling snow covering the outdoors.

Of course, it was hard work for her parents, but Bessie had never been asked to help with the shoveling or tried to drive on snow-covered roads. Now she couldn't help but feel as if a light dusting would make her Thanksgiving feast even more special. She'd checked the forecast, though, and Saturday was meant to be cool and rainy, typical Manx winter weather.

She arrived back at her cottage at the same time as John's car pulled into the parking area. "Goodness, I was enjoying my walk so much I almost missed you," she laughed as John and Doona got out of the car.

"We'd have waited for you," John assured her. "Or come looking."

Bessie unlocked her cottage and the trio went inside. "No Hugh, then?" Bessie asked after switching on the lights.

John started opening food containers as Doona found plates and cutlery. "He's on his way," he replied. "I sent him to pick up pudding."

The words were barely out of his mouth when someone knocked on the door. Bessie opened it and greeted Hugh with a hug.

"Come in out of the cold," she instructed him.

He handed Bessie a bakery box and removed his coat. "I couldn't decide what would be best," he said in an apologetic voice. "So I got a little of everything."

"That sounds about right," Doona told him, laughing.

They all filled plates and then settled in at the kitchen table. While they ate, they chatted about the weather and the plans for Saturday. Bessie was very aware that everyone was avoiding the very topic that they'd come to discuss.

After Doona cleared away the plates, Hugh put the bakery box in the centre of the table. He opened the lid and everyone looked inside.

"You weren't kidding," Bessie said happily.

Inside the box were chocolate and vanilla fairy cakes, thick and gooey brownies, a selection of cream cakes and a handful of tiny fruit tarts.

"I can't believe they fit it all into one box," Doona said.

"I'm not sure we'll be able to get anything out," John remarked. "There isn't an inch of space left."

They ended up taking the box apart in order to get to the treats inside.

"We'll just have to start with the things on the outside and eat our way into the centre," Hugh said, grinning widely.

"Maybe we should just attack it with forks," Doona suggested.

Bessie tutted her disapproval. "I shall give you all plates and you shall put what you want on them," she said sternly. "There's more than enough to go around, even with Hugh here."

As everyone dug into his or her own favourite, Bessie looked at John. He was nibbling at his fairy cake, but seemed distracted.

"Is it time to talk, then?" she asked with a sigh.

"I think so," John told her. "I have to go and see Fenella and Eoin later and I'd like to talk everything through with you before I go."

"I was going to ring you, anyway," Bessie told him. "I spent an hour at the farm this afternoon and had an interesting conversation with Fenella on the drive home. She was here when Eoin rang to tell her about her father."

John sighed. "I wish the circumstances were different," he said. "I'm sure they aren't going to want to talk to me."

"What do you mean?" Bessie asked.

"Anna spent an hour with Niall this afternoon," John told her. "She questioned him extensively and she's convinced that he confessed to killing Jacob Conover. She wasn't able to work out a motive, but she's prepared to close the case with him on record as having confessed."

"He wasn't in his right mind," Bessie argued.

"His doctor was with him the entire time. He said that he thought Niall was more lucid than he's been in years," John replied.

"Please don't tell me that Anna gave the poor man a heart attack," Bessie exclaimed as the idea crossed her mind.

"According to Anna, he was fine when she left," John said. "Apparently, a short time later his heart simply stopped."

"Maybe, having confessed, he was finally at peace," Doona suggested.

"What did he say, exactly?" Bessie demanded.

John shook his head. "I haven't seen Anna's report yet. She's submitted it directly to the Chief Constable and he's going to rule on whether the confession is valid or not."

"Poor Fenella," Bessie said.

"But what happened at the farm today?" John asked. "Did Nicholas remember Jacob?"

"He claimed he didn't, at least not really," Bessie replied. "But I think he was lying. Perhaps, now that Niall is dead, everyone up there will start being more honest."

"They all think Niall killed him, then?" John asked.

"Fenella does," Bessie said, feeling sad. "She even supplied a motive."

"Did she now?" John pulled out his notebook. "Go on."

"You know how Jane Harris said that her brother was looking for a wife? Apparently he was planning on taking Fenella back with him," Bessie said. "He was going to collect her at the farm after he left the pub, but he never arrived."

"And her father knew about it?" Hugh wanted to know.

"Yes. She said he was very upset."

"Maybe just upset enough to get into a fight with the man," Doona suggested. "Maybe he killed him accidently in a fight."

"I don't think we'll ever know exactly what happened that night," John said. "But I like that scenario better than cold-blooded murder."

"Fenella doesn't want anyone to know about her and Jacob," Bessie said. "She doesn't want to upset Eoin. He isn't well."

"I'm not sure how we can keep that a secret," John said. "But maybe, with Niall dead, it doesn't really matter."

"If he did confess, and the confession is valid, then maybe everything else can be kept quiet," Bessie suggested.

"I'll make sure I talk to Eoin and Fenella separately," John told her. "I can try not to mention motives to Eoin."

"I'm having a hard time with this," Bessie said. "I knew Niall for a great many years. I can't see him killing anyone."

"Jacob was going to take away his precious daughter," Doona said. "And maybe he didn't trust the man to actually marry Fenella."

"That's an interesting point," Bessie mused. "If he did want to marry Fenella, why couldn't they get married here, before they went across?"

"Would it have been a huge scandal?" Hugh asked. "If she'd run off with him and they'd not ended up getting married?"

"Oh, yes," Bessie replied. "Girls didn't travel unaccompanied with men in those days. Fenella would have been taking a huge risk, going with him like that. If he'd ended up casting her aside later, goodness knows what might have happened to her."

"Surely she would have just come home," Hugh said.

"If her father would have let her," Bessie said. "Some parents would disown daughters that behaved in such a immoral way. She may have been too embarrassed to try, though, as well. She might have ended up alone somewhere across, maybe even pregnant. It could have been a very sad situation."

"I'm glad those sorts of attitudes have changed," Doona said.

"It seems like a valid motive to me," John said. "Whatever Niall told Anna, this certainly increases the case against him."

"So what happens now?" Bessie asked.

"The Chief Constable is going to go over Anna's report and make a decision about the confession. I'll have to add my report after I've spoken to Fenella later tonight, but it seems likely, if she confirms what you've told me, that the Chief Constable will accept Niall's confession and close the case."

Bessie nodded. "I suppose that's for the best," she said, "especially if you can close the case without mentioning Fenella's relationship with Jacob to anyone."

"I can't believe she kept it a secret in a village as small as Laxey," Doona remarked. "It seems like every time I do anything everyone on my street knows about it."

"The farm was far enough out of town that they were able to meet without being seen," Bessie said. "And Jacob did take out just about every other girl in town. If he had been seen out with Fenella, we all probably would have just assumed that she was his latest passing fancy, not that there was anything serious going on."

"I would like to know just how serious it really was," Hugh said. "Did he seem like the type to get married and settle down?"

Bessie thought for a moment. "I don't know," she said eventually. "The man I remember was loud and flashy and had a different woman on his arm every night. But his sister claims he was definitely looking for a wife, and she knew him much better than I did. Fenella certainly believes that he was serious about marrying her, anyway."

"I'd better get up to the Clague farm and get my interviews done," John said after he'd glanced at the clock. "I want to have my report to the boss before midday tomorrow."

"I'm not sure Fenella will be up to answering questions," Bessie said. "She was very upset when she left here."

"I have to try," John told her. "Fenella has already told Anna that she isn't welcome on the farm again. I believe Fenella blames Anna for her father's sudden death."

"As well she might," Bessie said. "I know murder is a terrible thing, but I do rather feel as if Inspector Lambert pushed poor Niall too far."

"That's another matter for the Chief Constable," John replied. "I'm just keeping my focus on doing my own job."

After John left, taking Doona to drop off at her home before heading to the farm, Hugh helped Bessie with the dishes and tidying.

"You must take all the extra cakes and things," Bessie told Hugh. "Take them over to Grace's tomorrow evening or something."

"I will," Hugh said. "Unless I eat them myself tonight."

Bessie laughed. "Will you ever stop being hungry all the time?" she asked the man.

"I hope so," Hugh replied. "But it hasn't happened yet."

Bessie let him out and watched as he drove away. She was tempted to take another walk, as her mind was feeling unsettled again, but the cold and dark night felt unwelcoming. As Hugh's taillights disappeared up the hill, a heavy rain began to fall.

"I suppose I won't take a walk," Bessie muttered to herself as she shut the door tightly. She locked it and then wandered into her sitting room. Her latest half-finished novel held no appeal. After a while, she decided to head to bed with little hope of actually sleeping.

Her sleep was restless as Bessie tossed and turned, unable to direct her thoughts away from Jacob Conover. By five o'clock, she gave up on sleep and took a long shower. It didn't help much, but three cups of coffee seemed to take the edge off of her exhaustion. All of the caffeine left her feeling restless though, so she quickly headed out for her morning walk somewhat earlier than normal.

The beach was dark, cold, and deserted as Bessie made her way past the holiday cottages. She'd brought a torch with her, and now she used it to help her avoid tripping over driftwood and rocks. She walked as far as Thie ny Traie and then leaned against the cliff and stared out at the sea. No matter how hard she tried, she simply couldn't see Niall killing anyone. Sighing deeply, she turned and headed for home. She had to go and talk to Eoin and Fenella again; she had no choice.

It was far too early to go visiting or even ring the farm, so Bessie busied herself with little chores around her cottage. When she found that she was cleaning her bathroom mirror with furniture polish, she decided that she'd be better off just sitting still until she was able to make the phone call she needed to make. She flipped through a magazine she'd already read, staring at the pages without seeing anything, until nine.

"Ah, good morning," she said as brightly as she could. "This is Bessie Cubbon. I was just ringing to make sure that everyone is okay," she said when the phone was answered at the farm.

"Oh, hello, Bessie. This is Sarah. We're all doing as well as can be expected, I suppose," was the reply.

"I thought maybe I'd come and visit. I could bring some food or something," Bessie said.

"Oh, you don't need to bring anything, but you're welcome to come over," Sarah told her. "I think Fenella would probably like to see you. She's taken the news very hard."

"I'll be there in about an hour," Bessie promised.

She quickly rang for a taxi and then wondered what to take. When the car arrived, with her favourite driver behind the wheel, Bessie instructed him to take her into the village centre first.

"I need to pick up some sandwiches and snacks," she told Dave.

The little café by the police station had the order Bessie had placed by phone all ready for her. A few moments later, she was on her way to the Clague farm. Sarah answered her knock.

"I've brought some sandwiches and salads," Bessie explained, handing the woman one of the boxes. "Everything can go in the refrigerator and people can just nibble when they have an appetite."

"How incredibly thoughtful of you," Sarah said. "That's exactly what we need. Please come in."

Bessie followed the woman into the kitchen, carrying the other box of food. Together they managed to fit everything into the refrigerator.

"That was very kind of you," Sarah said.

"Do you think Fenella would like to see me?" Bessie asked.

"I can go and see," Sarah offered.

Bessie sat down at the table while she waited. She didn't want to upset Fenella any further, but she also didn't want the wrong person blamed for murder. A moment later, the door behind Bessie swung open.

"Oh, I didn't know you were here," Eoin said from the doorway.

Bessie turned and gave him a sympathetic smile. "How are you?" she asked.

"I'm fine," he said. "Niall was like a second father to me, you know. I'm going to miss him, although he's been gone a long time already, really."

Bessie nodded. "It's such a shame his health was so bad these last few years," she said.

"Aye, it was hard on Fenella, going to see him and him not remembering her," Eoin replied.

"And that made it hard for you, because you love her," Bessie said.

"I do," Eoin nodded. "I've loved her since the first time I laid eyes on her, when she was only about twelve and I shouldn't have been looking at her."

Bessie smiled. "You had to wait a long time before you could tell her, then," she suggested.

"I did," Eoin nodded. "I waited until she was eighteen to start courting her properly and it took me nearly two years to win her heart. It was worth it all, though."

"You would have been devastated to lose her," Bessie said softly. "If she'd found another man before you'd spoken up, for example."

Eoin sat down next to Bessie at the table. "I knew you'd worked it all out," he told her. "But you mustn't tell Fen. I'll be dead soon. It can all come out after I'm gone. It won't hurt anything, waiting a little bit, will it?"

Bessie stared at the man, feeling an uncomfortable mix of anger and compassion. "You killed Jacob Conover," she said softly.

"He was going to take her away," Eoin replied softly. "She was my whole world, even if she didn't know it then. I had everything planned out. We were going to get married and have a dozen kids and run the farm and look after Niall. It was going to be perfect."

"And then Jacob came along and swept Fenella off her feet."

"That man," Eoin said bitterly. "He didn't really care about her. He just wanted a hard worker to help run his father's farm. All while he was filling her head with nonsense, he was going around with every other girl in Laxey. I tried to warn Fenella about him, and I warned Niall, too, but neither of them paid any attention."

"How did you know about them? Fenella thought no one knew."

"He used to sneak up here every night, or nearly every night," Eoin said. "They would meet in different places and sit and talk about their plans. I was nursing a sick cow one night in the cattle barn. They didn't even know I was there."

"And you told Niall?" Bessie asked.

"Not right away. I started watching Fenella more closely after that. It had never occurred to me that she might meet someone else, but now I realised that I needed to keep a close eye on her. It was almost like a game, watching her and trying to work out where she might meet the man next. They had a sort of routine, anyway, and Fenella always had chores to do as well, so that made it easier to work out where they might be."

"So you heard all about their plans," Bessie said.

"I did. He was going back across, back to his farm. His father wanted him to start taking over after his extended holiday. Fenella was going to go with him. He said he was going to marry her as soon as they arrived in Cumbria, but I don't know if that's true. He seemed like the type to just take her along and then discard her when he grew tired of her."

"You wanted to protect her," Bessie suggested.

"Of course I did," Eoin nearly shouted. "I loved her, even if she was involved with another man. I'd have done anything for her."

"So what happened?"

"I was at the pub that night," Eoin said, his eyes unfocussed as he remembered. "I had a few drinks and I bought him a few as well. I told him that I really liked Fenella and asked him to leave without her. He laughed and told me that he wasn't going to give up a good thing like Fenella without a fight."

"So you fought him?"

"No, I laughed and told him he was crazy, that Fenella wasn't worth fighting over, then I offered to give him a ride up to the farm. He'd already sold his fancy car, and he had his suitcases with him, all ready to get on the boat."

Bessie didn't want to hear the rest of the story. She stood up. "I think maybe I should go and see what's keeping Fenella," she said, trying not to sound as anxious as she felt.

Eoin shook his head. "I may as well tell you the rest. It's such a relief, telling someone. I've been keeping it a secret for so long. It's the only secret I've ever had from Fen. We've been through a lot together, but I don't know how she'd feel if she knew what I did that night. I'd like to think that our years of happiness prove that I made the right choice, getting rid of Jacob, but I don't know if she'd agree."

"Maybe you should talk to her about it," Bessie suggested.

"I can't," Eoin replied. "I can't tell her that I drove Jacob up here in my truck but stopped at the lower barn. I told him I needed to check on something and asked him to come and give me a hand. He didn't want to do it. He was really lazy and hated getting his hands dirty, you know."

Bessie didn't trust herself to speak. She sat back down and looked at Eoin. He was pale and haggard and Bessie felt certain that he knew he didn't have long left.

"I don't know for sure what I was planning," he said now. "I wanted to beat him senseless, I know, but I don't know if I planned to kill him or not. I only hit him a couple of times, before he stopped getting back up."

A soft gasp came from the kitchen doorway on the opposite wall. Bessie looked up to see Fenella standing there. Eoin didn't seem to have heard her, and she was out of his line of sight. As Bessie stared at her, she slowly shook her head.

"I didn't realise he was dead for a while," Eoin continued. "I sat down and waited for him to wake up for hours, but he never did. Then I realised that I needed to get rid of the body. No one ever spent much time in the lower barn, anyway, so I dug a hole under the boxes that Niall had put there when Marion died and dropped him in it, and then put the boxes back on top. Once it was all over, I was certain I'd get found out. I've spent my whole life since waiting for the police to come for me."

"And yet you married Fenella," Bessie blurted out.

"I loved her. I did it for her," Eoin replied. "Jacob wouldn't have made her happy. He probably wouldn't even have married her. He never wrote to his sister about her; that's very telling, isn't it? I've done everything I can for my entire life to make Fenella happy. Getting rid of that man was for the best, really it was."

Bessie could hear the desperation in the man's voice as he tried to persuade himself that he'd done the right thing.

"Anyway, please don't tell Fen. I'll write it all down in a letter and you can give it to the police after I'm gone. It won't be long now, anyway. Maybe the police can just keep quiet about it. That would be for the best, really. Fenella would never have to know."

"She thinks her father killed him," Bessie said quietly.

"He might have," Eoin said. "He was very angry about her leaving. Maybe, if I'd brought him to the house, Niall would have killed him."

"You don't believe that," Bessie said. "Niall always wanted Fenella to be happy. Even if he didn't want her to leave, if it's what she wanted, he would have let her go."

"He was furious," Eoin replied. "He might have taken a swing at Jacob and killed him accidently, just like I did."

"Maybe," Bessie said, not wanting to argue with the man.

"I'll write out my confession and give it to you," he told Bessie. "Promise me you won't give it to the police until after I'm gone."

Before Bessie could reply, Fenella walked into the room. "Don't promise him anything," she said angrily.

"Fen? Please tell me you weren't listening," Eoin said plaintively.

"I was listening," she told him. "I loved Jacob so much, and you killed him."

"He wasn't good for you. He was seeing a dozen other women. He probably would have thrown you aside within a month."

"You didn't even know him," Fenella said, her voice low. "He loved me and we would have had a wonderful life together. We might even have been able to have children."

Eoin looked at her and his face crumpled. "I'm sorry," he said quietly. "I wanted to protect you."

"I wasn't yours to protect," Fenella said, tears flowing down her face.

"You were already my everything," he told her.

"But you weren't mine," Fenella replied. She turned and walked out of the room, leaving Eoin sobbing behind her. Bessie hesitated for a moment and then followed Fenella out.

"Can I do anything to help?" she asked the woman, who'd stopped a few paces away and was now leaning against the wall crying.

"Ring John Rockwell and ask him to come and get Eoin," Fenella said. "I don't want to see him ever again."

"Maybe I should ring your doctor," Bessie said. "Do you have any friends who can come and sit with you?"

Fenella shook her head. "I have Nicholas and Sarah," she replied.

"Maybe you could tell them what's happened? I don't feel like talking right now."

Bessie nodded. "Where's your room? Maybe you should go and lie down, and I'll find Sarah and send her to you."

"I think I'd rather go and lie down in my father's room," Fenella said. "He hasn't stayed there since just after the house was built, but we've kept it exactly the same. There's nothing of Eoin's in there."

Bessie took the woman's arm and helped her up the stairs and down the corridor. Fenella opened a door and led Bessie into a large bedroom. It was clearly a man's room, with large and dark furniture. Bessie helped Fenella into the bed, which was made up with dark blue sheets and a matching duvet.

"My father loved this room, when the house was first finished," she said softly.

"I'm so sorry," Bessie said.

"I can't quite take it all in," Fenella told her. "I've had so many years to get used to losing Jacob that I'm almost not angry about that anymore. It feels worse to me that Eoin was prepared to let my father take the blame, even if only for a short time." She rested her head on the pillows and sighed. "I think maybe I do need a doctor," she told Bessie. "I think I'd quite like to be heavily sedated for a few days."

"Do you want me to stay for a while or should I go and find Sarah?" Bessie asked after she'd rung Fenella's doctor.

"I think I'd like to have Sarah," the woman replied. "She's very nice and very motherly in a way. That's probably what I need."

Bessie headed towards the door. She hadn't rung John yet, but that didn't seem as urgent as getting help for Fenella. Sarah was standing just outside the room, watching the door when Bessie opened it.

"What's going on?" she asked in a whisper.

"Eoin's confessed to killing Jacob Conover," Bessie told her. "Fenella overheard and is, obviously, very upset. I've rung her doctor and he's on his way."

"Nicholas had his suspicions," Sarah said. "He didn't believe that Niall had anything to do with it, but he couldn't say anything against Eoin, of course."

"Someone needs to ring the police," Bessie said uncertainly.

"Perhaps that's what Eoin was doing when I came upstairs," Sarah said. "He was on the phone with someone."

Bessie walked back down to the kitchen and found Eoin and Nicholas sitting silently together.

"I've rung the police and asked for John Rockwell," Eoin told Bessie. "He's on his way."

"Fenella's doctor is on his way as well," Bessie told him.

"I never meant to hurt her. I never would," Eoin replied.

To Bessie he looked even smaller and sicker than he had an hour ago. She couldn't help but think that he would never make it to a murder trial.

CHAPTER 15

When Bessie woke up on Saturday morning, she wasn't feeling much like having a Thanksgiving feast. Events at the Clague farm continued to upset her, and even a long walk along the beach did little to help. When she got home from her walk, Doona was parked in front of her cottage. She greeted Bessie with a hug.

"I thought you might like some company," she told Bessie.

"I'm going to have plenty of that today," Bessie replied.

"I thought you might like some quiet company before the chaos," Doona amended her remark.

"I don't think I'm very good company at the moment," Bessie replied. "I understand Eoin is in hospital and the prognosis isn't good."

"John said they are giving him weeks at most," Doona said.

"Maybe that's for the best," Bessie sighed. "I've also heard that Fenella hasn't been to see him."

Doona shrugged. "Maybe we should find something else to talk about," she suggested.

Bessie forced herself to smile. "You're right," she said. "My Thanksgiving feast is one of my favourite days of the year. I need to put the whole sad story out of my mind for today."

"I brought a bottle of wine, if you think that might help," Doona told her.

"It's not even eight in the morning yet," Bessie said, shaking her head.

"It's a special occasion," Doona laughed.

Bessie hesitated for a moment and then smiled. "Go on then. Let's have a glass of wine. Just the one, though."

Bessie was taking down the glasses when she heard another car pull up by her cottage. Doona opened the door to Hugh and Grace.

"Pull out a couple more glasses," she called to Bessie.

"Wine? Isn't it a bit early?" Hugh asked after he'd given Bessie a hug.

"It's a holiday," Bessie explained.

"Hugh's driving, but I'm not," Grace said. "I'll join you for sure."

Doona poured wine into four glasses, giving Hugh just a small amount. "You can drive us all to the feast, can't you?" she asked him as she took a large sip from her own glass.

"Of course I can," Hugh replied. "I'd be happy to."

"But what brings you here this morning?" Bessie asked the pair.

Grace glanced at Hugh, who shrugged. "We just wanted to see how you were doing," she said after a moment. "I know that you've had a lot going on lately and I was afraid it all might interfere with your enjoyment of today."

"Hence the wine," Bessie said.

"Wine was a good idea," Grace told Doona. "We just brought pastries."

Bessie smiled. "What would I do without my friends?" she asked as Grace piled croissants, muffins, and doughnuts onto a platter.

An hour later the wine was gone. Hugh hadn't drunk much, but he'd made up for it by eating most of the pastries.

"I really need to head to the restaurant now," Bessie said, feeling the warm glow that the wine, good food, and great friends had brought.

"Let's go, then," Hugh said. "Maybe they'll need someone to taste-test things for them in the kitchen."

Everyone laughed and then they all climbed into Hugh's car and headed for Ramsey.

"Bessie, we have everything under control," Lisa assured her when they arrived at The Swing Bridge. "The turkeys are roasting, the pies are cooling, and the bread rolls are rising."

Bessie grinned. "I know I didn't have to be here this early, but I decided I might as well pace and fret here as at home."

"You have nothing to fret about," Lisa said. "Everything will be perfect."

Upstairs in the banquet room, Bessie surveyed the scene. White tablecloths were set with plain white plates. Centerpieces filled with autumn flowers matched napkins in a variety of deep autumnal colours.

"Look at the gorgeous colours," Doona said.

"I didn't know you could get all these different flowers this late in the year," Grace said.

"The whole effect is just about perfect," Doona told Bessie.

"It does look rather nice," Bessie agreed. "But it seems like an awful lot of places. I didn't think I invited this many people."

Doona laughed. "I suspect you invited many more people than this," she said. "Luckily, some of them couldn't come."

Bessie blushed and then laughed. "You could be right," she said sheepishly. "Once I got started, I couldn't seem to stop myself."

"What can we do to help?" Grace asked.

"I have place cards for everyone," Bessie said. "I thought that might be easier than having people trying to find their own seats. But now I'm not so sure. Maybe, if everyone can sit wherever they choose, people will be able to make new friends."

"I think either way will be good," Doona told her. "I'm quite happy sitting with the people I already know, but I know that anyone who is friends with you will be nice and interesting."

"What do you think?" Bessie asked Hugh.

"I think I want to sit with Grace," Hugh said. "But beyond that, I'm happy anywhere."

"As long as there's plenty of food," Grace added for him.

Hugh laughed. "She knows me too well," he told the others.

"I don't really mind, either way," Grace told Bessie. "I'll sit anywhere."

"In that case, I think we'll do away with the place cards and let everyone find their own groups," Bessie said.

"Just don't you worry about everyone," Doona said. "You relax and have fun. It's going to be a great afternoon."

Bessie nodded, but she felt a pang of uncertainty. She'd never hosted this many guests before, and there was quite a mix of people from all around the island. "I just hope it all works out," she muttered as Lisa brought them glasses of wine.

"It's going to be wonderful," Lisa assured her.

A couple of hours later, Bessie had to agree. The room was packed with people and everywhere that Bessie looked she saw a friendly face. Some of her friends from Manx National Heritage were chatting with Ruth and Muriel from the flats on Seaview Terrace. Doncan Quayle and his wife were laughing with Spencer Cannon and Beverly, whom Bessie had liked instantly. John Rockwell's children seemed to be having a wonderful time playing games with Liz Martin's two toddlers, and Doona was keeping Mary Quayle company while George wandered around, talking to everyone.

She looked over at Henry and grinned. He was shyly introducing his friend, Laura Meyers, to everyone. Laura was in her late forties or early fifties and had just moved to the island after being offered a job with Manx National Heritage. Bessie thought she seemed perfect for Henry, and from what Bessie had seen so far, it appeared that Henry felt the same way.

It was nearly time for the food to be served when Mark Blake found her.

"Bessie, I was wondering if you'd be willing to join a committee that I'm putting together," he said after an initial greeting.

"What sort of committee?" Bessie asked warily. She always felt at a slight disadvantage with the people from Manx National Heritage. They were all smart and well educated, and Bessie never forgot that she was simply an enthusiastic amateur when it came to studying history.

"We've come up with what we hope is a brilliant idea for a fundraiser," Mark told her. "It's going to be called *Christmas at the Castle,* and we'll be holding it at Castle Rushen."

"That sounds interesting," Bessie said, curious to hear more.

"We thought it would be a chance for not only Manx National Heritage to raise some money, but also other charities on the island. Any group that would like to take part is going to be allowed to decorate a room at the castle for the holidays, to some sort of theme of their choice," Mark told her. "We haven't planned out exactly how it's going to work, that's where the committee comes in, but what we want to do is find ways to help out all of the charities that get involved."

"I'm intrigued," Bessie told him.

Mark laughed. "That's good," he said. "I just hope the rest of the island is as well. We're trying to get a strong planning committee together that can bring a wide variety of ideas and experience to the event. I thought of you right away."

"I don't know," Bessie said. "I've never been involved in anything like this before."

"But I'm sure you'll have some wonderful ideas," Mark countered. "Marjorie has already agreed to help and so has Mary Quayle. I'd like your thoughts on who else to add to the committee as well."

"Let me think about it all," Bessie replied. "Things are a little bit hectic today."

Mark nodded. "I'll ring you towards the end of next week," he said. "That gives you some time to think it through. I'd be really grateful if you'd do it, but I'll understand if you can't." He gave here a quick hug and then disappeared into the crowd.

Before Bessie could give the matter any thought, the restaurant staff began to fill the long buffet tables with food. Wonderful smells began to fill the air and Bessie's mouth began to water.

With two identical buffet lines, it wasn't long before everyone was finding places to sit with their full plates. Bessie ended up at a table with Doona, Hugh, Grace, and John Rockwell and his children. She smiled to herself. No one else need know that that was exactly where she'd wanted to be.

After everyone had found seats, John stood up. "Before we all enjoy this wonderful meal, I believe it is traditional in America to give thanks. I just wanted to take a moment to say how thankful I am for the friendship that Bessie has shown me since we first met. She's a wonderful woman and a true friend and I'm very thankful that I met her."

Shouts of "hear, hear" and "hurrah for Bessie" filled the air. Bessie's eyes filled with tears as she looked around the room. It had been a difficult and trying year with many tragedies, but today, surrounded by the friends who were her family, she felt that it had been worth it. She loved her island, and even more, the people who lived there.

GLOSSARY OF TERMS

MANX LANGUAGE TO ENGLISH

- **kys t'ou** — How are you?
- **ta mee braew** — I'm fine.

HOUSE NAMES – MANX TO ENGLISH

- **Thie yn Traie** — Beach House
- **Treoghe Bwaane** — Widow's Cottage (Bessie's home)

ENGLISH/MANX TO AMERICAN TERMS

- **advocate** — Manx title for a lawyer (solicitor in the UK)
- **aye** — yes
- **biscuits** — cookies
- **booking** — reservation (at a restaurant)
- **boot** — trunk (of a car)

- **car park** — parking lot
- **chips** — french fries
- **comeover** — a person who moved to the island from elsewhere
- **crisps** — potato chips
- **cuppa** — cup of tea (informal)
- **fairy cakes** — cupcakes
- **fairy lights** — Christmas lights
- **fizzy drink** — soda (or pop)
- **flat** — apartment
- **hire car** — rental car
- **holiday** — vacation
- **jumper** — sweater
- **lift** — elevator
- **lorry** — truck
- **midday** — noon
- **pavement** — sidewalk
- **plait** — braid (in hair)
- **pudding** — dessert
- **queue** — line
- **shopping trolley** — shopping cart
- **skeet** — gossip
- **starters** — appetizers
- **telly** — television
- **till** — check-out (in a grocery store, for example)
- **torch** — flashlight
- **trainers** — sneakers

OTHER NOTES

CID is the Criminal Investigation Department of the Isle of Man Constabulary (Police Force).

"Noble's" is Noble's Hospital, the main hospital on the Isle of Man. It is located in Douglas, the island's capital.

When talking about time, the English say, for example, "half seven" to mean "seven-thirty."

When island residents talk about someone being from "across," or moving "across," they mean somewhere in the United Kingdom (across the water).

In the UK you enter a building on the "ground floor," and the floor above that is the "first floor." The numbers go up from there. In the US, it is typical to count the ground floor level as the "first floor."

Boxing Day is the day after Christmas (December 26th) and was traditionally the day that servants would get a present (their Christmas box) from their employers. It is a Bank Holiday (Public Holiday) in the UK. (And my birthday, if anyone is interested.)

A cattle grid is a grid of bars or tubes set into the ground to stop cattle (or other livestock) from leaving or entering an area. The gaps between the bars are far enough apart that the animal can't safely walk across them, but they don't impede vehicles from passing over them.

The Inland Revenue is the UK tax authority, similar to the US IRS.

ACKNOWLEDGMENTS

As ever, I have a great many people to thank.

My editor, Denise, who keeps my biggest mistakes away from my wonderful readers.

Kevin takes the beautiful photographs that make my covers so special.

Thanks to Charlene, Janice, Ruth and Margaret for being the best beta reading team in the world.

And, last, but never least, thank you, readers, for enjoying Bessie's adventures along with me. I am so grateful to each and every one of you.

Aunt Bessie's adventures continue in...

Aunt Bessie Joins

An Isle of Man Cozy Mystery

Diana Xarissa

Aunt Bessie joins the planning committee for Manx National Heritage's new fundraiser, *Christmas at the Castle.*

Bessie is delighted that her friends, Marjorie Stevens and Mary Quayle are also both on the committee. Carolyn Teare is a less welcome addition. When Carolyn insists on hiring an expensive designer to "improve" everything, Bessie is even less happy.

Aunt Bessie joins Mary and Marjorie in fighting against Christopher Hart's suggested changes to the beautifully decorated rooms.

But when Christopher ends up dead, not liking his design style seems a pretty slim motive.

Aunt Bessie joins forces with Inspector John Rockwell and his Douglas counterpart, Pete Corkill as an act of vandalism and a second dead body threaten to get *Christmas at the Castle* cancelled altogether.

ALSO BY DIANA XARISSA

The Isle of Man Cozy Mystery Series

Aunt Bessie Assumes

Aunt Bessie Believes

Aunt Bessie Considers

Aunt Bessie Decides

Aunt Bessie Enjoys

Aunt Bessie Finds

Aunt Bessie Goes

Aunt Bessie's Holiday

Aunt Bessie Invites

Aunt Bessie Joins

Aunt Bessie Knows

Aunt Bessie Likes

Aunt Bessie Meets

Aunt Bessie Needs

The Isle of Man Ghostly Cozy Mysteries

Arrivals and Arrests

Boats and Bad Guys

Cars and Cold Cases

Dogs and Danger

The Markham Sisters Cozy Mystery Novellas

The Appleton Case

The Bennett Case

The Chalmers Case

The Donaldson Case

The Ellsworth Case

The Fenton Case

The Green Case

The Hampton Case

The Irwin Case

The Isle of Man Romance Series

Island Escape

Island Inheritance

Island Heritage

Island Christmas

ABOUT THE AUTHOR

Diana grew up in Pennsylvania, moved to Washington DC and then found herself being swept off her feet by a handsome British man who was visiting DC on vacation. That was nearly nineteen years ago.

After their wedding, Diana moved to Derbyshire, where her new husband had his home. A short time later, the couple moved to the Isle of Man. After more than ten years on the island, now a family of four, they relocated to the outskirts of Buffalo, NY, where Diana keeps busy writing about the island she loves and driving her children everywhere.

She also writes mystery/thrillers set in the not-too-distant future under the pen name "Diana X. Dunn" and fantasy/adventure books for middle grade readers under the pen name "D.X. Dunn."

She would be delighted to know what you think of her work and can be contacted through snail mail at:

Diana Xarissa Dunn
PO Box 72
Clarence, NY 14031

Find Diana at:

www.dianaxarissa.com
diana@dianaxarissa.com

Made in the USA
San Bernardino, CA
10 July 2017